# A DANCER
# IN THE DUST

# Books by Thomas H. Cook

FICTION

Blood Innocents

The Orchids

Tabernacle

Elena

Sacrificial Ground

Flesh and Blood

Streets of Fire

Night Secrets

The City When It Rains

Evidence of Blood

Mortal Memory

Breakheart Hill

The Chatham School Affair

Instruments of Night

Places in the Dark

The Interrogation

Taken (based on the teleplay
by Leslie Boehm)

Moon over Manhattan
(with Larry King)

Peril

Into the Web

Red Leaves

The Cloud of Unknowing

Master of the Delta

The Fate of Katherine Carr

The Last Talk with Lola Faye

The Quest for Anna Klein

The Crime of Julian Wells

Sandrine's Case

NONFICTION

Early Graves

Blood Echoes

A Father's Story
(as told by Lionel Dahmer)

Best American Crime Writing
2000, 2001 (ed. with Otto Penzler)

Best American Crime Writing
2002 (ed. with Otto Penzler)

Best American Crime Writing
2003 (ed. with Otto Penzler)

Best American Crime Writing
2004 (ed. with Otto Penzler)

Best American Crime Writing
2005 (ed. with Otto Penzler)

Best American Crime Writing
2006 (ed. with Otto Penzler)

Best American Crime Reporting
2007 (ed. with Otto Penzler)

Best American Crime Reporting
2008 (ed. with Otto Penzler)

Best American Crime Reporting
2009 (ed. with Otto Penzler)

Best American Crime Reporting
2010 (ed. with Otto Penzler)

# A DANCER
# IN THE DUST

## THOMAS H. COOK

The Mysterious Press
an imprint of Grove/Atlantic Inc.
*New York*

*Published simultaneously in Canada*
*Printed in the United States of America*

FIRST EDITION

ISBN 978-0-8021-2272-8
eISBN 978-0-8021-9268-4

The Mysterious Press
an imprint of Grove/Atlantic, Inc.
154 West 14th Street
New York, NY 10011

Distributed by Publishers Group West

www.groveatlantic.com

14  15  16  17    10  9  8  7  6  5  4  3  2  1

*What we think, or what we know, or what we believe is, in the end, of little consequence. The only consequence is what we do.*

John Ruskin
*The Crown of Wild Olives*

*The crimes of evil are well known to history. It is the crimes of goodness that go largely unrecorded.*

Martine Aubert
*Open Letter to Foreign Friends*

For Susan Terner and Justine Cook,
with the overflowing measure of my love

# PART I

The circle of life is often a noose. But it isn't that particular risk I consider as my plane banks to the left and begins its descent toward Rupala. It is Martine I remember, along with the fact that, on any given day, the right thing can seem so wrong and the wrong thing so right that we easily become lost, to use Poe's exquisite phrase, in a wilderness of error.

And surely among those errors, I have learned, there is none deeper, nor more fraught with peril, than to believe that your world, your values, your sense of comfort and achievement, should be someone else's, too. Such is the grave understanding of things that came to Martine early, but came to me too late.

The airport at Rupala is a swirling bazaar of noises and smells, all of which are amplified by the sub-Saharan heat inside the terminal. Wires dangle like black snakes from the ceiling just as they had years before, when I'd first arrived in this country, carrying my bubbling good intentions as if they were bottles of champagne. In fact, the only thing that has changed since my last visit is that the enormous paintings of Abbo Mafumi, the Lion of God and Emperor of All Peoples, have been taken down, leaving ghostly rectangular outlines on the cracked and peeling walls where they'd once hung. Abbo had been Mafumi's birth name, but since its lowly meaning of "condiment" had not befitted Lubanda's

3

Supreme Commander and Ruler for Life, he'd changed it to Balondemu, "Chosen One," before the final assault on the capital. After that, he'd ruled the country as the lead character in a grisly operatic farce, adorning himself in plumed hats and bloodred togas, a mock Lubandan Caesar who'd ridden a chariot onto the soccer field, where he'd started the game by throwing a spear into a warthog tethered to a metal stake. Such buffoonery is laughable only if you are not a victim of it, of course, but Lubanda for the previous twenty years had been very much a victim of Mafumi's moronic clownishness.

But Mafumi is now dead, and Lubanda has a new president. For that reason change seems possible. It is with a full understanding of the nature of that change that I've returned here, bearing my gift of hope.

"What is your business in Lubanda?" the passport agent asks when I reach his booth. His eyes are on my passport, but he has not opened it. I have seen this purposeful lethargy before. Trapped in his sweltering booth, he can keep me waiting in the same unbearable heat, and by his indifference to my comfort and presumed urgency he can carry out a petty act of self-assertion. I have experienced this crudely orchestrated inconvenience a thousand times on my many trips to the world's mendicant nations, and so I recognize it as the sole pathetic power of the supplicant and the dependent, the beggar's hatred for the one who drops a coin into his hand.

"I'm here to help Lubanda," I tell him frankly.

Such an assertion means nothing to him, but he doesn't care that it is meaningless. He is long accustomed to people unlikely to divulge the true nature of their business. I am just the latest member of that familiar crowd, another foreigner who has come either to take something from or impose something upon his country. At worst, I am after his homeland's gold or diamonds or rare animal skins. At best I will insist that his children learn a language steeped in foreign arts and sciences, and judge them by their ability to do so. This thought returns me once again to Martine, particularly to her belief that a people's inner life could be nurtured only by its own waters, and is the product of millennia, not the object of an alien surge.

The airport agent finally opens my passport, sees my name, and is immediately animated. Without doubt he has been told to expect me, to expedite every procedure, welcome me with eager eyes and a big smile.

"Ah, Mr. Campbell, sir," he says with exaggerated warmth. "Welcome to Lubanda." He stamps my passport with a newfound briskness. "There are people waiting for you," he adds, "through that door."

The freshly painted door has been stenciled with the letters "Diplomatic Entrance." It is an ordinary door that has been tarted up for my benefit. Two uniformed men stand on either side of it and both snap to attention as I approach. The uniforms are green, the berets black with a bit of gold piping. The men themselves are probably the not-yet-replaced members of the recently deceased Emperor's private security force, Mafumi's version of a Praetorian Guard. It is possible that they will not be replaced at all, because under the new president there is to be a spirit of reconciliation. A recent amendment to the country's constitution has enshined this in law, and as a result, Mafumi's bodyguard has not been disarmed, a situation I deem very risky for the new president of Lubanda.

"Mr. Campbell?" one of the faux Praetorians says.

I nod.

"This way, sir."

A late-model Mercedes idles in front of the terminal, another holdover from the Emperor, one of the seventy luxury cars he is reported to have owned. The driver, dressed in a white shirt, black pants, black tie, opens the door for me.

"Good morning, sir." He smiles cheerfully. "The air-conditioning will feel good. It is hot in Lubanda."

The drive to the palace takes me through the usual throng, a sea, as they say, of humanity. Everyone is either out in the open or sprawling beneath whatever manner of shelter or shade can be found or improvised. I notice an old man in the ragged remnants of what had once been flowing orange robes. He is squatting beside an enormous mound of car bumpers, doors, windshield frames, and the like. Here, surely, is one of the last of the Lutusi, the nomads of the savanna who'd once roamed freely, their erect figures walking slowly with their staffs, herding their animals before them. Until now, I had never seen a Lutusi in Rupala and so, as my car moves past, I look at him more closely, note the anxiousness in his eyes, the way he searches the crowd of children who have gathered by the long-defunct railway station.

"Rupala is overrun with orphans," my driver tells me.

"Yes, I can see that," I answer, then turn from the old man and stare straight ahead, into a country whose chief industry is salvage and whose capital city seems built of scavenged materials: cardboard, plywood, corrugated iron, flaps of cloths, shards of glass, snaking coils of copper, the shoddy remains of countless earlier importations, a largesse that had once flowed into Rupala, and that now gives it the sense of a project earnestly begun and then abruptly abandoned.

We arrive at the palace, with its great gate. It had once been topped with a menacing sculpture of crossed machetes, the symbol of Mafumi's ironfisted rule, but this naked display of merciless power has been taken down by the new president.

"Welcome, Mr. Campbell," a man in neat civilian dress tells me when I step out of the car. He introduces himself, then says, "Come with me, please."

I am escorted up the wide, carefully swept stairs. Everything has been spruced up, every surface polished. I am aware that in other countries temporary walls, usually of plywood or sheets of corrugated tin, have often been built to hide the slums from such passing dignitaries as myself. At other times, more extreme measures have been taken. When such people came to Addis Ababa, for example, Haile Selassie would order the city's beggars rounded up, herded into trucks, and driven out into the desert. If the dignitaries were to stay two days, they would be driven the distance of a two-day trudge back to the capital. If the dignitaries were staying three days, then the distance would be a three-day walk. Many, of course, could not survive the trek back to the capital, but the desert is wide and the vultures are efficient, and so their sunbaked corpses would quickly disappear. The dignitaries would not have known any of this, of course, which had been the point of Martine's having related this grim bit of Ethiopian history on one or another of the many evenings I spent with her.

*Oh, Martine,* I think, as I tighten my fingers around the handle of the briefcase I have brought with me to Rupala, *I have come at last to help the country whose risks you'd known too well.*

"Welcome to Lubanda."

The man who says this wears a gray suit, white shirt, narrow black tie. He smiles warmly, but the bulge beneath his shoulder indicates a readiness for trouble.

"Thank you," I reply.

We are standing in the marble foyer of the Imperial—now the Presidential—Palace. Overhead, the recently adopted Lubandan flag hangs from the second-floor gallery, and a bust of George Washington has been placed in a small alcove to my right, its base swaddled in an American flag. Years before, at Lubanda's independence, and under the leadership of its first president, a considerable effort had been made to help Lubanda. Aid workers from the United States and other donor nations had poured into the country, starting all manner of projects. Mafumi's shamelessly racist, psychopathic rule had put a stop to all that, the result being that an economy and infrastructure almost entirely dependent upon aid had collapsed at its abrupt withdrawal.

"So," the man says as he sweeps his arm toward the gracefully curving stairs, "Shall we?"

As we move up the stairs I consider the heart-stopping risk I carry in the briefcase that dangles from my hand, the as-yet-untested strategy I have brought to Lubanda, and which, after much painful thought and experience, I feel to be its best hope for the future.

At the top of the stairs, I am directed to the right, where I see large twin doors, beautifully carved with various jungle scenes. There are lions, rhinos, giraffes, and the like. Several of these animals (polar bears, for example, and giant sea turtles) cannot actually be found in Lubanda, since, after all, it lies below the Sahara and has no coastline. But fantasy always trumped reality in Mafumi's fevered mind, so why shouldn't the doors that lead to his office do the same?

"This way, sir."

Now I am moving down the corridor toward those doors.

On the way, I think of Isak Dinesen and Olive Schreiner, women who worked African farms just as Martine had. But unlike Martine, they'd written books and then returned to their native lands, Dinesen permanently to Denmark, Schreiner back to England for long periods. Neither in mind nor heart had they ever truly left Europe, so that when they dreamed, it was of that continent's carefully pruned gardens or wide boulevards. My error had been in believing that Martine's dream had been the same as theirs.

We are now nearing those fantastically carved doors, so that I can see the unreal jungle romance they portray in more detail, wooden versions of a harmonious vision Henri Rousseau made famous, idyllic jungle scenes painted by a man, as Martine once pointed out, who never left France.

Soon those great doors will open to me and my task will come that much closer to its end. At some point the new president will receive me. We will chat cordially, in voices each finds amiable and familiar. Then I will open my briefcase and present him with my offer of hope for Lubanda, and with that offering, render my last tribute to Martine. With that act, and after only three months, my mission will come to an end in a way far different from the way it began, with the snap of a briefcase latch rather than the jangle of a phone.

# New York City, Three Months Earlier

# One

"Hello."

My tone was wary because for a professional risk assessment and management consultant calls are never welcome, since they are usually from people terrified that they have made the wrong choice and now must face the consequences. The simple, contradictory fact of life is this: human beings, victims, as they sometimes are, of sudden misfortune, easily lured into misadventure, and in all things bound by time, nonetheless dream of certainty even as they roll the dice.

"It's Bill Hammond. It's been a long time, Ray."

The tenor of his voice was considerably more somber than I remembered, and coming from so far in the past, it had the alarming effect of a board cracking beneath me.

"It has, indeed," I said.

Bill had never been one to come slowly to his point, so I added, "What's on your mind?"

"A murder."

*Murder.*

The word itself is unnerving. Like bankruptcy or default, it suggests a hard road ahead for the simple reason that a line that should have been avoided at all cost has instead been crossed. For that reason, I felt that simultaneous sense of tightening and emptying that accompanies any mention of an act whose consequences, though surely serious, remain for the moment unclear.

"It's someone from the old days," Bill added. "When you lived in Tumasi."

Tumasi was the name given to the vast savanna that stretched east to west across central Lubanda, as well as the village that rested near its center and served as its primary market. I'd lived in the village there for almost a year, but I hadn't heard its name spoken in a very long time. Even so, I'd often thought of the place, along with the winding red dirt road that connected it to the capital in Rupala. I had driven down that road in joy and sorrow, and once with a mind animated by a purpose I never should have had, and whose result was far different and more serious than I'd been able to predict.

"Seso Alaya," Bill said.

Seso would have been a middle-aged man now, I calculated, but I recalled him as a youth of eighteen, thin, wiry, his smooth skin so black that in high sun it had given off a blue sheen. He'd had the keen eye of a boy who'd lived by his wits. Early on I'd noticed that everything he looked at, he immediately sized up in the starkly unforgiving way of the wild: *Do I eat it or does it eat me?* Those supported by family money or social guarantees do not feel the insistent pinch of this particular kind of fear. Come what may, in boom or bust, they will not go hungry or without shelter. But for those who must support themselves or fall to ruin, deep worry is a life companion. Seso was of this latter estate. For him a job was not just a job; it was a lifeboat in a storm-tossed sea, and for that very good reason he had gone about his service to me with determined care, shining shoes that would only track through dust, heating stones to warm my bed on those few chill nights, rising immediately when I approached him, his keen eye to these tasks and gestures not at all slavish, but rather, a manly attempt to survive in a country where survival of any kind was not guaranteed. To think it otherwise, as Martine had once observed, was but one of the many errors into which foreigners like me, people who had come to help Lubanda, inevitably fell not because we *did not know* the people we wished to aid, but because we *could not know* the depths of both good or evil in their hearts. We could and did romanticize them, as Martine once pointed out, and we could and did cut them all kinds of slack, which, she said, was just another form of abuse. But we could not know them.

"You went back to Lubanda some years ago, didn't you, Ray?" Bill asked.

"Ten years ago," I told him.

It had taken nearly two days to make it halfway to Tumasi, where in a seizure of spiritual cowardice, I'd turned back toward Rupala. There'd been the expected ruts and washouts that bedeviled Lubandan travel, but to these inconveniences there'd been added thirteen separate roadway stops, all of them manned by khat-chewing thugs, often armed with nail-spiked clubs, or pangas, the country's ubiquitous tool, a wide-bladed, wooden-handled machete, light and easily wielded, but still heavy enough to lop off a man's head or a child's arm.

During my last journey up Tumasi Road, the thugs, usually para-military gangs armed by Mafumi's Revolutionary Army of Lubanda, had called their stops "border inspections," but the only border was a chain stretched across the road, motionless as a puff adder, until a vehicle neared. Then, two "customs inspectors" would lift the chain waist high and wait, either grim-faced or with sinister smiles, as the car approached.

"That's dangerous travel, Ray," Bill said. "Why'd you go back?"

"To visit the scene of the crime," I answered flatly. "I thought it might be good for my soul."

15

"I see," Bill said quietly. He was clearly reluctant to venture further into the moral minefield of this subject. "Anyway, it was dangerous in Lubanda when you made that trip."

Indeed it had been dangerous, though I'd had only one tense moment on the road. It had occurred at one of those thirteen criminal customs stops. This time a couple of burning tires had been dragged into the road, and there'd been ten or so "inspectors" whose ages had ranged from early to late teens, years when simmering maleness easily boils into sudden, annihilating violence.

"Where you from, bwana?" the Kalashnikov-wielding leader of this band asked me as he peered about the interior of the Jeep I'd rented in the capital.

The malignant glimmer in his eyes made it clear that the "bwana" was meant as mockery. In Ethiopia it might have been *farangi* and in Kenya it might have been *mukiwa*, but universally it meant you were the pale-faced enemy, the destroyer of some idealized precolonial paradise that had never in the least existed. By this reckoning, you and you alone were responsible for the derelict world whose mad contortions were now so extreme they could only be addressed by swinging clubs and hacking pangas.

"New York," I answered.

His grin revealed teeth sharpened to a point. The Wagogo in Tanzania did this, and the Congolese pygmies; others too, perhaps, but I'd never seen it in Lubanda, and so I assumed it to be some new badge of terror, man merged with crocodile.

"You see *Lion King*, bwana?" he asked.

From a few feet away, a knot of boy-men laughed and the skinniest of them slapped his panga against what had clearly once been a much larger man's boots.

"No," I answered.

"Where you going, bwana?"

"Up Tumasi Road," I answered.

"How far up?"

"To the end."

He looked surprised, and a little suspicious. "There's nothing up Tumasi Road," he said.

"There once was," I told him.

This was true, for Tumasi had once been a thriving village, its market stocked with locally grown produce. I'd seen mounds of sweet potatoes and jars of honey, along with stalls selling various local grains and cured meats and pots fashioned from the local clay. There'd been wooden carvings for sale, and kindling gathered from the savanna, and everywhere, stacks of cassava. Such had been Tumasi from time immemorial, its fundamental needs met by fundamental means.

"It is a long drive to Tumasi, bwana," the man said. "Bad road. Hard on the body." He pronounced bad "bahd," and body was "buddy." He nodded toward a pile of pillows and blankets, some of which were stained with various body fluids. "We sell cheap. Make you more comfortable for the bad road."

I shook my head. "No, thanks."

"You sure, bwana?"

He wore desert-camouflage pants and a bright tie-dyed T-shirt of the kind you might have bought on Venice Beach thirty years before. His cap said "Red Sox," and as he watched me, he took out a long cigarette holder, inserted a hand-wrapped cigarette taken from a crumpled Gauloises box and lit it. "Many bad people on the way to Tumasi." He waved out the match and tossed it to the side. "Maybe you like a paper for safe passage." He grinned. "I give you special price."

"I don't need a paper from you," I told him stiffly, because I knew there would be no end to this extortion once the first advantage had been gained. "I already have safe passage."

The man laughed as if I'd made a bad joke. "Oh, yeah? Who give you that?"

"The Emperor of All Peoples," I said.

To call Mafumi by so exalted a title was, in itself, one of Lubanda's grim jokes. He'd been nothing more than a warlord who'd built a largely tribal army across an artificial border drawn by a British bureaucrat, then invaded on the pretext that President Dasai was in league with "the old colonialists," determined to bind Lubandans once again in those mythic chains. He'd beaten this drum so loudly it had drowned out Dasai's gentlemanly defense, and for that reason it had taken Mafumi little more than two years to march on Rupala, take the capital, then do what he liked with the rest of the country, which had been mostly to terrorize it.

I had never met the Lion of God, of course, and certainly he'd not given me clearance to drive up Tumasi Road. For that reason, using his name was a risk whose consequences I'd considered, and which, for a few seconds, as the guard grinned at me with his crocodile teeth, I'd feared a bad idea. But by then I was in too deep, and so I doubled the bluff.

"Here, I'll show you," I said, then reached for the backpack on the seat beside me, where I'd placed an official-looking paper, complete with a starburst seal. It was only a car warranty, but few people in Lubanda could read, and so the risk was rather slight that it wouldn't buttress my claim of an Imperial safe passage.

"Hmm," the man said as he gazed at the paper. He moved his lips in imitation of reading, but this movement didn't match the words on the page, so I knew he was illiterate. When he finished this charade, he handed the paper back to me.

"So, may I go?" I asked.

He looked at me sternly, but the air was out of him, the midday sun was growing hotter, his mushy chew of khat was losing its kick, and nothing was coming of this customs inspection. So it was time to end it, as I could see—end it and wait for the next car, in anticipation that no paper would be produced that might call into question the little kingdom of this boy-man's fanged blockade.

He flipped a few flakes of ash from his cigarette. "Go."

With that, he banged the stock of his rifle on the bumper of the Jeep, a signal for the burning tires to be dragged out of my path.

I pressed down on the accelerator and moved ahead slowly, resolutely, with my head up, but not arrogantly, only a man on his way. The skinny soldier in the big boots stepped out from among the others and sighted me down the chipped blade of his panga, laughing as he faked repeated chops and then, even more pointedly, drew it slowly across his neck.

"As I recall, you told me that you didn't make it all the way down the road to Tumasi."

Now it was Bill who was asking me questions, his voice thin and metallic over the phone line, but strong enough to pull me out of Lubanda and return me to the present.

"That's right," I answered. "I found it too disturbing."

Instead, I'd stopped the car and stared ahead, my gaze fixed on the red road that lay before me. As my soul emptied, I'd turned back toward Rupala.

"What a sad country," Bill said starkly.

"Not always," I said.

Bill seemed hardly to hear me. "Jesus, it was just horrible what happened to Dasai," he said. "And Gessee, too."

I recalled photographs I'd seen of their bodies, Dasai's hung like a side of beef, Gessee's slumped against a post, clip after clip having been emptied into it, the tire around his neck still burning.

"Mafumi watched it all," Bill added softly.

In these same photographs, the Emperor of All Peoples could be seen peering down at these murderous orgies from a balcony overlooking

Independence Square, a rogue who had not yet achieved his near-legendary status as Lubanda's malevolently farcical dictator. Soon after, he'd become the chief instrument of terror throughout the country. He'd also been quite ingenious in his methods. An Amnesty International report had made a good deal of the fact that he'd had vents dug from the Security Police's basement torture chambers to street level so that the cries of those belowground could clearly be heard by anyone passing by. One scream, he was reported to have said, can shut a thousand mouths.

"But now Mafumi, too, is gone," Bill said.

With that reference to recent changes in Lubanda, I returned to the actual content of his call. "So, tell me, what do you know about Seso's murder?"

"At the moment, it's pretty much a blank," Bill said. "He just turned up dead, you might say."

"Turned up where?"

"Here in New York," Bill answered.

"I presume you don't know what he was doing here? How he was making his living, for example."

"Correct," Bill said.

"So it's possible his murder was purely random," I said.

"Oh, come on, Ray," Bill said. "I mean, what would be the chances of that?"

"Around one in two hundred and fifty thousand," I answered in the matter-of-fact voice of a seasoned risk assessor. "That's admittedly a very low risk, but random killings do occur."

"Seso's murder wasn't random," Bill told me firmly. "That's the one thing I'm sure of."

"Why are you sure of it?"

"Because he was tortured," Bill answered. "On his feet. With bars. What's the word?"

"*Bastiado*," I said.

"Right. So can you meet me tomorrow, Ray?" Bill asked. "I need a . . . risk assessment."

His request suddenly sounded more urgent, something important clearly at stake.

"All right," I said.

"The Harvard Club, nine a.m.?"

"Okay."

"Thanks, Ray. See you then."

The click of Bill's phone as he hung up was loud and oddly jarring, like a pistol shot.

*A murder,* I thought, and suddenly felt somewhat like Fowler, the jaded British journalist, when he learns that Alden Pyle's body has been found floating in the Saigon River. *The Quiet American* had been one of the books I'd read on that first plane ride to Lubanda, and I'd so reveled in its exotic atmosphere that its warning about the risks of inexperience, of entering, even with the best of intentions, a country one knows nothing about, had drowned in the waters of my youth and naïveté.

Those risks had long ago made themselves clear, however, and so for a moment, I went back over the conversation I'd just had with Bill. It was a habit of mine, going over things again and again, putting one piece of data with another. Risk assessment is mostly connecting the proverbial dots.

*Someone from the old days,* I heard Bill say again. *When you lived in Tumasi.*

The old days, when I'd been young and fiercely determined to do good, and nothing, least of all my soul, had seemed at risk.

I thought of my first meeting with Seso, how I'd found him standing alone in a small, airless room not far from the capital, the way he'd introduced himself very formally as "Mr. Seso Alaya." He'd stood extremely straight, and though the collar of his shirt had been frayed and his pants too short, he'd had the dignity the great explorer Richard Burton had found in those who'd served him in India, made yet nobler, as he'd said, by their raggedness.

Seso informed me that he'd been assigned to be my translator and general assistant, and with that he'd reached for my bag, which I'd refused to give him because to do so would suggest that I was his master; and I'd come to help the Lubandan people, not to rule them. Seso had read this gesture for what it was, and smiled. "It is my job to be of service," he told me. "I am not ashamed to work."

Thus had ended the first exchange I'd had with Seso. After it, he'd taken my bag and followed me to the white Land Cruiser that was to be at my disposal for as long as I remained in Lubanda. We'd driven to Tumasi that same day, out of Rupala and up a road that took us past those storied scenes of Africa, small townships, then the villages of the bush, and from there across that broad savanna the Lutusi had immemorially roamed, and to which I believed myself to be bringing my earnest gift of hope.

# Two

There are three principal factors in risk assessment, I reminded myself not long after ending my conversation with Bill Hammond: the amount of the loss, the likelihood of incurring it, and in the event of loss, the subsequent possibility of either full or partial recovery. The first two may not be equally weighted, however. For example, the amount of loss might be very great but the likelihood of incurring it very slight. Or it may be that the loss is slight but the likelihood of incurring it is quite high. In all risk assessment there are only two invariables: that loss is possible, and that some things, once lost—innocence, for example, and sometimes hope—are irrecoverable.

For a few minutes after receiving Bill Hammond's call, I spent some time pondering the considerably less ominous risk of meeting him the next morning. He clearly had some request to make of me, but I reasonably assumed that it was one I could grant or refuse. Either way, there was little risk that my life would change. The odd thing was that Bill's call had returned me to Lubanda in a way that lingered through the night, so that I again recalled myself as the young man who, some twenty years before, had arrived in the sedate capital of a languid country whose arid central region had for a long time remained pretty much undisturbed.

At that time, Lubanda's president was a Western-educated intellectual whose idea of social organization and economic development had been a form of pastoral anarchism, derived, as he freely admitted, from the lessons he'd learned from utopian novels, and which he called Village Harmony. His name was Kojo Dasai, and he was round and huggable, with a huge smile and one of those rich chuckles that immediately put everyone at ease. He'd encouraged his fellow Lubandans to call him "Baba," which means "Father," but Bill Hammond had early dubbed him "Black Santa," and indeed, President Dasai had remained quite jolly, chuckling softly almost to the day he'd been hung upside down by Mafumi's renegade soldiers, stripped of his signature bright yellow dashiki, and hacked to death in Independence Square.

A gruesome video of his murder could still be bought on the streets of the capital when I'd last visited it. In it, the first flag of Lubanda waved at the far end of the square, a huge sunflower against a background of light blue, the design chosen by President Dasai. The flag had later been hauled down, trampled, spat and pissed upon. It was this filthy, reeking bit of cloth in which the president's body, or what was left of it, had been wrapped, placed on a cement slab, doused with gasoline, and burned. The sound of his sizzling fat had been clearly audible on the video, and it was this detail, according to the hand-lettered sign in the shop that sold the tape, that "made it juicy."

Unlike Dasai's murder, Seso's death had not made news. But in fact, little having to do with either Lubanda or Lubandans had made news after that particularly savage assassination, the sole exception to this general indifference having been the slaughter of the animals held in the national zoo.

I'd long been back in the States, a graduate student at Wharton Business School, successfully studying the risks inherent in almost everything, when I'd heard of it. And although Mafumi's renegades had repeatedly demonstrated their love of brutality, nothing could have prepared me for the footage by then available on the Internet.

A year after Lubanda's independence, a wealthy London matron named Charlotte Hastings had decided that what this newly minted nation needed was a national zoo, and so, at her own considerable expense, she'd had one built.

It was small by Western standards, but it housed a collection of deer, goats, a few lions and other big cats, two elephants, and four or five giraffes, along with a small aviary and a pool of snoozing crocodiles.

A few days after President Dasai's death, Mafumi had declared a "White-Out"—twenty-four hours of celebratory destruction that included the ripping down of "white" advertisements and the looting and torching of "white" buildings and residences. Its culminating act was to be the demolition of Charlotte Hastings' "white zoo."

A mob of about two hundred had carried it out, mostly with pangas, but also with knobkerries, which had proven particularly effective on the birds of the zoo's tightly enclosed aviary. In the films, these airborne clubs could be seen hurtling toward the panicked birds, knocking them from the limbs to which they'd fled. As for the crocs, they'd been roped and cut to ribbons, mostly by teenagers using box cutters. A few of the larger and more dangerous animals had simply been riddled with automatic weapons fire, but the smaller ones had suffered a far more painful and protracted death, their legs hacked off, after which, mere groaning torsos, they'd been slashed and clubbed to death while the zoo's liberators danced the *toyi-toyi* around them, the women ululating in a strange, bloodcurdling ecstasy as the pangas rose and fell, sending droplets of blood raining down upon the crowd.

These were horrid images of the madness that had befallen Lubanda in the years following my brief stay there. Bill had once said that the road that led from loving Lubanda to hating it was short and straight, and in a sense, I realized as I thought of Seso and opened myself to a dark cavalcade of memories, it was a road I'd taken to its cold dead end.

At precisely that moment, I also came to understand that Bill's call had sounded in me like a fire bell in the night. Something of that distant, tragic year still floated inside me, insistent, accusatory, reminding me that a grave error is like a rogue star, eternally polluting the vastness with its smoldering trail of miasmic wrong, crashing into this or drawing that into its unforgiving gravity, but always moving, on and on into the vulnerable and unsuspecting expanse.

As if fixed in a mental circuit I could not escape, I went back to that first day, when I'd gotten off the plane and been whisked to an orientation meeting where I was treated to a brief history of Lubanda under French, German, and at last British rule, then directed to a room whose door had been fitted with a neatly hand-lettered sign that said "Tumasi," surrounded by a circle of paper sunflowers.

I waited in that room for almost ten minutes before a slightly overweight, curly-headed young man entered, thrust out his hand, and introduced himself as Bill Hammond. He'd worked in the Peace Corps before coming to Lubanda, he told me, and had expected to be in the country for only a couple of years. But to his surprise, he'd "developed a crush" on the place, and so had signed on with an NGO called Hope for Lubanda.

"And you?" he asked. "What's your story?"

"There's not much to tell," I admitted. "I'm from a small town in the Midwest. I went to the University of Wisconsin. After that, I moved to New York and got a job teaching."

"Let me guess, a ghetto school?"

I nodded.

"So you're the type who, in the sixties, would have been down South working in voter registration drives, that sort of thing."

"I suppose so."

"English major?"

"With a concentration in the classics," I said. "Mostly Greek theater and the Greek myths."

Bill handed me a large envelope. "You'll find a few orientation pamphlets in there. Most of it is routine stuff, but you should make yourself very familiar with the Lubandan Constitution, because when you meet government officials, it impresses them if you've taken the trouble to learn its provisions and amendments. It's a show of respect."

I smiled. "I'll commit it to memory."

Bill glanced toward the window, where, just beyond the outskirts of the city, the Lubandan vastness spread out and out, all its mountains and its plains, the twining river that circled the capital, the great savanna over which the nomads roamed.

"It's strange how the die is cast, Ray," he said. "The fact that if rhinoceroses could have been domesticated, the Africans might have ridden them to Calais." He looked at me and smiled. "They'd have been Sherman tanks against those puny little European horses." His smile turned down slightly, a movement that betrayed his darker line of thought. "Tumasi is in the middle of the bush. Mostly nomads wandering around. There are only a few farms up that way. Strictly subsistence." He plopped down in one of the metal chairs, swung his arm over the other, the posture of an amiable traveling salesman. "So, is this your first time in Lubanda?" he asked.

"Yes."

"You'll never forget it."

I'd always known that there are short goodbyes and long ones, but with Bill's call I'd discovered that there were certain things no farewell can put behind you, that we are made, in the end, by the things we can't forget.

On the heels of that recognition, Martine returned to me in the peculiar, disjointed way of memory. It was not a vision of the first time I'd seen her, nor the last, but of somewhere around the midpoint of the time I'd known her.

In this memory, she is standing in her spare field, a hardscrabble farmer if ever there was one. We have just walked the land line of her acreage, where she's pointed out the plowed earth and told me what she's planted. The bright light of the sun turns her red hair to flame. She looks away, then faces me again, staring at me so intently I feel like a small animal in the crosshairs of her gaze.

"What are you thinking, Martine?" I ask her.

She gazes at me a moment, then bends forward, takes up a handful of soil, and looks at it as if, for all the world, she is part of the earth she now lets stream from her spreading fingers. "It's very odd, I know," she says with a sudden, radiant smile, "but when I walk these fields, or into the village, or out into the bush, l feel the strangest joy."

Joy. Yes, that had been it, I thought now as I recalled that moment. Martine had found joy in the very look and feel and tastes and sounds of Lubanda, and amid those richly sensual delights, she had awakened each day as if it were Christmas morning and there, before her, arrayed beneath the glittering tree, bound in bright colors and ribboned with gold, had lain the richest of life's pleasures to unwrap.

This memory lingered awhile before I returned myself to the risk-aversive world I'd chosen after leaving Lubanda. I knew that had I gone on to have a normal life after Tumasi, been able to forget what happened there, what I did there, I might later have married a woman who, at this critical moment of risk assessment, would surely have asked worriedly, "Why, Ray? Why open yourself up to all that again?"

I knew what my response would have been.

*Because I have to.*

"And why is that?"

My answer would have been simple: *Because it is long and sad and red with blood, my tale of Lubanda.*

And yet, even as I imagined such an exchange, I knew that although my story was Lubandan in the sense of having taken place during my Lubandan interval, Martine's tale, at least in the larger sense, was not Lubandan at all. Rather, it was the story of one who'd believed she had a home only to discover that she didn't, believed that love was enough, when it wasn't, believed that he who'd loved her most would have understood the singular joy that had been hers and helped her keep it. I had no doubt that to believe such things strongly, and follow them courageously, as Martine had done, should have bestowed a measure of victory upon her final act. But that day, as I confronted my year in Lubanda once again, it seemed to me that instead of crowning her with laurel, Martine's good faith—the very substance of her unique and precious happiness—had merely opened the door to a far more tragic fate, and in doing so proved yet again how lonely are the brave.

# Three

"Some people think the elephant head was given to the club by Teddy Roosevelt," Bill told me as we entered the main hall of the Harvard Club, "but it was really a guy named William Sewall, Class of 1897, who shot it." He glanced about at the other animal heads that adorned the paneled walls. "Along with some other unfortunate creatures."

I noticed a moose and an ibex, with its gracefully curled horns. There were warthogs and reindeer, too, along with a wapiti. The guns of Harvard worthies had fired on these animals in North America and Asia, in Kenya and Tanzania. There must have been a time, I thought, when they'd felt their reach infinite. Perhaps they still did.

"There's always some politically correct talk of taking down these trophies," Bill continued. "But so far, the board has voted no."

With that, he turned and escorted me into the dining room, where we chatted briefly before a waiter came forward with pad and pen. "Gentlemen?" he asked quietly.

"Have whatever you like, Ray," Bill said. "The trust has deep pockets."

I ordered a cup of fruit. Bill had the works. He'd always been portly, but now he was hovering near obesity, which made him look a bit sloppy despite the Hickey Freeman suit. It was hard to look at him without calculating the many risks his eating habits had accrued: high cholesterol, gout, blockages of various arteries, fatty liver. By no standard could he be judged attractive, and yet he had the distinct air of a man well acquainted with remote places and peoples, and the table talk of such people is always spiced with the exotic and the faintly dangerous, neither of which had been part of my life for a very long time.

"So, still a bachelor?" Bill asked.

"Marriage is risky," I said with a quick smile, "and parenthood is riskier still."

"Risk management is theoretically a good thing, of course," Bill said. Then he added with a hint of warning, "But in real life, you have to take risks, don't you?"

"Not really, no," I answer. "For that reason, first base will always be the most crowded."

"I thought you were a classicist," Bill said with a laugh. "What's with the sports allusions?"

"My clients like them," I told him truthfully.

"Your clients," Bill repeated. "So, tell me, what do you do for them exactly?"

"Mostly I advise investors looking to buy a failing business on the chance they can turn it around," I said.

"What do you tell them?"

"To calculate the assets, subtract the debt, then take a leap into the dark."

"It's the darkness you stress, I'll bet."

"Risk is always risk," I said.

"No doubt," Bill agreed.

After leaving Lubanda, he'd landed a job in the State Department, the African desk, never an important position and probably a career dead end, nothing but famine and AIDS, warlords and atrocities. The good news was that he'd parlayed his brief experience at State into a cushy job of funding aid programs throughout the continent. He was now at the top of the heap, the Mansfield Trust being a kind of holding company for a large number of charitable institutions and NGOs. At its recommendation, billions in aid might or might not pour into any particular country. Its decisions were closely followed by senators and representatives, as well as by the USIA, the International Monetary Fund, and a host of less muscular organizations. The stamp of the Mansfield Trust was a green light to open the dam and let aid cascade in. If Mansfield turned off the tap, other means would have to be found to deal with a nation's problems, abject supplication having failed.

"Do you still have plenty to spend?" I asked. "I would have thought the last downturn might have narrowed the pipe a little."

"No, the people with the big bucks always have big bucks," Bill said. "The problem is that they generally prefer to give to the opera or the art museum, cultural stuff that gets their name in the program or guarantees invitations to prominent events. That's the kind of giving that makes them feel like big shots. But they also respond to pictures of kids with bloated bellies and flies on their faces."

"Which is what you give them?"

Bill was not at all defensive. "Sure, but not enough to gag a maggot. And as you know, Ray, there's always the unpredictable thing that turns off the spigot. That business in Mogadishu, for example. A dancing, cheering mob dragging American soldiers through the streets. Talk about fund-drive hell. People close their wallets when they see shit like that. They don't say it, of course, but they watch that howling mob and they say, 'Fuck those goddamn savages.' So they punish a whole continent for what a few thugs do."

When I made no response to this, Bill said quite pointedly, "You're not like that, are you, Ray?"

"I don't know what you mean."

"I guess I'm asking if you're still an idealist."

"Well, the answer is, I'm not," I told him.

Bill looked anything but surprised. "Truth be told, I'm not either, really," he said. He looked at me quite seriously. "Once you give human nature a seat at the table, the progressive horizon narrows right away." He leaned back slightly. "But that sense of mission, that feeling that brought you to Lubanda back in the day, is there any of that left in you?"

My expression answered for me.

In response to it, Bill smiled, but sadly. "Well, hope is easy to lose. Especially in a place like Lubanda."

"We could afford to lose hope," I reminded him. "We had someplace to go."

He knew I was talking about Martine.

"A tragic case," he said. "You can't have a balanced life if you don't love your country. Isn't that what one of your precious Greeks said?"

He was referencing Plato, of course. "Martine loved her country," I told him. "The problem is that her country didn't love her back."

Bill was silent for a moment. I suspected that he was trying to find an appropriate return, something that would put a soothing perspective on Martine's fate. But there was no way to do that, as he clearly discovered, so he simply gave up and turned to the matter that had brought me here.

"Seso was found in one of those cheap hotels the African street vendors live in," he said. "Not much more than an SRO, but big enough for them to squat with their phony Rolex watches and Gucci bags." He smiled in that sardonic way of his. "Made in China, of course. Nobody makes anything in Africa anymore. They don't even make sisal. Not for themselves or anybody else."

"Nylon came along," I said. "Who buys sisal?"

"Plenty of people, actually," Bill answered. "Brazil produces two hundred fifty thousand tons. Kenya doesn't produce a tenth of that."

He waited for me to make some argument against this dire assessment of the continent's lack of productivity, but I had none to offer. Everything had gone wrong. The three C's of devastation: corruption, crime, chaos. Add the rampant spread of AIDS to that mix and the road to hell was fully paved. Of course, it was easy to lay all this at the foot of that fourth demonic C, colonialism. At a conference in Cape Town, I'd even heard an academic apologist claim that rampant black-on-black rape was caused by the anger of African men in the wake of colonialism, a causal link that seemed farcical by almost any standard.

Bill appeared to see some part of this going through my mind, and so he said nothing more on the subject, but instead drew a photograph from his jacket pocket, lay it facedown on the table, and slid it over to me.

"Seso," he said.

I picked up the picture and felt an unexpected tremor of emotion, one of those silent gasps the soul makes quite involuntarily, as if to remind you that it's still there.

In the photograph, Seso lies in a littered back alley. He is on his back, his arms folded over the orb of his stomach. As for dress, it was strictly African street vendor: a long sleeved shirt, cheap pants frayed at the cuffs, a cracked brown belt. The shirt's open collar revealed a deep but slender line around his throat.

"Garroted," I said. "Piano wire?"

"Mafumi's favorite, wasn't it? He liked to draw them up slowly, as I recall, using a hand crank operated by the victim's wife or children."

Such had been the tale. I had no idea if it was true.

"Where'd you get the picture?" I asked.

"The cops gave it to me," Bill answered. "It seems they found a paper with my name and phone number in Seso's room. A detective by the name of Max Regal came to my office. He showed me the paper, and yes, there it was, my name and number."

"Why would Seso have had your name and number?" I asked.

Bill hesitated, but only briefly, then said, "Seso called me last week. He said he had something to show me, but he wouldn't tell me what it was."

He saw my doubtful look and lifted his hand. "Swear to God, Ray, I have no idea what he had."

"Did you tell the cop about the phone call?"

"Of course I did," Bill said. "This is a murder investigation."

I looked at the photograph again, Seso in his ruin, a picture that called up Lubanda with a vividness that seemed undimmed by time, so that I again saw him as I'd once known him, Watusi-tall, dressed in the flannel trousers and white cotton shirt he'd bought in Rupala and which, for Lubanda, passed for business dress.

Bill folded one beefy arm over the other. "Mind if I ask when you last heard from Seso?"

The question brought me back to the paneled stateliness of the Harvard Club.

"When I was in Lubanda ten years ago," I answered. "Before my unsuccessful attempt to make it back to Tumasi. We met in Rupala before I headed north."

"He was living in Rupala?" Bill asked.

"Yes," I answered. "He had a government job."

"Working for Mafumi?"

"He worked in the archive. I wouldn't call it 'working' for Mafumi."

"Okay, so you met in Rupala. Tell me about that."

"We just sat and talked for a while in Independence Square," I said. "There'd just been a public execution. Some prostitutes. Six of them were still hanging from the gibbet."

Bill looked at me doubtfully. "Since when have prostitutes been hanged in Lubanda?" he asked. "Mafumi preferred them, as I recall."

"These prostitutes were men," I told him, "And 'prostitution' was just the charge."

"Gay in Lubanda, what could be riskier than that?" Bill took a sip of coffee. "So this work Seso was doing. Did he talk about that? The job in the archive, I mean."

I folded my napkin and placed it neatly on the table beside my plate. "Actually, you could hardly call it an archive because it was just a few rooms where papers were stashed," I said. "There was no order to it. Seso was just going through the papers."

"Looking for what?"

"Money, of course."

"What does that mean?"

"It means that Mafumi's people thought President Dasai and his cronies had stashed funds outside the country," I said. "He had that Third World fantasy of a Swiss bank account, so he set people like Seso, people who could read and do arithmetic, to work finding it."

"How did Seso seem when you met him?"

"He was guarded, which was natural enough," I answered. "He said he'd married, and that his wife was expecting. When I got back here, I wrote him a letter, but he never wrote back and I never heard from him again."

"Those Lubandans have a way of vanishing, don't they?" Bill said with a kind of dark nostalgia.

I glanced toward the far end of the room, the animal heads that hung in the distance. "So, what do you want from me, Bill? Why this meeting, all these questions? I'm not a cop or a private investigator."

Bill glanced down, then looked up again, his gaze now quite full of purpose. "I'd like for you to nose around a little, see what you can find out about Seso." He allowed a moment for this to sink in, then added, "I know I'm asking a lot." He was silent for a time, his gaze unaccountably directed toward the great elephant head, a creature too magnificent, its death too tragic, to be memorialized this way, the masthead of an entrance hall. "Lubanda was hard on everybody."

"It was hardest on Martine," I said.

I suddenly saw her just as she'd first appeared to me, her hair tucked beneath a checkered scarf, leaning over a basket, glancing up as I approached. How like Martine that first glance had been, a no-nonsense expression, but somewhat quizzical. Everything she looked at, she questioned, as if the only thing she could be sure of was herself.

Bill released a breath that seemed weighted with bad memories. "I sometimes wonder how different things might have been if Martine had just—"

"Stop," I said sharply. I glanced away, then, after a moment, turned back to Bill. "Just . . . stop," I repeated softly.

And he did, his eyes darting from table to table before he settled them once again on me.

"So, will you do it, Ray?" he asked. "Will you make a few inquiries into Seso's murder?"

Before answering, I asked a question of my own. "Why do you care about this? You haven't seen Seso in years."

"Well, the truth is, the Mansfield Trust is poised to offer a great deal of aid to Lubanda," Bill answered. "And if we do that, so will everybody else. It could change the country."

"What does Seso's death have to do with whether the Mansfield Trust opens the money chute?" I asked.

"It probably doesn't," Bill answered. "But it's a loose end that bothers me. I like all my ducks in a row." He smiled. "Mixed metaphors. Sorry." His tone grew serious. "Think of it in terms of your business. I don't want to risk missing the mark with regard to Lubanda. If Seso had something I need to see, then I want to see it."

"You're afraid not to see it," I said.

"Life's a trickster, Ray," Bill said. "I like to know if there's a rabbit in the hat." He looked at me in the way of one who'd shared a searing experience. "It's always the thing we don't know that destroys us."

A staple truth of risk assessment came to mind: the fear of loss is sometimes all that is needed to incur it. Certainly the awful knowledge of what I'd done in Lubanda had kept me from going back to Tumasi, Martine's farm, my one year of living dangerously. Save for the single failed attempt I'd made ten years before, I'd avoided the risk of going back there, or even of thinking about it, the error of my own actions still more than my self-protective soul could take.

"Well?" Bill asked.

Classicist that I remained, I suddenly thought of Artemisia, how fiercely Xerxes' only female commander had fought at Salamis. It was a bravery the king had found merely ill-fated rather than inspiring, however. "My men are become women and my women become men," he'd said, and with that stark admission retired from the field. Martine was like that fabled woman warrior, it seemed to me, and should have received Lubanda's praise, rather than its ire.

"I need an answer, Ray," Bill said, though softly, fully aware of the weight of his request.

As if there were a dark insistence that I could no longer avoid the verdict that honesty required, I sank the photograph Bill had given me into the pocket of my jacket. "I'll do what I can," I said.

# Four

After leaving the Harvard Club, I took the subway to my office on Rector Street.

"Mr. Douglas will be here at eleven," Gail said.

Gail was my only employee, a woman who regularly retreated to the street for a cigarette, always returning with the smell of its smoke on her clothes and in her hair. She was overweight, made no attempt to exercise, and ate anything she wanted without regard to either calories or nutrition. As the welcoming face of a risk management firm she was wildly inappropriate, but there was something in Gail's willing acceptance of statistically unacceptable risks that appealed to me. Perhaps she reminded me of that long-ago time when I'd taken the ultimate one, bet everything on a single chip and spun the wheel.

"And you've got Mr. Carter at two," Gail added as I swept past her desk and stepped into my office, where, rather than taking my usual place behind my desk, I turned to the window. From that perch I'd once been able to see the upper stories of the World Trade Center. Their sudden, cataclysmic collapse had added an unexpected urgency to the notion of risk assessment, but the magnitude of their fall had faded with time, and my clients had returned to the more mundane risks inherent in shifting markets and floating currencies.

People can rarely pinpoint the forces that shape them, but I'd always known that I'd chosen a career in risk assessment in the wake of my Lubandan experience, the dark surprise it had brought to my life. For twenty years I'd lingered in its shadows, but Seso's murder now made reliving it more urgent, so that I found myself once again drifting back to my time in Lubanda.

For the most part it had been very pleasant, at least at the beginning. I'd been given a Land Cruiser and directions to Tumasi. As I pulled into it that first afternoon, I saw a group of small concrete buildings not far from the market. They were painted different colors: white, green, bright orange. A few had wooden shutters, but most of the windows were nothing but square openings into the interior, without glass or anything else to hold out rain or noise or whatever insects or animals might find their way in. I'd been told that mine was painted green and had a white door, and sure enough, there it stood, just off what appeared to be the market square. I remembered thinking, *home,* and feeling a wonderful excitement at the prospect of just how far away I was from anything I'd previously experienced. There was exhilaration in that feeling, a sense of adventure combined with service, a heady mix if ever there was one, since there is no better, nor riskier, amalgam than pleasure mixed with purpose.

The market wasn't particularly busy, though a few people strolled about the stalls, tradesmen and customers with whom I would become familiar during the next few months. Quite a few had stopped whatever they were doing and turned to look at me, or perhaps the Land Cruiser, though none of them approached, and most resumed their usual activities almost immediately.

For my part, I simply stood for a moment and took the place in— the stalls, the chickens roaming free, a couple of camels, an old woman who squatted under a tree. The market was animated, but not what a Westerner would call lively. No one appeared hurried.

I'd started to turn back to the Land Cruiser and unpack my gear when I gave a final glance into the market and she was suddenly, strikingly there.

I'd not seen a white woman since getting off the plane in Rupala, and this one—tall, slender, her skin only slightly tanned—seemed more like a vision. She was standing near one of the stalls. There was a basket in front of her, and she was fiddling about with whatever was inside it. I'd no doubt made quite a display upon entering the village, a cloud of red dust behind me, but she had not been one of those who'd turned to see it.

At that moment, I might have unloaded my gear and gone directly to the building that had been designated as my home in Tumasi. Why didn't I? The answer is simple. Whether she was American, Dutch, French, German, or anything else, I'd instantly pegged Martine as a woman, as it were, of my tribe.

She surely guessed this as well, for she seemed not at all surprised when I came toward her, though she looked up from her basket only after I'd closed most of the distance between us. It was then I'd noticed her most distinctive characteristic: eyes so luminously green they seemed lighted from behind.

"Hello," she said when I reached her.

"Hi," I said. "I'm Ray Campbell."

She offered her hand, and the instant I took it, I realized how very different it was from the other female hands I'd touched. Those other, far less tested hands had been creamed, oiled, moisturized, daily soaped and showered. Martine's hands had never known such pampering. They were not only rough, they were damaged, wounded by brier and scarred by thistle. Heat had parched them, and dust had dried them just as it had the hands of the village women I was later to know in Tumasi.

"Martine Aubert," she said.

She was tall, with broad shoulders, and looked to be about my age, which was twenty-five. Her skin had darkened in the sub-Saharan sun, but even so, it was only a shade darker than my own. A line of freckles, very small and light, ran from just beneath her right eye over the bridge of her nose to the left one. In another place she would have looked like that fabled girl next door. Here, however, the color of her skin and the texture of her hair rendered her as out of place as a traffic light.

"Tourists don't usually come to Tumasi," she said.

"I'm not a tourist," I told her. I nodded toward the little concrete building that was to be my house in Tumasi. "I'm moving into that one."

"How long will you be here?" she asked.

"I'm not sure," I told her. "A year. Maybe more. How long do you expect to be here?"

Something in her eyes suggested how indulgent she was of my question, as if it had been posed by a little boy on his first day in class.

"I will never leave," she said. "I am Lubandan."

*Never leave? Lubandan?*

Until that moment, and despite the evidence of her hands, I'd thought her a fellow aid worker, citizen of some donor nation to which she would certainly return to regale dinner parties with tales of her Lubandan experience. But as I now noticed, her clothes were indistinguishable from the long skirts and loose blouses of the other women of Tumasi. She wore the same colored scarf on her head and the same crudely made sandals on her feet. The basket before her was identical to those carried by the other women and a quick glimpse inside it showed me that its contents were typical of those bought by anyone else at the market.

"You are American?" she asked.

I nodded.

"Many of you are coming here, I suppose," she said. "To Lubanda, I mean."

Her accent had a characteristic Lubandan lilt, a soft fluidity to it, a sense of words strung together like small wooden beads. For some reason I'd expected to hear a British accent, but there were no soft a's, no "cahn't" or "tomahto." As I later learned, her first language had been the French of her Belgian father, but he'd also taught her English, which she spoke slowly, with a measured gait, in a manner that was quite precise, but formal, too. She rarely used contractions, for example, and there were times when her English took on the syntax of her native French. She always said, "May I pose a question?" rather than "May I ask a question?" There were also times when specific English words eluded her and she would search for them, sometimes finding them, sometimes not. I would always remember that one of them had been "atonement."

"I hope that you will enjoy your time in my country," she said. "And also, I hope that when you return to your country, you will speak well of Lubanda . . . as it is."

She did not elaborate on the meaning she so obviously attached to those last three words, but simply returned to arranging the things in her basket, though now it appeared more like an inventory.

She was still going through the basket when a tall man in orange robes approached her. Martine stopped what she was doing and turned to him. For a moment they spoke in what I presumed to be the local dialect, then Martine reached into her basket, brought out a bag, and gave it to the man. He nodded, turned, and walked away.

"What was that all about?" I asked.

"We have made an exchange," Martine said in that same slow, deliberate way, as if she had to think of the words before she said them. "I give him something he needs and he gives me something I need. To me, he is giving wood. It is a wood that is from the north. It is good for carving."

"I didn't see him give you any wood."

"This is because it is valuable," Martine explained. "He is a Lutusi, and if something is of great value, he does not show it until he knows what I will give him in return."

"Where's the wood then?"

"It is hidden," Martine said, then went back to sorting things out in her bag. "He will bring it to me in time." She stopped and looked at me. "That is the way of the Lutusi."

She said this with neither admiration nor distain for this custom, an attitude I would come to know well in the coming months. Nor did I ever hear her romanticize Lubanda itself nor declare special powers for its people. She gave them no higher moral authority than anyone else, nor did she make any claim that their view of life was superior. Lubanda was what it was, a place she neither demeaned nor glorified.

I glanced about the market. Most of that day's customers were dressed in the same orange robes as the man who'd just walked away. They moved slowly among the sheds and stalls, eyeing the goods.

"The Lutusi live by herding," Martine said matter-of-factly, when she noticed me watching them. "They are nomads. They bring things here that they gather in their travels." Her smile was delicate, but there was a strange force in her eyes. "When they are in this part of Lubanda, Tumasi is where they come to trade."

I glanced back toward the road that led out of the village.

"Where does the road go?" I asked.

"Into what you call 'the bush,'" Martine answered.

She returned to her basket and was still rifling through it when a young man approached us. He was dressed in brown slacks and a white, short-sleeve shirt. His gait was slow, but arrow-straight, and his stride was long.

"Fareem," Martine said without looking at either of us, "this is Ray Campbell. He is from the United States."

Fareem nodded softly, but said nothing. He was very tall and very thin, and I instantly thought of him in terms of Hollywood myth, one of the Zulu warriors who'd attacked the English forces at Isandlwana, slashed their way through the sort of men later portrayed by Stanley Baker and Michael Caine, and delivered a defeat that had stunned Imperial England.

Martine finished arranging her goods inside the basket. "It is for balance," she told me without my asking. "That is why I must put things in the basket just so." She smiled again, this time quite warmly. "Welcome to Lubanda."

"Thank you."

She placed the basket on her head, where it seemed immediately to find purchase, then turned and headed toward the road. Once there, she stopped and looked back at me. "May I pose the question, who sent you here?"

"I am working for Hope for Lubanda," I said.

She nodded toward my Land Cruiser. "Is it true that Rupala now has many cars like that one?"

"Quite a few, yes."

"So many like you are coming?"

I nodded. "Lots of people are trying to help, yes," I said. "Lubandans are the last people to get their independence and so—"

"So we Lubandans should learn from the history of our neighbors," Martine interrupted. Now her smile transformed itself into something other than a smile, and I saw a hint of uncertainty in her eyes. "If we can." She looked at me in what I would come to know as that searching way of hers, like someone trying to bring a distant shore into focus. "Come to my farm for dinner tonight," she said, "You are a stranger, so it is customary among Lubandans that we give you food. My farm is at the end of Tumasi Road."

"Thank you," I said. "What time?"

"Before sunset."

With that, she turned and moved up the road. I watched for a time, then snapped back to attention and realized that Seso had remained at the Land Cruiser, leaning against it. He was watching the orange-robed Lutusi move through the market, a curious sadness in his face, as if he were looking at old photographs of a time gone by.

"We should unload," I called to him, and we immediately set to work. Within a little while we'd unpacked our supplies. We'd brought very little to Tumasi because the house had already been furnished with bedding, a desk, furniture, and I expected to buy my weekly supplies in the market, where, as I saw, there was plenty of grain, meat, milk, and whatever else I'd need.

"There's more here than I expected," I told Seso.

He nodded. "There is enough for everyone," he said as one from another country might have said. "There is plenty."

I told him about Martine's dinner invitation, but he didn't want to go.

"No, I will stay here," he said, and offered no further explanation.

"All right," I said.

Toward evening I arrived at a farmhouse that was considerably smaller than what I expected and which I'd already imagined as roomy, with tall windows and comfortably graced by a spacious porch. In fact, Martine lived in what seemed the bush version of a house: unpainted, sloping oddly, ill-suited to endure anything but heat. A single tree sprouted in the front yard. Otherwise there was nothing but plowed fields all about save for a small fence behind which a few goats lazily roamed around, nibbling at the spare vegetation.

I brought the Land Cruiser to a halt, creating a cloud of red dust that drifted, then curled over and fell back to earth. Even this seemed strange, as if the dust had been unaccustomed to such violent disturbance and had quickly returned to its ancient rest.

The door of the house was open, but I saw no one inside.

I tapped at the door. Still nothing.

Suddenly, Martine came around a corner, carrying a basket of grain on her head.

"So you have arrived," she said.

"It was easy, since there's only one road," I told her.

She took the basket from her head. It had no handles, so she held it in her arms.

"Please, come in," she said as she stepped up on the porch and gestured toward the door.

It would be too late before I fully understood the meaning of Martine's house, how completely it had both mirrored and expressed her character. In fact, my first thought was no more complicated than the simple observation that she was the opposite of a hoarder. There were a few chairs and a couple of small tables. Two cots, one of which had been done up to serve as a sofa, rested on opposite sides of the farmhouse's single room. A gray cord made from sisal hung just below the ceiling, and a curtain had been fashioned that could be drawn across the length of the room, presumably for privacy. To these Spartan furnishings, Martine had added a clay oven, and beside it, a stack of wood. All light came from candles, and the only bathroom, as I learned later, was an outhouse whose contents Martine and Fareem emptied by turns.

In fact, there was only one exception to the spare nature of these furnishings: an old gramophone with a black crank.

"Does it work?" I asked.

Martine nodded. "It is the one thing my father brought with him from the Congo. Not the only thing, no. There are some records. Most

47

of them cannot be played on the machine anymore. The heat is bad for them. And the dust. But with a few, it is possible."

"Do you ever play them?"

"Not so much," she answered, then turned back toward the center of the room. "Would you like a drink? I make it from fermented honey that comes from the hives. It is strong."

She walked through the back door of the house, then returned with two bottles of a thick, amber liquid.

"So, how did you happen to come by this farm?" I asked after the first sip.

"My father was the first to come here," Martine answered. "He was very young. For some time, he worked in Rupala, in the coatroom at the French consulate. While he was in Rupala, he learned a few Lubandan dialects, as well as English. In fact, an Englishman had told him about this farm. None of the whites had wanted to stay in Lubanda. They had come for gold and other mythical riches that didn't exist. With no natural resources of value, land in Lubanda was cheap, particularly in the savanna. He bought the farm with the little money he had saved, and settled it with a Belgian girl he had met one day in the park."

"My guess is that she had red hair," I said airily.

"No, my father did," Martine said. "It is he who raised me."

She appeared quite pointedly to avoid any further discussion of her mother, and so I didn't make any further inquiry in that direction.

She shook her head, then took a sip of her home brew. "Do you like it?" she asked with a nod toward the bottle in my hand.

I did. It was sweet, but the kick was strong.

"Another glass of this and I wouldn't make it back to Tumasi," I said.

Martine smiled. "If you are drunk, you can leave the road and sleep under the stars. No one will bother you." She pointed across the room to shelves that lined the wall, laden with scores of books and what looked to be official reports of one kind or another.

"My library," she said. "Come."

We walked over to the shelves and Martine stood silently while I perused them. There were around a hundred books, most of them in French, a few novels, mostly Balzac and Stendhal. But the great preponderance of her books appeared to deal with African history, much of it recent. True, she had several volumes having to do with the "scramble for Africa," the history of its colonization. But most of her histories chronicled the continent's varied struggles for independence, the achievement of nationhood, then what had happened after it had either been gained or granted, the grim narratives of Zimbabwe and Uganda, Kenya, and the like.

"Have you read much about Africa?" Martine asked.

"Just some preparatory stuff," I told her. "And I just got a packet of material from the agency—the Lubandan Constitution and a few other government documents. Back in college I read Mary Kingsley's book about coming to West Africa." I laughed. "It was quite funny in places. I remember how she is told to make quick contact with the Wesleyans because they are the only ones with feathers on their hearses."

"Hmm," Martine breathed in that vaguely meditative way of hers.

"And that book of useful African phrases she reads," I went on. "I remember that one of the useful phrases was, 'Why is this man not yet buried?'"

I'd expected Martine to be amused by these little anecdotes, but instead she shook her head at their absurdity.

"It is hard to be a foreigner," she said. "I would never want to be one."

She smiled briefly, then became quite solemn and in that mood took a book from the shelf and handed it to me. "This book is a history of the *Force Publique*." She watched me silently for a moment, her gaze quite penetrating, as if trying to discover if this meant anything to me. "My grandfather did very bad things in Congo when he was a member of the *Force*." She nodded toward the book. "You should read it as a warning of the evils foreigners can do."

"Well, foreigner or not, I intend to do good things," I assured her.

She looked at me somberly. "Of course you do." She glanced toward the open front door, where Fareem suddenly appeared. "Now we can have dinner," she said. "I hope you like goat."

I had never eaten goat, but found it quite tasty. The table talk that went with it was mostly about farming in Tumasi, an area of Lubanda that had little water. At that point, since I was in search of a project, I seized upon the idea of irrigation, a suggestion neither Martine nor Fareem appeared to find particularly noteworthy, though neither offered any reason for this.

Still later, we talked a little about President Dasai—his popularity in the West; the fact that with his administration now running Lubanda, the country would likely be the beneficiary of a steady stream of aid.

"That will make Lubanda ripe for the picking," Fareem said.

I looked at him quizzically.

"Bad people will suddenly have an interest in Lubanda," he explained.

"Bad people?"

"Warlords, you call them," Fareem said. "They will see all these foreign things coming in, and they will think, *Hmm, I could take all that. It could all be mine.*"

Martine placed her napkin on the table in a gesture that was almost violent. "Dinner is not for politics," she said, then rose and walked out onto the porch, leaving Fareem and me alone at the table.

"She is afraid," Fareem told me.

"Of what?" I asked.

50

"The future," Fareem answered. "What will happen in Lubanda."

He looked at me with the anxious gaze of a man who had much to protect. "She may need a foreign friend," he confided in a tone I found unexpectedly intimate. "Will you be that friend, Ray?"

I looked out toward the porch, where Martine stood alone, leaning against one of its wooden posts. There was no way I could have imagined ever betraying her or causing her the slightest harm. And so with full confidence, I turned back and looked straight into Fareem's passionately inquiring eyes.

"Yes," I said. "I will."

# Five

It was Gail's voice that broke through this recollection.

"Mr. Douglas is here," she said.

I nodded, and on that signal she escorted him into my office, where we exchanged pleasantries, then got down to business. The shakiness of the Eurozone had put my client into a sweat. He wanted reassurance that one of the world's largest economies wasn't about to crumble. Unfortunately I could offer him no such certainty.

"Some events are too large to predict or evaluate," I told him. "The fall of the Soviet Union, for example, or the attacks on 9/11."

I would normally have supported this statement with up-to-the-minute references to this book or that paper, a show meant to demonstrate that I was fiercely in the moment when it came to the latest research. One aspect of risk reduction has to do with trusting your source, and in my field, I'd long ago discovered that there is nothing like a dazzling display of citations to shore up the confidence of a skittish client. But honesty is also important in risk management, and the starkest and most obvious of all life's truths is that its course cannot be reliably predicted. One afternoon, while drying off from a swim in the pool, you notice an unslighlty blemish. Six months later you're dead. *Such,* as the fabled Australian criminal Ned Kelly declared in his final words from the gallows, *is life.*

"The simple fact is that world-transforming events can never be factored into a risk assessment," I told my client, "save to posit the possibility of their sudden and unexpected arrival."

"So, what am I paying you for, Ray?" Walter asked half-jokingly, though undoubtedly with a keen eye to my fee.

"You pay me for reassuring you that you've done all you could do to protect yourself against the unexpected," I answered truthfully. "That no matter what happens to your assets, you can't be blamed or accused of malfeasance. You pay me to protect your soul from moral hazard."

Walter looked at me oddly, as if he'd suddenly glimpsed a fissure in my rock-solid character.

For that reason I should have stopped, taken a breath, and gotten back on track. But something in me would not be held in check.

"The greatest risk anyone runs is to be found wanting, inadequate, not up to the job," I added, the pace of my voice quite measured, almost stark, a one-man Greek chorus. "It is reducing the risk of that kind of ultimate, end-of-game failure that we all seek."

Something in Walter's gaze deepened.

"Where did you learn about risk assessment?" he asked, almost warily, as if I'd changed shape before him.

*In Lubanda,* I thought, but I didn't say this to Walter. Instead I got ahold of myself and nimbly shifted to my studies at Wharton, where I seized a few anecdotes about the professors I'd encountered there, the risk management tidbits of wisdom they'd dispensed, all of it designed to regain his briefly endangered sense of my personal and professional solidity, as well as to secure the illusion that this get-together was mostly a matter of reaffirming our hail-fellow-well-met companionability. It worked, and a few minutes later he was chuckling at some joke of mine or nodding appropriately when I made a point. This was followed by a farewell handshake, and I was once again alone in my office, staring silently out my window, seeing not Manhattan beyond the glass, but the arid reaches of the savanna that spread out on either side of Tumasi Road, recalling that upon arrival I'd known nothing of the place beyond what I'd read in a pamphlet published by Hope for Lubanda, its pages adorned with pictures of cheerful Lubandans singing and dancing. "The hope of Lubanda is in the hearts of its people," the pamphlet had proclaimed in its ludicrously inspirational final line, "and you are here to help them realize that hope."

Even so, it was true. I had, indeed, come to help, though with few skills anyone could have considered useful, unless a certain acquaintanceship with classical literature might prove vital to building a school or sinking a well or growing maize among a people who would ultimately resist its introduction as a staple crop, this because, as it turned out, and as Martine had later written in her *Open Letter*, "The minds of we Lubandans are neither as open nor as malleable as you imagine them to be."

How true this had proven to be, I thought, and instantly found myself in the village again, returned to my first day in Tumasi, watching Martine make her way up the road, walking with a basket on her head, Fareem strolling beside her. I could no longer say just how long I'd peered down the road, focused upon and oddly mesmerized by Martine as she continued on and on. I knew only that I'd watched until the horizon had at last consumed her, and she was gone.

The vision of her vanishing lingered throughout the day as one client followed another. In fact, it trailed me into the afternoon, by which time I felt as if I were being carried on a wave that was determinedly bearing me ever more deeply into the past, back to Martine and Fareem and Seso, to that long-ago trial by fire that had, in different ways, seared us all.

*Seso.*

Thinking of his murder brought to mind one of the central truths of risk assessment, namely, that the correct calculation of a risk rises in proportion to the accuracy, variety, and scope of obtainable information. It is for that reason that any risk assessment worthy of the name must rest upon a multitude of sources.

With regard to Seso's death, however, I had only one source, Rudy Salmon, a Wharton classmate who'd landed a job at One Police Plaza, then risen in the department's administrative ranks. He now held one of those posts that adhere like barnacles to the great lumbering ship of New York's municipal bureaucracy.

I knew no one else in the Police Department, however, and so it was to Rudy I made the call.

"Seso Alaya," Rudy said slowly, so that I knew he was writing down the information I'd given him, namely the victim's name, the location of the murder, the fact that a friend of mine's name and telephone number had been found in the dead man's room, and that my friend had been visited by the police as a result.

"Got any idea who paid this visit?" Rudy asked.

"A detective named Max Regal."

"And this was a homicide two days ago, at the Darlton Hotel on East Twenty-seventh Street."

I could hear the tap, tap, tap of Rudy's computer. "There was a homicide in that hotel, yes," he said after a moment, "What's your interest in this guy, Ray?"

"He had something he wanted to show to a client of mine," I answered. "Naturally, with Mr. Alaya now having been murdered, my client would like to know what he had."

"We're not talking guns, drugs, something of that sort, are we?" Rudy asked. "You can't say African without thinking contraband."

"I think the risk is very low of it being contraband," I answered truthfully.

"Okay," Rudy said. "Give me a few minutes. I'll call you back."

And he did.

"Well, Max Regal is still handling the case," he said. "Max and I go back a long way. He'd be more than happy to fill you in on what he knows—which isn't much, by the way."

"It's a start," I said. "Thanks, Rudy."

"Max can meet you tonight."

He gave me the name of a bar on Ninth Avenue, the old Hell's Kitchen, now one of the city's hot neighborhoods, its streets filled with young people, all of them distractedly texting as they walked, and thus quite oblivious to the risk of running into a fellow pedestrian.

Max Regal was seated at a table in a back corner. He was short and round, and had the tired look of a man who'd take the first deal he was offered for early retirement. His suit wasn't new, but it was less worn than his shoes. But *spanking* new wouldn't have mattered because Regal had the sort of disproportionate body that defeats off-the-rack tailoring, and for that reason he would always look as if he were wearing someone else's clothes. The good news was that the risk of appearing shabby appeared never to have occurred to him. He had an air of physical self-confidence, of being able to face a man, even a larger man, and make him blink.

"So, you're an amateur sleuth," he said with a vaguely cop-land swagger, as if to say, *You have no idea, my friend.*

"Not exactly," I said with a friendly smile. "But perhaps close enough."

I'd had little to do with policemen after leaving Lubanda, perhaps because that particular experience had been so fiercely troubling that I'd avoided all further contact with law enforcement of any kind.

"Thanks for seeing me," I said.

Regal nodded, then immediately got down to business. "Seso Alaya," he said. "We figured he was just another African trader who'd pissed off the competition. Then we found a name and a phone number

56

in the squat where he was living, and the name turned out to be a big shot. Rudy tells me that this big shot is your client?"

"Both a client and an old friend," I said.

"Well, as it turned out, your 'old friend' couldn't help us very much," Regal said. "Just told me that he'd gotten a call from the dead man, and that the dead man had something to show him."

"That's as much as he told me," I said.

"So what are you after?"

"Mr. Hammond thought I might be able to find out what Seso Alaya had to show him," I answered in my best professional voice, cool but cooperative.

When Regal said nothing, I added, "So, I'm just curious as to whether you have any leads."

"A couple," Regal said. "For one thing, we found some kind of pin in his mouth. The sort of thing you might stick in your lapel. Two swords crossed over each other. Any idea what that might mean?"

"Not swords, crossed pangas," I said. "Under its last ruler, a tyrant named Mafumi, they were the symbol of Lubanda. They were on the flag. It was Lubanda's version of a swastika."

"Where is this Mafumi character now?" Max asked.

"He's dead," I answered. "Lubanda has a new president now."

"So why would somebody put this pin in Alaya's mouth?"

"I don't know," I said. "I suppose it's possible that Seso was killed by a Mafumi agent. They don't just go away, the people close to a dictator."

"Could the pin have belonged to Alaya?"

"It's possible," I said. "Under Mafumi everyone in the government had to wear a crossed-pangas pin. It was part of the uniform. And since Seso worked for the government, he would have had a pin."

"What did he do for the government?" Regal asked.

"He worked in the archive," I said. "Sorting through old records."

"What else do you know about him?"

"He once worked for me," I answered. "In Lubanda years ago."

"When was the last time you heard from him?"

"We met in Rupala ten years ago. Nothing since."

"So you have no idea why he was in New York?"

"Other than to give my friend whatever it was he had for him, no."

"What was his connection to your friend?" Regal asked.

"I'm sure you asked him that," I said.

"Yeah, but it's always good to have another source, right?"

"We were all in Lubanda together. But until that call, Mr. Hammond hadn't had any contact with Mr. Alaya for over twenty years."

A waiter approached. Regal ordered a beer. I had a white wine.

"So," Regal said as the waiter stepped away. "Here's what I know about the case."

There wasn't much, and Regal went through it routinely and with surprisingly little attention to order, mentioning this or that as the mood struck him, sipping at his beer, pausing to tell a joke or make a comment on whatever came to mind. But disorganized though Regal's narrative was, a few spare facts came through: A janitor had found Seso's body in the alley behind the hotel where he lived. He'd obviously been murdered, but not before he'd been tortured. Regal had no idea where either the murder or the torture had occurred.

"The Africans have places where they do things," he said. "Places where blood feud grievances can be settled, for example. Their own courts. So I'm guessing they have special places for hurting people."

This might have as easily been urban myth as not, I thought, but it pointed to the fact that as far as Regal was concerned, Africans existed at a different place on the immigrant spectrum, their habits as unknowable as their motivations.

"They're never really *here*, you know?" he added. "They're always back *there*."

"What else do you know about Seso?" I asked.

"Well, the autopsy showed that there were no drugs in his blood," Regal answered. "And we couldn't find any prior criminal activity."

As to the reason Seso had been murdered, Regal hadn't found it.

He shrugged. "It could be anything from screwing someone else's woman to owing money." He sat back and stared at me pointedly. "You met him in Africa, I take it."

"In Lubanda," I answered. "I'd gone there to make some improvements in an area around the village of Tumasi. Seso was assigned to me. He was my translator, but he also did whatever needed to be done. Cooking. Odd jobs."

"It doesn't look like he ever improved his lot," Regal said. "Wrinkled pants. Ragged shirt. He could have been any of those traders you see around town." He paused briefly before offering his final assessment of the case. "We almost never get to the bottom of any of these killings. You got family feuds and tribal feuds, all kinds of stuff we know nothing about. I hear the Somalis are the worst when it comes to tribal murders."

"Seso wasn't Somali," I reminded him.

"Anyway, from Africa," Regal said, dismissively shrugging off the entire continent.

It was a grim assessment, but in terms of Africa's recent history, I couldn't entirely contradict it. As Martine's *Open Letter* had enumerated, in nation after nation the trajectory had been remarkably similar. The struggle for independence had first lifted the great father figures: Nkrumah, Kenyatta, and the like. These had been followed by the Amins and the Bokassas, the Mugabes, the Mobutus, rulers so psychopathic, their tyrannies so operatically over-the-top, they'd brought a funhouse mirror into Hell.

59

"I presume you canvassed the hotel," I said.

"Did you get your knowledge of police procedure from television or do you have some experience on the job?" Regal asked with a slightly mocking smile.

"Strictly television," I answered. "Did anybody talk?"

"One guy," Regal answered. "He lived across from the victim, and they had a few talks here and there, but according to this guy, Alaya was very closemouthed."

"Would you mind giving me this man's name?" I asked.

Regal hesitated. "You know, dipping your toe into a murder investigation could be dangerous. I presume Rudy told you that."

"He wouldn't have to," I said, "but I'll take my chances."

Something in the tone of this answer seemed to convince Regal that I'd figured these risks and accepted them. He took a notebook from his shirt pocket and flipped through it before he found the man's name.

"Dalumi," he said. "Herman Dalumi. Room 14-A."

"Thank you."

Regal closed the notebook and returned it to his pocket. "There's one more thing." He drew a paper from his jacket pocket and handed it to me. "It's a picture of the tattoo we found on the victim's back. The ME said it was done right before the murder."

I looked at the photo and suddenly felt not nostalgia, but its chilling opposite, not a sweet or even bittersweet return of old feelings, but a wrenching, aching one.

"Is the tattoo some kind of symbol, like those machetes?" Regal asked.

"I don't know," I answered softly.

"It seems to strike a chord," Regal said. "Like you recognized it."

I nodded. "It's an oyster shell," I told him. "There was a woman in Tumasi who used to carve shells like that out of wood. She would tie one to the other, so that they could be clicked together like castanets. She gave them to children who passed by her farm, and in return, the nomads always gave her something. A little cheese, maybe. Some goat's milk or a gourd."

In my mind I saw Martine on one of those scorching afternoons, a group of Lutusi gathered in the front yard of her farmhouse, the children dancing around her, clicking the wooden shells she'd just given them. An old man, wrapped in flowing orange robes, had strolled over to her with something covered in a sack. She'd taken it and bowed to him, then turned toward me. "The Lutusi do not accept handouts," she said in that softly pointed tone of hers. "They always give something in return." With that she unwrapped the cloth to find a small pot that clearly delighted her, turned, and spoke to the man in the Lutusi dialect.

"What did you tell him?" I asked, once he had returned to the other Lutusi lingering beside the road.

"I told him that what he gave me is useful," Martine answered. She turned the pot in her hands. "And it *is* useful."

A scraping sound brought me back to the present. It was Regal's chair as he scooted it forward. "So, what was this woman to Seso?"

"He knew her," I said. "That's all."

Regal looked disappointed. "So, that's a dead end then, that tattoo?"

"Probably."

We talked on for a time, though mostly about other cases Regal had known, odd ones he'd never solved or had solved by accident. He clearly believed Seso's case would be one or the other. During all of this, I sat silently, my mind focused on the tattoo, the fact that it unexpectedly raised the possibility that Seso had died in some mysterious aftershock of the same quake that had shattered me.

"So you got any other ideas?" Regal asked.

"No," I answered.

This was true. I couldn't imagine why Seso would possibly have come so far, a trip that surely must have cost him every dime he had. Toiling in Mafumi's basement archive could not have paid much, and even such low work would have been done under the watchful eyes of the Emperor of All Peoples' spidery agents.

So why had Seso come to New York, and what had he brought with him? Because I had no way to answer this question, I found myself simply remembering him, fondly for the most part, his year of loyal service, and in particular, the time he'd saved my life.

I'd been in-country only a few weeks at that time. We'd been walking through a part of the savanna I was considering as a possible location for a well. There was dried vegetation all about, along with a scattering of termite mounds that looked, at least from a distance, like the ancient towers of a long-abandoned city. Such was the favored abode and hunting ground of the black mamba, the continent's most dangerous snake.

I had no inkling that I was casually strolling a typical mamba habitat, of course. Seso knew it quite well, however. The closer we got to the mounds, the edgier he'd become, and he finally grabbed my hand when, like a little boy, I picked up a long stick and playfully began swinging it around.

"You should not do this," Seso said. "You should put down the stick."

"Why?"

"You are calling the mamba," Seso said. "It does not run. It attacks. And it is very fast."

Very fast indeed, I later read, clocked at twelve miles an hour, a snake so swift and deadly it could kill not just an occasional, unfortunate hyena, but an entire pack of them at a time.

"In my village, one of them killed five dogs," Seso told me. Then with a forwardness very unusual for him, he took the stick from my hand and dropped it on the ground. "It is good I warn you."

*It is good I warn you.*

It struck me suddenly that all during my time with Seso, he had continually warned me of this peril or that one, to avoid this place or that animal. He had warned me not to trust Gessee, and on a particular evening, when he'd seen the dreadful signs, he'd warned me not to fall in love with Martine. Looking back now, it struck me that his most important service had been to lower my risks.

If that protective impulse was still fundamental to his character, then perhaps it was for that reason that Seso had come to New York, I thought, bearing whatever he'd brought with him from Lubanda . . . as a warning.

# Six

Another risk management maxim occurred to me as I made my way home after talking with Max Regal. It states that the window of speculation narrows as proven facts accumulate, the final goal of risk assessment being the complete closure of that window. The problem, of course, is that indisputable facts remain open to highly disputable interpretations.

For example, the shell tattoo. The very sight of it had called up a critical element in Seso's character, how protective he'd been of me, of Fareem, and most certainly of Martine. This had led to my speculation that he'd come to warn Bill about something, an idea I'd found quite convincing at the moment it had occurred to me, but which my training in risk assessment now demanded that I call into question.

True, Seso had chosen a symbol that would have meant nothing to anyone who hadn't known Martine, but darkly suggestive—a potent symbol indeed—to anyone who had. Even so, I couldn't remotely be sure of the tattoo's meaning. Perhaps Seso had had his own reason for having it done. Perhaps it was the symbol of some cult he'd joined or some secret organization. Surely it was possible that it had nothing to do with Martine, save that Seso had, in coming here, felt himself no less doomed than she had been.

I had only the memory of a particular night to argue that Seso had always considered himself something of a marked man. "I am an outcast," he'd said on that occasion. He'd said this grimly, his words weighted with fatality, and he'd never seemed more a boy of the bush than at that moment, a boy who'd seen just how a pack of hyenas surround their isolated prey, their cackling and their cries, the nipping at the flanks of their exhausted victim. There is nothing kind in nature, as anyone who lives at its mercy knows, and Seso had certainly lived that unforgiving life. Even so, I'd come to believe that as he'd lived alongside me, he'd become more trusting not only of me but, dare I say it, of his fellow man, perhaps even his institutions. More's the pity that he'd abruptly found that trust both unwarranted and dangerous.

I'd been in Tumasi for only a couple of weeks when it happened, and on that particular day I'd been driving about the savanna in an attempt to come up with a helpful project. While I was gone, an official from the Agricultural Ministry who'd stopped in the village had returned to his car to find his binoculars missing. He'd seen Seso loitering about his car and had immediately accused him. Seso had stood silently and with great dignity as the official hurled insults at him. "You are an outcast," he'd yelled, "a thief like the rest of your kind." At that point the official had more or less arrested Seso, then taken him to Nulamba, where the National Police had an office.

It was Fareem who'd told me all this when I got back to Tumasi late that same afternoon. He'd been in the village when Seso was accused and had waited there until my return so that he could tell me what had happened. He agreed to go with me to Nulamba, where we'd found Seso locked in a back room of the small, tin-roofed building that served as headquarters for the district police. In a room that doubled as a storage closet, Seso sat on the floor in a humble, squatting posture, surrounded by a bramble of brooms and mops and plastic buckets. He seemed utterly reduced and humiliated, like one whose best efforts had come to nothing.

"They are accusing me," he said as he lifted himself from the floor, "but I did nothing. I work hard. I am not a thief."

It was the cry of a young man who'd done everything he could to better himself. To be locked up like a common criminal in this sorry backroom depository of plastic jerry cans and buckets seemed almost more than he could bear. "I am not a thief," he repeated brokenly. "I do not steal."

It was seeing noble, hardworking Seso in such a condition that had emboldened me at that moment, so that I'd marched back into the constable's office and demanded his release.

"I am sorry, but he must be questioned," the constable said.

He wore no badge on his plain, olive green uniform, so there was nothing to suggest his authority save the decidedly innocuous sunflower pin on his cap, one that would be replaced by crossed pangas a few years later. This shaved-down form of official dress had also been part of President Dasai's ideology of Village Harmony. In Lubanda, even the attire of authority was to be soft, pliable, unthreatening. That the constable currently wearing it would shift his allegiance to Mafumi when the time was right, get a much-sought-after promotion, and later help to carry out the Janetta Massacre, would never have occurred to Lubanda's soon-to-be-filleted chief of state.

But the constable's capacity for violence was plenty clear to me. I could almost see the shadow of jackboots creep over his saintly sandals. He started to get up, then thought better of it, and eased back into his chair, where he rested like a big cat in the corner of his cage. "This prisoner has been accused of stealing, Mr. Campbell," he explained. "This is a serious crime in Lubanda."

"Seso is not a thief," I told him.

The constable smiled. "I have only brought him here. I have not denied him food or water. Father Dasai does not wish any of his children harm. Negritude forbids it."

I recalled that the Lubanda Constitution had emphatically and repeatedly stated its faith in Negritude, the concept that no black man could do to another black man what white colonists had done, but I'd never heard the word used by a government official.

"Surely you know this," he added pointedly.

"Of course I do," I assured him. "I know Lubanda's Constitution very well, and on the basis of that knowledge, I think it's fair for me to ask when Seso will be released."

"This I cannot say, Mr. Campbell," the constable told me. "There are certain problems."

"What sort of problems?"

"Where he was when the theft occurred," the constable answered. "He was near to the official's car."

"Tumasi is a market," I said. "I'm sure there were lots of people near the official's car."

The constable didn't answer, but we both knew the truth. Seso had been accused because of his tribal origins. It was the old, old story of guilt by association, and Lubanda was sunk as deep in that reeking mire as any other place.

"He admits he went near the agricultural inspector's car," the constable said.

"So what?"

The constable looked at me with the motionless eyes of the seasoned interrogator he would later become as district commander for the Ministry of Internal Security.

"I cannot say more at this time, Mr. Campbell," he said, after which he offered a wide, Lubandan smile, all white teeth and cordiality, but in his case, with something steely in it.

"I will come to you with any later questions," he added, then glanced over to where Fareem stood in a corner, his hands folded in front of him, the posture of a valet.

"Who is this?" he asked me. "One of your . . . servants?"

"No," I said. "A friend."

The constable appeared to find this mildly amusing. "You were in Tumasi when the theft occurred?" he asked Fareem.

Fareem nodded.

The constable looked at me. "He will stay."

"Stay?"

"He will stay here," the constable repeated. "To be questioned."

I looked at Fareem. There was a fierce supplication in his eyes: *Please do not leave me with this man.*

"No," I said. "If you need him later, let me know. I'll bring him in myself. You have my word on that."

For a moment the constable stared at me with those same motionless eyes. He was obviously trying to calculate the risk, if there was any, in insisting that Fareem remain behind.

"I will take your word, Mr. Campbell," he said at last. "You may take your man with you." His eyes shifted over to Fareem, and I saw in them the faint sparkle of contempt that would later shine so brightly in the eyes of Mafumi, as well as in those of all his officers and minions, his followers and hangers-on, the ululating women who danced at his rallies, the boy army that committed his outrages, a smoldering hatred so intense it was all but blinding.

But that dreadful wave had not yet inundated the country, and so I simply nodded to this officer who had not yet transformed himself into the murderous factotum of a tyrant, glanced at the sunflower pin that winked from his cap, and said, "Good, then we can go."

With that I waved Fareem toward the door, then turned to leave myself. I had just reached the door when the constable called me back.

"One moment."

I turned to face him. "Yes."

"You know that woman, yes? " he asked.

"That woman?"

"The white woman. The one who has a farm at the end of Tumasi Road."

"Martine Aubert? Yes, I know her," I said. "I met her my first day in Tumasi."

The constable stared at me evenly. "So she also is a friend of yours?"

"Yes, she's a friend," I told him.

His large eyes were dark and still. "Good," he said, quietly, though with a curious edge. "It is good that she has a friend."

He meant a white friend, as we both knew, and by that he meant someone with influence. Even so, his remark had less than an amiable tone, the suggestion being that Martine would soon be in need of such a friend, and that quite naturally that friend, like Martine, would be white.

"Why is that?" I asked.

The constable only smiled, then nodded toward the door. "Be careful on your way back to Tumasi. It is a dangerous road."

We walked out of the building, got into my Jeep, and headed back toward Tumasi. Fareem was clearly shaken, and for a long time he said nothing. Then, quite suddenly, he said, "It is as I thought. They are after Martine."

"Who?"

"The big men in Rupala," Fareem answered. "She got a letter from them. They want to evaluate her farm."

"'Evaluate'? What does that mean?"

"I don't know, but it is never good when they come here, the people from the capital."

I tried to reassure him. "Everything is going to be fine," I said. "It's probably just some sort of survey. Governments are always taking surveys."

The sun was going down when we arrived at Martine's house an hour or so later. She was sitting on the porch as we came to a halt, but rose quickly and was almost upon me by the time I got out of the Land Cruiser.

"There is something wrong," she said the instant our faces came into view.

I told her what had happened—the theft, Seso's arrest, our journey to Nulamba, what had transpired there.

"The constable wouldn't release Seso," I said at the end of the narration. "But he looked fine. He hasn't been harmed. I expect that he'll be released very soon."

I started to buttress this conclusion with some unfounded notion about legal procedure, the rule of law, the present government's commitment to these decidedly Western principles, but before I could speak, I happened to glance out and, in the distance, across the plain, I saw a long line of slender figures moving slowly at the far reaches of the bush, their animals moving with them: goats, cattle, camels, a dog or two. It was a group of Lutusi on their way to some watering hole perhaps forty or fifty miles off, slowly and gracefully moving at their own pace.

"It's beautiful," I said by way of lightening the mood. "The way they move."

The tenderness of Martine's reply touched some previously untouched part of me.

"The Lutusi have their own pace," she said in that way of hers, with neither admiration nor condemnation, but only as a matter of fact. They had their own time, and it was at one with their immemorial course, immutable as an ocean current. It was neither good nor bad. It simply, intractably . . . was.

At that moment, as we three stood together watching the line of Lutusi at the horizon, Martine seemed at peace with her homeland, a country so perfectly hers that I could not have foreseen the fury with which it would turn against her, nor that, in the face of that fury, she would set a course down Tumasi Road where, at some terrifying instant, she must have heard a rustling in the brush, then the rhythmic clack, clack, clack of the shells as they sounded behind her, then in front, then tightening like a clattering noose all around.

# PART II

Einstein is said to have welcomed death because it put an end to risk. I have to admit that I'm not quite as sanguine about it. Death doesn't appeal to me, but sometimes killing does. "The reek of human blood smiles out at me," one of the Furies says as they close in upon Orestes. I have known that smile, and I must confess that at this moment, I know it once again. The unavoidable truth is that there are times when the rigors of forgiveness defeat us, and we wish only to do damage.

Even so, why could I not have let Seso's murder go, returned to my secure little office and my safe little life? I think it was because each time I thought of Seso facedown in that alley, I thought of Martine facedown on Tumasi Road, a swarm of black-winged vultures already circling overhead.

"Please stand over there, Mr. Campbell," a second man tells me as he ushers me into a large room. "Someone will come for you very soon."

The man who gives me this instruction wears a dark green suit with a yellow tie whose brightness reminds me of the sunflower flag of that earlier Lubanda. But for all that, I suspect that he is a holdover from the old regime, perhaps one of Mafumi's bodyguards. I make this admittedly unproven assumption because his eyes have the look of one whose acts long ago turned his heart to stone. For that reason, I can't help but wonder how many times he's reached for the pistol I glimpse beneath his jacket as he sits down a few feet from me. It is probably a 9mm Browning Hi-Power, Mafumi's weapon of choice for his Praetorians. Clearly, Lubanda's new president has not chosen to reduce the lethal firepower of those who are supposed to guard him. But given that they once protected Mafumi, can he really believe that they will as ardently protect the man who all his life opposed that now dead tyrant? Surely not, I tell myself. But then, my life, as well as my profession, has taught me that the greater part of man's self-created sorrow is caused by his failure to trust the right people. It is our errors of judgment in precisely this regard that insures our deepest doom.

A second man now emerges from an adjoining room. He smiles as he comes toward me. "Please take a seat anywhere you like," he tells me. "The president offers his apologies. I'm sure you understand." With an even bigger smile, he says, "He wishes you to be comfortable. We have bottled water. May I bring you some?"

"No, thank you," I tell him. "I'll just take a chair. The flight was long, and I'm a little tired."

He waits while I stroll toward the fifteen or so ornate chairs that line the opposite wall. Until recently this was Mafumi's library, where those in his favor waited to be received by him. I peruse its shelves, the hundreds of pulp fiction paperbacks the Emperor of All Peoples preferred, novels spiced with sex and fueled by rip-roaring action. Mafumi could not read, and so he was read to by a relay of young girls, the Emperor so aroused by the sex scenes that these reading sessions often ended on one of the zebra skin carpets that cover the floor.

Across from me, I notice a portrait of the current president, now a little heavy and with sprinkles of gray in his hair. He wears gold-rimmed glasses and is dressed in suit and tie.

It is said that the desk this new president has inherited from Mafumi once belonged to Mussolini. The Emperor of All Peoples had been a collector of such morally tainted relics. He owned a pen taken from Hitler's bunker, it is unreliably reported, and a lamp that once rested on one of Stalin's bedside tables. I have no idea if the current president has rid himself of these other seamy artifacts, though I suspect he has, for he would be careful in such matters, and he would certainly know that any official emissary from the Mansfield Trust, which is what I am now, would find them offensive.

I glance toward the door at the far side of the room. There is an anteroom behind that door, as I have seen in drawings of the palace. More than one assassination plot has unraveled there, but that was years ago, when Mafumi was still new to power and the forces against him had not yet been killed or imprisoned or driven into exile. The first failed resistance fighters were reported to have been skinned alive, but who knows if this is true. One thing is clear, however: for the last fifteen years of Mafumi's rule no internal hands were raised against him, because such hands had been severed by pangas early on.

A man in a dark suit enters the room, and as if signaled by his appearance, a great cheer arises. It comes from beyond the tall windows at the other side of the room, which the guards instantly open so that these young voices fill the airy space. The cheering continues as the man in the dark suit comes to the window, peers out, then turns to me and in a friendly gesture waves me over to the window.

"I am Joseph Abutto," he says as he offers his hand. "the president has appointed me minister of orphan affairs." His hand sweeps out toward the window. "Orphans are our great problem now," he says. "Those below are just, as you say, the tip of the iceberg."

I look out into a large courtyard where scores of children have gathered, women in nurses' uniforms moving among them, handing out cookies and dispensing milk from large plastic buckets.

"They receive mid-morning snacks," the minister tells me. "They are the children of the nomads."

"Where are their parents?" I ask.

"They starved to death," Abutto tells me. "There have been many years of drought in Tumasi."

"Which isn't good for coffee," I remark, remembering Martine's fatal choice. "Drought doesn't hurt teff all that much, but it is very bad for coffee."

"Teff," the minister says. His smile is fully appreciative. "The president has told me that you know Tumasi well."

"As well as any foreigner can, I suppose."

Below, the children are quiet now as each awaits his or her portion. Watching them, I recall the mute and nearly motionless waiting I have seen among the crowds outside food warehouses and in refugee camps, people with nowhere to go and nothing to do, so that they wait in silence to be fed, clothed, sheltered, their stoical patience not so much impressive as simply dependency's mark of Cain, the admittedly complicated fact, as Martine said, that handouts stifle reach.

"These children would have died, but we brought them here to be fed and sheltered," the minister tells me. "We are bringing more every day."

"And they're to stay in Rupala?" I ask.

"Oh, no," the minister tells me. "We intend to return them to their native region." He smiles benevolently upon this sea of waifs. "And if we can do this, then these children will become the future hope of Lubanda."

I find it fitting that I am the official now charged with helping the country realize this noble ambition, since years before, I'd made a similar, though far less exalted, effort to help Lubanda. How strange that year had been, it seems to me now, and how far I thought I'd traveled beyond it before I was returned to it by Seso's murder—a crime that has now brought me back to Lubanda in a final effort to do what I failed to do so many years before, offer to this sweet, long-suffering country a genuine gift of hope.

"Our president will see you soon," a voice from somewhere across the room assures me.

I nod, grip the handle of my briefcase . . . and wait.

# New York City, Three Months Earlier

# Seven

Memory is sometimes like an unlucky traveler, the type who needs only board a train for the bridge that lies before it to collapse. It can attack a man at any point, and mine attacked me at full force in the days following my brief meeting with Max Regal. The classicist returned, and I recalled that King Darius had given one of his servants the specific task of reminding him that Athens had to be destroyed. My mind now acquired a similar servant, this one tasked with insistently returning me to Martine. *She was Lubandan,* this dutiful servant repeated, a remark inevitably followed by a vision of Martine in her last days, set upon her course, her reasoning quite plain: *In fighting for my land, Ray, I am fighting for my country.*

Given the force of such a statement, and the tone of her voice when she'd made it, how could she not have returned to me with startling vividness, so that I'd seen the plain blue scarf that bound her hair, the tattered skirt, the frayed sandals. How could a crystal wineglass not have returned me to her dusty bottles of home brew? After all, shouldn't the many who risk nothing continually remind us of the few who risk everything?

And so it struck me as perfectly natural that in the wake of Seso's murder I would often find myself adrift in time, remembering Martine in the glow of a sunset, the silhouette of the Lutusi moving across a red horizon while we sat beneath a scraggly tree, peering out over the savanna. Baboons would sometimes slink out of the darkness, grab whatever they could find, then dash off into the bush, squealing with what seemed a raucous joy. Martine never chased them or made much of their thievery, since the food stocks were secure and beyond them there was nothing of great value.

But my memories didn't always return me to Lubanda itself. One evening as I sat alone in my apartment, I abruptly recalled a conversation I'd had with Bill Hammond shortly after his latest visit to that ill-fated country. By then, the bloody event that the press had dubbed the "Tumasi Road Incident" was almost ten years behind us. Even so, it seemed still to be reverberating in both our minds, perhaps all the more so in view of what had happened since—the fall of Rupala, Mafumi's savage rule.

"Lubanda is a mess," he said.

We were at a bar on Bleecker Street. Bill had only recently assumed his position at the Mansfield Trust, and I'd just opened up my consulting firm for risk assessment and management. Though I'd not returned to Lubanda after my abrupt departure, the awful state of things Bill described had not surprised me. I was well aware that under Mafumi the country had descended into nightmare, its "stability" now maintained by force of arms, along with the archipelago of police barracks and makeshift prisons and little concrete torture chambers.

"Mafumi actually encourages crime against any foreigners crazy enough to stumble into the country," Bill added.

"Why shouldn't he?" I asked. "He's a thief who came to seize the aid warehouses and stayed to empty them."

Bill appeared genuinely puzzled by Mafumi's extremism. "But what kind of fool would believe that once he'd emptied the warehouses, we'd just fill them again?" he asked.

"It's been done before," I reminded him. "Remember Goma?"

The largest relief effort in human history had been carried out in Goma, Congo, a city that lay just across the Rwandan-Congolese border. It was later shown that vast amounts of this aid had gone to the Hutu *genocidaires,* who'd only recently massacred, mostly with clubs and pangas, nearly a million Tutsi. With this aid, they'd set up restaurants stocked with donor food and established a black market in donor goods, the profits for which had gone into bars, nightclubs, whorehouses, and the automatic weapons necessary to maintain this vast criminal enterprise.

"Besides, Mafumi went to a convent school when he was a boy," I said. "They tested all the students there. His IQ was seventy-three." I shrugged. "All he knew was what a panga can do. But he knew that really well."

The grave nature of this fact clearly made Bill uncomfortable.

"Anyway, crime is rampant in Lubanda now," he said. "The guy who picked me up at the airport . . . Christ, Ray, you wouldn't believe the equipment he had to keep his car from being stolen." He shook his head at the nightmarish life that had descended upon Lubanda in the wake of Mafumi's triumph, and for the first time I saw some hint of his own regret at the part, marginal though it was, he'd played in its doomed trajectory. "In addition to the usual electronic alarm, the kind that kills the engine if someone tries to hot-wire it, he's got a lock on the wheel, a lock on the stick shift, and another lock on the accelerator." His gaze became quite sad. "Poor Lubanda. People can't live normally with crime like that. If property isn't secure, nothing is."

"Isn't that what Martine believed and said in no uncertain terms?" I asked him pointedly. "That tyranny gains power by taking your property and holds it by taking your life."

He looked at me candidly, like one facing a friend who knows all his secrets. "She did, indeed, make her opinions known."

I saw that even after all these years, his memory of Martine remained both raw and painful, and so I moved to a different subject. "Did you meet with Mafumi while you were in Rupala?" I asked.

He nodded. "Of course. I could hardly ignore him. He controls everything." He shrugged. "I even got his excuse for one-man rule, namely that Lubandans can only be ruled by a chief."

"Mobuto said that about Africans in general."

Bill looked at me solemnly. "You know, Ray, when darkness fills my soul, I sometimes think it might be true."

I shrugged. "All I know is that there was a time when Lubanda had hundreds of chiefs, and most of them were pretty decent to their people."

As if to shore up some small collapsing wall within him, Bill took a sip from his Grey Goose martini. "True enough," he said with the sympathetic look I recalled from years before. Then, to my surprise, he returned to Martine. "I recently read a line that reminded me of Martine," he said. "As a classicist you've probably heard it. It's what Zeus says about Athena, that she had a wondrous way of bringing men to grief." Now his expression filled with warning. "It's risky to fall in love with a woman like that."

He waited for me to respond to this, but when I didn't he glanced out the window, where the usual Saturday night street life was flowing by: NYU students on their way to jazz or blues clubs, tourists looking for Positively 4th Street.

"Do you think she ever trusted Dasai?" he asked.

"I don't know," I answered. "But she tried to help him."

I remembered the dusty afternoon when President Dasai's modest little Nissan had rolled into the northern village of Shintasa. He'd come to make his pitch for Village Harmony, and he'd asked Martine and Fareem to join his entourage because he'd wanted to showcase Martine, a decidedly white Lubandan, and coal black Fareem, two people working a farm that sat pretty much at the geographical center of Lubanda, a position that, he said, was symbolic in itself. Surely if black and white Lubandans could work together, then so could members of the country's various tribes. Martine had had her doubts about lending herself to this mission, but had finally decided to do it.

Bill had subsequently asked me to go along with Martine and Fareem. It would, he said, be a good opportunity for me to see more of the country. "Just remember, Ray," he'd jokingly written, "you're an ambassador for Hope for Lubanda, so no cursing, brawling, or bedding native girls."

Shintasa's villagers were Visutu, the same tribe as Mafumi. It was typical of the upper savanna, a scattering of mud huts only a few miles from the country's northern border. There was the usual cassava, along with a few staples of subsistence farming. For meat, there were goats, chickens, and a few cows, along with grubs that were eaten, still alive and wriggling, in a red sauce.

We arrived in the afternoon after a bumpy journey along roads that were little more than trails, perfect for herding animals but very hard on the president's car, which was covered with the region's pale yellow dust by the time we pulled into the village.

Once there, Dasai gave the villagers his big, jolly laugh, then drew groups of children into his cuddling arms so that the folds of his bright yellow dashiki seemed to capture them in a golden light.

"These little ones are the future of Lubanda," he proclaimed grandly, in response to which the villagers smiled as widely as Dasai himself.

The president and his entourage were then offered the usual village entertainment. Girls danced before us, hopping and twirling to the beat of drums played only by the boys. The president responded enthusiastically, of course, his eyes sparkling with delight.

As a scene, it was picture-perfect, so I quickly reached for my camera, only to find that the battery had died. This was a major problem because Bill had specifically wanted me brought along to take pictures that could later be used in Hope for Lubanda's promotional material. I had not yet presented him with a project, and now I had even failed at taking a few publicity shots.

"You can use mine."

It was Fareem, and he was offering me his camera.

"It's old and has a crack in the lens," he added. "But perhaps it will do."

The crack was in the left-hand corner, a distinctive starburst pattern that was certainly large enough to appear quite prominently in photographs, but perhaps not so prominently that it couldn't be cropped out.

"Thanks," I told Fareem, then began shooting as President Dasai drew one child after another onto his ample lap.

For the next few minutes I chronicled the president's visit, snapping pictures of him with Martine on one side, Fareem on the other, each of them looking somewhat embarrassed by his designation of them as "the embodiment of Village Harmony." And yet at the time, they'd seemed exactly that: two Lubandans, different in sex and race, who'd managed to share a farm, make it work.

I'd taken more pictures over the next hour or so, President Dasai shaking hands with villagers, walking through their small gardens, watching women as they pounded cassava. With one and all, he'd played the black Santa, smiling, laughing, dispensing advice and encouragement, assuring the Visutu villagers that he would look out for their interests despite the fact that he was of a different tribe, the Besai, of the south.

"We are no more different peoples," he proclaimed just before he got into his car for the trip back to Rupala. "We are all Lubandans, children of the same village."

"He means it, don't you think?" I asked Martine as we stood together, listening to the president's speech.

"Nyerere said the same thing," Martine answered. "That the country's tribes could live quite well together as long as they were all members of the same political party." She drew a handkerchief from the pocket of her blouse and ran it across her brow. "Nyerere's party, of course." She shrugged. "Lubanda could go the same way."

This struck me as a darkly pessimistic remark, a product of the many books and reports Martine had studied, and which I'd seen in her farmhouse a month before. How many nights had she pored over them by candlelight, I wondered, tracing the history of postcolonial Africa from one failed state to another?

"Unless it finds another way," she added now.

A few yards distant, President Dasai ended his talk, then led the villagers in a ragged version of the country's national anthem. Few of them had learned the words.

After that, we were on our way back to Rupala, the president with his advisors, Martine, Fareem, and I following behind in my Land Cruiser.

"He doesn't have much security," Fareem said at one point. He looked out toward the scrub brush that rose in thick patches as far as we could see. "And Mafumi's thugs are just across the border."

We rumbled on through the heat, the dust thickening as the brush thinned, so that we were soon driving over an isolated landscape, empty as the moon, with only a set of previously laid tread marks as a road.

The plan had been to stop midway to Rupala for another presidential visit, this time to a nomad encampment one of his aides had described as "picturesque," and where Bill had asked me to take yet more photographs of Lubanda's beloved president.

I'd expected all of this to go smoothly, but once we were out of the desert and into the more lush landscape of the south, I noticed Fareem becoming steadily more agitated.

"This would be the place," he said, then looked pointedly at Martine. "This would be the place to assassinate Dasai."

At first I'd thought myself the butt of a joke, Martine and Fareem engaging in a little game to frighten me. But when I looked at Martine, I saw that she'd taken Fareem's remark in deadly earnest.

"That's always the easiest way," she said darkly, "Just to kill someone."

There is the sadness one feels for one's own life, and there is the sadness one feels for all life, and it was this second sorrow that seemed to fall upon Martine at that moment, the bleak and dreadful fact that men were simply not up to the job of taking the harder, slower road to whatever vision of paradise possessed them.

"Always the easy way," she repeated softly, almost to herself.

As if to confirm her stark conclusion, at that very moment a loud pop, pop of rifle fire sounded from both sides of the road.

"Get down!" Fareem cried, then grabbed Martine, pushed her into the rear floorboard of the Jeep, and dove on top of her. "Fast, fast!" he yelled at me. "Go! Go!"

By then the president's lead car was speeding away as fast as the bad road would allow, but fast enough to spew a nearly impenetrable cloud of dust from its madly spinning rear tires. The president's driver had not been trained in evasive action, and so he simply shot forward as fast as possible.

Within seconds the firing was behind us, a distant, muffled series of shots that made it clear that this had been a stationary ambush, the president's would-be assassins on foot and thus unable to pursue him.

Minutes later the president's car came to a halt, and Dasai, quite unruffled, got out and strode back to where I sat, pale and shaken, behind the wheel.

"Are you all right, young man?" he asked.

I nodded mutely.

The president glanced to the rear of the car, where Fareem and Martine had now retaken their seats.

"And you, my dear?" he asked Martine.

"Fine," Martine said, though I could see her fear, along with the firm way she acted to control it.

Dasai's familiar smile spread once again across his face. "The perils of office, my child," he said with a soft laugh.

Suddenly, I blurted, "May I take a picture, Mr. President?"

"Of course," Dasai said. "Just let me slap some of this dust off."

As he did precisely that, I picked up Fareem's camera and stepped out of the Jeep.

"Where do you want me?" Dasai asked.

"There," I said, "with the horizon at your back."

Thus did I pose the president, standing proudly, and as if alone, a blazing sunset behind him, his fists pressed into his sides, his feet spread somewhat farther apart than usual, the stance of a man in full charge of his country, a picture so brimming with confidence in the future that only a month later it would adorn the cover of Hope for Lubanda's glossy new brochure.

It was a brochure I'd brought back with me when I'd left Lubanda ten months later, and which I still had, and which called to me that night so many years afterward, in the wake of Seso's murder. In answer to that call, I walked to a drawer where I kept my Lubanda memorabilia. There, among papers, a map, and one of Martine's carved oyster shells, was that very brochure, along with the original picture, never cropped, and thus still marked by the spidery crack of Fareem's broken lens.

I stared at that original photograph for a moment. How symbolic the crack in Fareem's lens now seemed of the fractured nature of Lubanda at that time. But there was nothing to be done about the terror that had later overrun it, so I returned the brochure to the drawer, then took out the map I'd used to plot the movements of the Lutusi across the savanna. I recalled the way Martine had stared at it, her gaze focused on the black lines that marked their wanderings. She'd said nothing, but I'd noticed the look of disquiet in her eyes.

Had that been the second time I'd visited Martine's farm, I asked myself now, or the third? I was surprised that such an insignificant detail mattered to me, though it was clear that I'd begun to go over my year in Lubanda with the curious sense of searching for small clues.

There is a certain element of investigation in all risk management, of course, but when one's own actions may increase the risk to another, then the thoroughness of that investigation becomes of prime importance. Had I known that simple rule of risk assessment all those many years ago, and applied it to life itself, I would have acted differently that day on Tumasi Road, facing Martine as she began her walk, the basket on her head bearing her few necessities, as well the *Open Letter* she was bringing to Rupala.

It had been found in her basket, then retrieved by authorities, one of whom, an army officer, had had it on his desk the day I was questioned. "Did she write this herself?" he'd asked as he nodded toward the paper.

I looked at Martine's *Open Letter*. The bloodstains had by then darkened and gone dry, crude evidence indeed that Village Harmony had grown decidedly inharmonious.

"Yes," I said.

"You weren't involved in writing it?"

"No."

"And the one she lives with on that farm in Tumasi." He glanced at a note on his desk, the name I could see written on it. "Fareem Nebusi. Was he involved in writing this . . . paper?"

"I don't know." I nodded toward the *Open Letter*. "May I have it?"

The officer hesitated only long enough to decide that there would be no further attempt to investigate this latest crime, and so no need to keep anything in evidence, least of all a worthless piece of paper. "Of course," he said finally, then handed it to me.

And I had it still, a dreadful souvenir of my time in Lubanda that now rested in this same drawer, rolled up tightly and secured with a rubber band. I had not thought of taking it out since last putting it there, but that night, only a few days after Seso's murder, thinking of Tumasi again, of Martine and Fareem and, of course, Seso, I drew it from the dark and unfurled it on the top of my desk.

There it was, the plea Martine had written on behalf of her country, then placed in her basket and set off with down the long, weaving road that ran from her farm to the capital.

In the years since then, I'd rarely thought of Martine making her way down Tumasi Road. Instead, I'd imagined her as evening fell and she left the road and headed out into the bush, where she rolled out her bedding and sat down, took a deep breath and a swig of water, then ate the bread she'd made from the grains she'd grown, and after that, stretched out, faceup, and peered into the overhanging stars. For years that vision had floated through my mind, but now as I thought of it, it arose through the screen of Seso's death, as if I were now searching not just for Seso's killer, nor even for whatever it was he'd claimed to have for Bill, but for that elusive, perhaps unknowable, but always painful line that in every life divides what we should have done from what we did.

# Eight

Before going to Lubanda, I'd known that there is an innocence of mind that experience can change, and you will be the better for it—less naïve, for example. The risk is cynicism, of course, a religion whose only sacrament is suicide. But if something, even cowardice, stays your hand from so final an act of hopelessness, you have no choice but to soldier on, a fact Seso's murder made clear. Besides, I finally decided, it was possible that Lubanda still had tricks to play, an experience, dark and bloody, that wasn't finished yet. I had no idea what those tricks might be, of course. I knew only that, like an unexplored river, its source lay behind me and its terminus ahead.

It was a Friday night when I made my way toward the Darlton Hotel, a busy evening for most of Manhattan. But Twenty-seventh Street has no clubs, and only a few restaurants, and so in that part of the city, a peculiar urban quiet descends with the failing light. It isn't the silence of a meadow at close of day, nor the whispering softness of a twilight field, and certainly it isn't the ancient silence that fell over the savanna on those evenings when we would gather on Martine's porch to watch the sun go down. An urban nightfall can have a sinister effect, as I'd noticed all the more vividly upon returning from Lubanda. In Lubanda all nocturnal things had lingered; here they lurked. There the perils of night had been at one with the scheme of things; here they seemed the product of a grim manufacture, a world of risks that were fundamentally man-made.

There were people on Twenty-seventh Street, of course, but by and large they were on their way somewhere else. None would be headed for a low-rent hotel populated by African traders whose customs and dialects might as well have come from Mars.

Both the street and the Darlton Hotel had the look of an after-thought. Much of New York had changed during the last twenty years, but this part of the city had remained remarkably the same. The buildings were shorter than most of Midtown, and the youthful energy of the Village, the vibrant restaurants of the old Hell's Kitchen, the clubs of the Meatpacking District here gave way to something gray and heavy. Even the buildings seemed to slump.

The Darlton had that same feel: old, tired, less a faded movie star than a faded bit player. It stood erect, but somehow on its last legs, like a man suffering from a long, debilitating illness, still alive but weakening by the hour. I had little doubt that its owners were waiting for one last wave of speculation, the building destined either to be torn down or completely renovated, nannies dragging their properly dressed wards down streets once reserved for people who'd come with nothing, acquired nothing, transients, runaways, men with unclear motives who faced uncertain fates . . . like Seso Alaya.

How different this later Seso was from the young man I'd known, impeccably dressed in black trousers and a white shirt. Max Regal had found a middle-aged man, destitute by all appearances, living in a derelict hotel, a man who'd come all this way for a reason I was trying to uncover.

On that thought I recalled that Seso had accompanied me to the airport on the day I left Lubanda.

"Maybe I'll come back someday," I told him, though with little confidence that I ever would. "Maybe things will be different and I can have a drink with you and Fareem."

"Fareem will never come back to Lubanda," Seso said. He shrugged. "He would have nothing to come back to."

"But where will he go?" I asked.

"To the north," Seso said. "Back to his tribe." For the first time since I'd known him, Seso offered a cutting smile. "Isn't that where you're going?" he asked. "Back to your tribe?"

I might have made some limp defense for leaving Lubanda, but the airport public-address system scratchily sounded at that moment, announcing the boarding of my plane.

"Goodbye, Seso," I said, and moved to embrace him, but he stepped away.

"Do not worry for me," he said. "We must now take up our old lives." He offered his hand. "You were always kind to me. I thank you for this." Now his smile became genuinely warm and generous. "It is not your fault that Lubanda is not your home."

The lobby of the hotel in which this noble man had died was a shadowy affair. The floor was covered with a dull layer of linoleum, and although the walls were wood-paneled, some of the panels had fallen away, leaving strips of bare wall behind them. There was a row of vending machines to the right of the reception desk, and on the other side a few worn chairs. Everything looked drained, a room on life support.

"What can I do for you?" the woman at the desk asked. She was wearing a brightly patterned dashiki and a large African headdress, but her accent was full-throttle Bronx.

"I'm here to visit one of your guests," I said. "Herman Dalumi."

"You a cop?"

"No."

"You with Immigration?"

"I'm a consultant," I said to quickly shorten the long list of unwelcome officials I might be. "I have nothing to do with any government, foreign or domestic."

"You can't go up," the woman said curtly, the queen of this dilapidated kingdom. "Herman will come down." One eyebrow arched upward like the back of an aggressive cat. "If he wants to."

"I understand."

The woman nodded toward one of the chairs. "Wait over there."

I did just that, watching silently as the denizens of the Darlton Hotel wandered in and out. They were mostly African traders, just as Max had told me. I'd seen them throughout the city, selling T-shirts and baseball caps, pocketbooks and backpacks, along with the usual array of knockoffs and counterfeits, everything carried in blankets that could be gathered up quickly and hauled away at first sight of a cop. In that way, they struck me as the opposite of the nomads Martine and I had once watched move with such unencumbered grace at the far horizon, erect, dignified, carrying what they owned, a poor people under Western eyes, certainly, but not a desperate one.

"You are looking for me?"

He was a man of around forty, I guessed, short, but with powerful arms and legs. The features of his face blended flatly, like a chocolate bar left out in the sun. Only his eyes had any sparkle, though it was the sparkle of alertness rather than of love or pleasure or even curiosity, save for what might await him at the dark end of a street. Here, I thought, is a man accustomed to high risk.

"Herman Dalumi?" I asked.

The man nodded. "I told Nasar I'd pay him on Wednesday," he said. "I'm good for it. I never run away. He don't need to send a man to make threats. He insults me doing this. He is lucky I don't pull the rag from his head and strangle him with it. You can tell him this."

"I don't know this Nasar," I assured him. "I'm here about the man whose body was found in the alley behind the hotel a few days ago."

Something played in Dalumi's eyes, though I couldn't tell what it was, save that it wasn't fear. He'd already sized me up and found me harmless. Whatever I'd come for, it wasn't to break his bones over an unpaid debt.

"His name was Seso Alaya," I said. "I knew him a long time ago. He worked for me when we both lived in Lubanda."

Dalumi said nothing, but he didn't have to. Even his silence was calculated. He clearly considered words dangerous, as people unaccustomed to speaking freely inevitably find them. To have license with language is a rarity on earth, a pleasure Dalumi seemed never to have enjoyed.

"Do you have any idea how he was supporting himself?" I asked.

He shrugged.

"Is it a matter of money?" I asked bluntly, "Is that what you want?"

He shrugged again. "A man does not feed the animal that eats him."

This was no doubt a home-country saying, but its meaning was clear: I was not his friend. He owed me nothing, least of all a favor.

I reached for my wallet, but Dalumi grabbed my hand, brought it forward, clearly expecting that I'd reached for a pistol or a knife.

"I'm unarmed, if that's what's bothering you," I assured him.

He reached around, plucked the wallet from my back pocket, then released me.

"I must be careful," he said. He added nothing else as he went through my wallet, first checking for ID, then taking out a few bills, which he waved in my face. "I will take only this much," he said like a man demonstrating how reasonable he was, the amount of his theft, he seemed to feel, hardly thievery at all.

When I offered no argument, he shoved the bills into the pocket of his shirt.

With the terms of this business transaction now met, I took the photograph of Seso's body from my jacket pocket and handed it to him. "Do you have any idea who did this?" I asked him flatly.

Dalumi stared at the photograph, then shook his head. "He was always alone. Sitting in the lobby. Sometimes we talked."

"What did he talk about?" I asked.

"Are you asking if he had gold, diamonds?" He laughed, then took a single cigarette from his shirt pocket and lit it. "He was a gloomy one." The laugh devolved into something less mirthful. "As we say in my country, such a man sometimes speaks of his goats, but only to tell you they are dead."

"Gloomy or not, he had something I'm looking for," I said.

"Uranium?" Dalumi said, a question that appeared to turn a small key inside him, open a tiny door. "Those Chinese fuckers are taking all of it out of Niger. Building a road to it with their own little yellow prison slaves, so there is no work for us."

*Ah, so that's it,* I thought. *We have our distrust of the Chinese in common.*

"So, you're from Niger," I said.

Dalumi neither confirmed nor denied this. "He was from Lubanda, this man who is dead. What could he bring from there?" He squinted as if to bring my motives into clearer focus. "How do you know he had something, and why do you want it? What was he to you, the dead one?"

"Seso called a friend of mine," I answered. "He said he had something for him. My friend wants to know what it was. He thinks it must have been important if Seso left his family to bring it to him."

"Seso had no family," Dalumi said quite firmly.

"Yes he did," I insisted. "He told me this when I last saw him in Rupala."

"All gone," Dalumi said with a dismissive wave of his hand, "The mother died giving birth to his son," he added in the offhand way his life had taught him to regard the lives of others, that they were transient, fleeting, quickly snuffed out, especially the lives of women and children, since their helplessness only increased their risk. "And the boy was stolen."

"Stolen?" I asked.

"By the Visutu," Dalumi told me. "That is what he told me. They are a—"

"They are Mafumi's tribe," I interrupted. "Did Seso get his son back?"

Dalumi shook his head. "He died where the Visutu took him."

So Seso had come to the city of dreams only after he'd had no dreams left.

"Did he mention anyone else from Lubanda?" I asked.

"Once he talked about a woman," Dalumi answered. "A farmer, he said. He did not say a name, just that she had a farm and that she was white."

This was obviously a reference to Martine, and so I said, "She was white, but she was Lubandan."

Lubandan, I repeated in my mind, and suddenly remembered an evening a couple of weeks after the attempt on President Dasai's life. Fareem, Martine, and I were sitting on the farmhouse porch when a convoy of trucks appeared. Some were civilian, some were military, but all of them had their rear beds crowded with men, women, and children.

"They are Besai people," Fareem said. "The president's tribe."

"Where are they headed?" I asked.

"To the northern provinces," he answered. "Dasai wants to move his people into that region. This is part of Village Harmony, to bring all the tribes together."

Martine peered out at the passing trucks but said nothing. I'd noticed this quiet before, but failed to realize how very deep it was, a statue-in-the-park stillness at her core that reduced the women with whom I'd been involved during college and after it to chattering magpies. Suddenly it seemed to me that I had spent my life pursuing window-shop mannequins when all the time, here in Lubanda, there was *this*.

"Dasai will end up like that Tanzanian trickster Julius Nyerere," Fareem continued. "When he was president of Tanzania, he would listen to the weather forecasts on short-wave radio, then go out and predict the weather."

Martine remained locked in her own inner quiet, her gaze now focused on the far horizon not like the gaze of one who dreamed of going beyond it, but one for whom it served as a completely natural border, the sky no more than the blue bowl that held the boundaries of Lubanda.

"Such things make us a laughingstock," Fareem said sadly. He took another drink. "Moving the Besai up north will only cause trouble. The Visutu will see the clothes from the West, and the food from the West, and they will want these things, and they will come south to get them." He followed the trucks as they grew small in the distance. "There is no way to stop it now, this . . . invasion."

Martine made no argument against this dark surmise, but something in her eyes deepened. Finally, very softly, she said, "Maybe not."

Had that been the moment? I wondered now, with Dalumi staring at me as if distantly investigating my long silence. Had that been the moment when she'd first conceived of her *Open Letter*?

"What did Seso say about her?" I asked Dalumi by way of returning myself to the present.

"That she was betrayed."

Because I knew the risk, I dared not ask by whom.

"What else did he say about this woman?"

"He said he worked for her."

"But that's not true," I said. "Seso worked for me the whole time I was in Lubanda."

"He did not mean he worked for this woman then," Dalumi said firmly.

"Then when else?" I asked.

Dalumi's answer could not have struck him as oddly as it struck me.

"Now," he said. "He said he is working for her now."

"He couldn't possibly have been doing that," I told him adamantly.

"Then he was a liar," Dalumi said with an indifferent shrug. "You want to see his things? They are still in his room." He nodded toward the woman behind the desk. "You will have to pay her," he added. "But maybe in the room you will find what you are looking for."

In every discovery, as I well knew, there is risk. Discover this, and you will withdraw your bet. Discover that, and you will increase it. Most such discoveries are technical, and few are profound. But the deepest discoveries are those that alter the prevailing colors of the moral spectrum, reveal that what seemed right was wrong, and what seemed wrong was right. It is these gravely transforming discoveries we avoid, I had long ago discovered, and yet, without them, I decided now, we forever roll the same stone up the same heartbreaking hill, and then, with heads hung low, follow it down again.

"I'll pay her," I said.

Dalumi looked pleased. "Okay . . . boss," he said in the way of one whose only power was disdain.

I walked over to the woman behind the desk, and quickly struck a bargain.

She grasped the bills with fingers that seemed more like talons, then nodded toward the elevator. "Go under the crime scene tape," she told me firmly. "Don't rip it. If you do, the cops will give me shit."

"I won't touch it," I assured her. The police had taken no such investigative precautions on Tumasi Road, I instantly recalled, had made no effort to preserve the scene from contamination nor discover and subsequently apprehend the criminals involved. Nor had any marker ever been erected to note what happened there. It was this failure to memorialize the "Tumasi Road Incident" that now struck me as an added measure of injustice. For the stark truth remains that there are those who shoulder the cross and those who don't, and that it is those who bear its splintery burden who hold the heart of the world and by that means provide humanity with its only claim to glory. For that reason, something should have stood in commemoration of Martine's sacrifice, I thought, even if no more than her name etched into a stone.

"You ready?" Dalumi asked by way of returning me to the present. I nodded.

"Okay, let's go," he said, and on that command jerked his head upward, toward the ceiling, his expression fiercely reluctant, dreading the journey, as if he believed what those fiery red Tumasi sunsets had later come to suggest: that hell hung above us, rather than yawned below.

# Nine

On the way up to the fourteenth floor of the Darlton Hotel, I considered how strange it was, Seso's remark about working for Martine. How could he have thought himself working for her? He had never worked for her, and certainly was in no position to do so now.

Even so, I couldn't help considering the curious thing Seso had said to Dalumi. In my usual style, I went through this spare information looking for some sort of linkage. This process got me nowhere save, by an unpredictable twist of mind, to another memory of Martine, the way she'd once remaked, "Once a classicist, always a classicist." This thought brought Hecate to mind, how her name meant "will" in Greek, and the way in which she'd often been described as a sorceress of inordinate power, having an infinitely far reach through space and time. I knew that Martine would have been amused by this strained comparison, though completely typical of the classical education I'd evidently considered sufficiently preparatory to my efforts in Lubanda.

She'd walked into the village a week or so after we'd lounged on her porch, watching the trucks loaded with Besai families move north. Fareem had been with her, and once again, as I watched them stroll into the village, it seemed to me that they shared a private vision of some sort.

I'd been sitting on the steps of my house, honing my proposal to dig a series of wells along the route the nomads traveled across Tumasi, when I'd seen Martine and Fareem, and it struck me that they might know the best location for these wells.

"The market is charming, isn't it?" I said cheerfully as I approached them.

"Yes," Fareem said with a curious smile. "Charming."

For a moment, Martine seemed reluctant to speak, then as if compelled to do so, she said, "Do you want to learn about Tumasi, Ray?"

"Of course."

She didn't appear entirely convinced of this, but she turned and pointed to a stall where various cuts of meat hung in the open air. "The Lutusi sell their animals to the people here in the village." She nodded toward other stalls, some with mounds of beads, others selling grains, cassava, bolts of hand-woven cloth. "The nomads buy from those stalls with the money they get from the meat vendors." She turned to face me. "This is what you would call the 'economy' of Tumasi. I am sure you find it very simple."

"Well, isn't it?" I asked with a small laugh.

"Of course it is," Martine said. "But it is fragile, too, and changing it would not be simple."

I might have asked a question or two about all this had Bill Hammond not suddenly come roaring up in his Land Cruiser. As usual, he was all smiles and self-confidence as he strode toward me, a large cooler under his arm.

"Hello, Ray," he said cheerfully. His eyes whipped over to Martine. "Bill Hammond," he said as he offered his hand.

"Martine Aubert."

"Where are you from?" Bill asked.

"Lubanda," Martine answered.

A less ebullient spirit might have felt rather embarrassed at having to entertain the possibility that Martine was a "native," but Bill pressed forward obliviously.

"Well, congratulations on being a citizen of this wonderful country," he said. "One that will be much more wonderful once Ray is finished with it." He laughed and slapped me on the back. "Right, Ray?"

"Right," I said softly, then watched as Martine's gaze slid away from me and settled on Fareem. "This is Fareem," she said to Bill.

Bill smiled and offered his hand.

"We'd better finish getting our supplies," Fareem said to Martine after shaking Bill's hand with a clear sense of keeping his distance.

"Well, I hope you'll join Ray and me for a beer afterwards," Bill said expansively. He slapped the side of the cooler. "Fresh in from the States." He indicated a group of wooden benches that rested a few yards from where we stood. "We'll be waiting right over there."

Martine and Fareem smiled politely, then moved away, leaving Bill and me at the edge of the market.

"Good-looking woman," Bill said as he watched her. "What's the story with the local?"

"Didn't you hear what she said? They're both . . . locals."

"I mean the black guy," Bill said. "Does he live on her farm?"

"Yes."

"Hmm," Bill mused with something of a verbal leer in his tone.

We walked a few paces, then stopped in a patch of shade, and in that stillness I became aware that Bill was watching Martine closely.

"Just how far do you think that woman has gone bush?" he asked with what was now an openly salacious grin.

"Martine hasn't 'gone bush,'" I told him. "She was *born* bush. That's what she meant when she told you she was Lubandan."

"Yeah, well, she's living a fantasy if she believes that," Bill said. His gaze drifted over to me. "Lubanda is a snake that knows its eggs, Ray."

"What does that mean?"

"It means that some people in Rupala already have their eyes on her."

"What people?"

"The people in the Agricultural Ministry," Bill answered. "They think she may prove to be an obstacle to the ministry's plans for the region, which is to grow cash crops."

"Why would Martine pose a threat to that?"

Bill smiled. "With your help, maybe she won't."

I didn't smile back. "I don't want anything to do with politics."

Bill's smile vanished, and he became dead serious. "Everything is political, Ray. Lubanda hasn't stabilized yet. In the north, that warlord asshole Mafumi is stirring up some serious trouble." He abruptly returned his attention to Martine. "But I'm sure she'll do the right thing." His attention remained on her for a moment before it returned to me. "Now let's go have that beer," he said. He draped his arm over my shoulder and guided me over to the bench that sat a few feet from my quarters. "So," he said. "Tell me what's on your mind, project-wise."

"I've been thinking of a well." I said. "Only one to begin with, then maybe others."

"Great," Bill said. "Let's hear it."

I reviewed the research I'd done, tracing nomadic routes, going over with him the calculations necessary to determine the likelihood of finding water at various depths, along with the always-considerable risk of finding none at all.

Bill paid great attention to all this, then said, "Okay, so, where do you plan to dig?"

I rose, walked into my house, and returned with a map of Lubanda. "Here," I said, and pointed to the x.

Bill nodded. "Good enough," he said. "Write up your project proposal and I'll review it, and if it's approved, I'll get you whatever you need."

We talked on for a few minutes, and after a time Martine and Fareem strolled over to where we sat.

"Ray's going to dig a well," Bill said ebulliently. He pointed to the mark I'd made on the map. "There." He smiled at Martine. "What do you think?"

Martine sat down beside me and for the first time, as our bodies touched, I felt a steady charge in her nearness. She was not classically beautiful, but something furiously sensual came from her, so that a hint of breast beneath her shirt was far more tantalizing to me than anything a *Playboy* could provide. Her voice, with its musical Lubandan rhythms, added to the mix, of course. And then there were those emerald eyes, soft yet resolute, with something in them that had been tested by heat and dust and long, hard labor. There is nothing more unfathomable than the sort of desire that has the seed of later love inside it. In the end, it has little to do with the flesh and so much to do with the heart and the mind. On a New York street I might not have noticed Martine because she would have been dressed like a million others, spoken like a million others, been framed by the city's immensity and lost in its faceless crowds. But here in Lubanda, sitting close beside me, she seemed quite suddenly to shimmer with a rough beauty no powder could smooth nor any rouge provide a false bloom of youth. I thought of the women who'd followed the westward trek of my own now distant country, who'd lived in sod houses and weathered the innumerable hardships of a land in which they could ultimately depend upon nothing but themselves. Martine had the sense of those older struggles about her, the dust of ages past still clinging to her hair. There was nothing cracked about her, nothing fragile. She was like a vessel whose every particle had been strengthened by a flame.

"Hmm," she said as she stared at the map, the place my well was to be located.

Bill's gaze remained fixed on Martine. "Good idea, don't you think?" he asked somewhat tentatively, as if he was already probing for both her strengths and her weaknesses. "To dig a well?"

When Martine drew her eyes up from the map, the look in them was neither quizzical nor hostile.

"Have you a pencil?" she asked.

Bill took one from his shirt pocket and offered it to her.

She took it, leaned forward, and drew a circle around the x where I'd positioned my proposed well. "The nomads will come to this well," she said, "and because of the water, they will have bigger herds. But to and from the well, these larger herds will eat more of the grassland, and so the nomads will have to move farther and farther from the well to feed their animals." She drew a second, wider circle around the x. "The grasses will be eaten clean first here." She drew a third, still larger circle. "Then here." Now a much larger circle. "Then here." She looked at Bill. "All their cows will die within the first circle." Now she looked at me. "The goats will die within the second circle." She handed Bill back the pencil, her gaze now fixed on him intently. "When that happens the nomads will have nothing to trade for the grains and materials they need. No meat or milk. Nothing to sustain them . . . but your water." She stared at us in that level, no-nonsense way of her. "You are friends of Lubanda, but even so, it is important to know the consequences of what you do," she added softly.

Bill looked at her sternly. "We're trying to do something good for Lubanda," he said.

"I am sure you are," Martine replied. "Honestly. I have no doubt that you are." She smiled in a way that was not at all superior or even unfriendly. "Did you know that in Nairobi, when the aid workers turn on the air conditioners in their compounds and houses and apartments, the lights dim or go off in the poor parts of the city?"

"And your point is what?" Bill asked with an icy smile.

"That everything is more complicated than you think," Martine said. "More connected to other things." She looked at me. "Like your well, Ray."

With that she politely said goodbye, turned, and walked away.

"Does she think I don't know about these contradictions?" Bill asked when she was out of earshot. "Does she think I don't know that at conferences on starving children, you'll find food and wine, all you can fucking eat?" His eyes whipped over to where Martine and Fareem were beginning their homeward journey up Tumasi Road. "It's easy to make aid workers look like assholes. But, Ray, those people stuffing their faces are getting more done for the world's poor than Martine Aubert, who is, after all, only taking care of herself." When he looked at me again, I saw the warning in his eyes. "Be careful, Ray," he told me, "because she'll undermine everything you say or do. She's a primitivist. If it were up to her, Lubanda would stop dead in its tracks."

"But do you think she's right?" I asked Bill. "Technically, you might say. About the well?"

Bill shrugged. "What I know is that she should keep her mouth shut," he said quite seriously.

With that he rose, motioned me forward, and the two of us headed back toward his Land Cruiser, silent all the way.

Then, once he was behind the wheel, a smile struggled to his lips as he tried to return to his more jovial demeanor. "Just dig your well," he said, "You're a good man and you've come here to do good. That's what really matters."

A harsh clatter of metal on metal loudly returned me to the present and I was back in New York, facing Herman Dalumi, a man who now seemed uncertain that he'd made the right decision in allowing himself to have anything further to do with me.

"You look like man in a spell," he said to me. "A bad magic spell."

The elevator door had opened to a bleak landing, a floor covered with a strip of linoleum that seemed never to have known a mop.

"The dead man's room is down there," Dalumi added as we stepped into the foul-smelling corridor.

I followed him down the hall, though with little expectation that I'd find anything of interest in Seso's room. Still, it was the way of movie cops and private eyes, a well-known route that generally led from clue to clue until the villain was discovered, and though in real life such an investigation would probably reveal nothing, I calculated that there was little risk in carrying it out.

We stopped at Seso's room. Dalumi inserted the key and eased open the door. "You first," he said as he stepped back and let me go ahead of him, careful to duck under the yellow crime scene tape.

Imagine a bare room, and then add to it the poorest trappings of necessity. There was a bed with a thin mattress, supported by creaking springs and an iron frame. It was unmade and the blanket, a girlish pink, lay crumpled on the plain wooden floor. There was a chest with two drawers. The mirror was cracked in the lower right corner and again about halfway up, so that the line crossed the forehead of an average-sized man but must have cut ominously across Seso's throat. There was no closet, only a metal rack like the ones used to transport clothes along the streets of the nearby Garment District and from which hung two plaid shirts, both long-sleeved, and a single pair of badly frayed trousers. A small radiator supplied the room's only heat, and a dangling bulb its only light. There was no chair, no desk, no adjoining bathroom. A few cans of food rested on the windowsill, but there was no hot plate. A plastic fork, spoon, and knife sprouted from a Styrofoam cup, the room's sole utensils.

I walked over to the window and looked out. Below there was a square courtyard littered with whatever had been thrown from the windows that overlooked it.

"Seso was a quiet man," I said softly. For a moment, I continued to stare at the brick wall Seso must have faced during the time he'd spent here. Then I turned to Dalumi and suddenly felt the urge to tell some small part of my story.

"I went to Tumasi to do something good," I began, "and so I studied the routes the nomads took across that part of Lubanda. They wriggled and curled back on themselves and zigzagged. A journey from one point to another that should have been a mile became two miles, or three, or ten. Because of that, the routes themselves made no sense."

Dalumi stared at me silently, his eyes glimmering in the dim light of Seso's room.

"I would never have understood these routes if Seso hadn't told me that the Lutusi wandered in this way in order to familiarize their young with all of their territory, not just to make a beeline to water."

"How did this man know any of that?" Dalumi asked. "He said he lived in Rupala."

"He knew it because he was a Lutusi," I said. "A nomad."

As I continued, I thought of Seso as he'd been so long ago in Tumasi, shy, rarely speaking to anyone, sitting for long hours simply staring out into the bush, his gaze never so focused as when he caught sight of a line of nomads wandering in from the far reaches of the savanna.

"The Lutusi send their boys out into the bush, then wander away from them," I went on. "It's part of their training. The boys must find the tribe. Seso got lost. He couldn't find his people. So after a while they looked for him. They found him in the village. He had just wandered in out of the bush. The people in the village knew he was Lutusi and so they knew his people would eventually come back this way. And they were right. The Lutusi came into the village, but they wouldn't take Seso back."

"They are crazy, those nomads," Dalumi said with the contempt city people generally have for country people, "bumpkin" being a designation that appears in almost every language.

"It wasn't because he'd gotten lost that they wouldn't take him back," I said. "It was because, while being lost, he had accepted help. A little food and water. He didn't ask for it, but it was brought to him, and he ate and drank." I shrugged. "So he ended up with me."

I suddenly felt the oddly contradictory elements of Seso's character come together, the correctness with which he followed my instructions merge with the joylessness with which he followed them, as if his care were itself a diminishment. He'd done his job well, but he'd done nothing beyond his job. He'd never once initiated anything or exhibited any real ambition. Perhaps all he'd ever wanted was to return to the Lutusi.

"When Seso told me this story, I pointed out the fact that he might have died out there," I said, "a young boy all alone in the bush. Seso agreed that this was true; he might have died. But he reminded me that he might also have found his people . . . and himself."

After a brief silence, Dalumi said, "You should finish looking now. The woman downstairs, she will not let you stay in this room very long."

I set to work immediately, but I found nothing in the drawers of the bureau, nor in the pockets of Seso's shirts or trousers. I even pulled out each drawer and turned it over, thinking that Seso might have taped some message there.

But there was nothing.

"Okay," I said. "We can go."

Dalumi didn't move. "You said this man never returned to his people."

"That's right."

"Maybe this is not true."

The look in Dalumi's eyes was unmistakable. He had a trader's instinct for the deal.

"It would cost you a little bit more," he said.

"And if it isn't worth it?" I asked.

Dalumi smiled. "That's a chance you take."

"How much do you want?" I asked.

Dalumi hesitated a moment, calculating the value. "I will say fifty dollars."

I nodded.

"I was here when the janitor found the dead one." He smiled at the opportunity this had presented to him. "Since he was dead, I came to see what he had. Why should I not do this? He was dead, so what did it matter, the things he had. Maybe a watch. Maybe a ring." He shrugged. "The police would take everything, or if not the police, the thieves who run this place, so I said to myself, hey, maybe there is something here I can use." He drew a small photograph from his wallet and handed it to me. "I found this, and now, it is worth fifty dollars."

I took the picture from him and looked at it, unsure that it was worth the money I'd agreed to pay, but reluctant not to keep it.

"Okay," I said. "The fifty's yours."

# Ten

"So in the end, Seso went back to his tribe," Bill said when I showed him the photograph as we sat in a coffee shop the next morning.

The photograph showed Seso in his midthirties. He was no longer dressed in shirt and trousers. Instead he wore the orange robes of the Lutusi, a staff in one hand, the other holding a little boy of three or four, also clothed in orange robes, and obviously his son. Another man stood beside Seso, dressed in shirt and trousers. He had one hand on Seso's staff, a sign of the great trust Seso had in him.

"I know the village where this was taken," I told Bill. "It's called Sura. Seso's best friend lived there. He's the other man in the picture. He was like Seso, a castout from the Lutusi. I met him several times. His name was Bisara."

Bill seemed barely to have heard any of this. His gaze was still fixed on the photograph.

"I'm surprised that the Lutusi took Seso back," he said.

"There was always a way to return," I told him. "It isn't easy, a real test of endurance, but it could be done. But once it's done, you could never depart from any of the Lutusi customs. Not in the slightest. If you did, they would never take you back."

"A hard people," Bill said.

"Or just a very careful one," I said. "Wary of outside corruption."

Bill handed me back the photograph. "Risk-aversive, you might say."

"The question is, why didn't Seso stay with his people, instead of coming here?" I said as I returned the picture to my jacket pocket.

We talked on for a time. I told Bill the little I'd learned from Dalumi, my conclusion being that I'd hit a wall quite as windowless as the one Seso had faced outside his room.

"Only one thing seemed odd," I said. "Seso told Dalumi about a woman in Tumasi. A white woman. He said he was working for her."

Bill's expression changed abruptly. "Martine?" he asked.

"Who else could it be?"

Bill looked genuinely puzzled.

"When I saw Seso in Rupala, he didn't mention Martine," I added. "It was as if he'd erased all that from his mind."

Bill shook his head. "It should have stopped with that first letter from Rupala, Ray," he said gravely.

In Bill's troubled features, I saw once again just how much the Tumasi Road Incident had changed both of us, called into question all the things we'd hoped for and trusted. Even so, it was hard for me to calculate just how deep the fissure ran in Bill, how lasting the damage of that human quake, what once sturdy structures it had leveled.

"That letter should have been enough," Bill said.

As I now vividly recalled, the letter had been delivered by a low-ranking military officer who'd given it to Martine with a big sunflower smile. He'd driven all the way from Rupala, and the letter had borne the equally winning sunflower seal of President Dasai's office. The president had even added a personal note: *I hope this finds you well, my child.*

"This came from Rupala," Martine said when she handed me the letter. "I have been expecting it."

I read the letter, and was quite confident that it was only a polite, and not at all unreasonable, request from Rupala.

"They just want you to consider growing coffee so that Lubanda can have a stronger place in the . . ."—I glanced down at the letter in order to quote it exactly—". . . global market."

Fareem suddenly appeared at the door. He looked far more worried than Martine, perhaps, I thought, because he'd already glimpsed the risk she was running by the simple act of being herself. "What do you think, Ray?" he asked with obvious urgency. "How should we answer the letter?"

"There is no need to answer it," Martine said before I could respond to Fareem's question. She drew the letter from my fingers. "The big men in Rupala do not care about my little farm. They are listening to the foreigners who want Lubanda to become part of the 'global market.'" A curious sadness fell over her. "And if we do not or cannot become what they want us to become, they will make us feel ashamed of what we are."

With that, she folded the letter, dropped it into her basket, put the basket on her head, and stepped out of the room, leaving Fareem behind.

"She is thinking of Nadumu," he said. "A young man she . . ." He stopped and shook his head. "It is not for me to say about this." He shrugged. "Anyway, Martine thinks something bad is coming and that this letter is only the beginning of it."

"But it's just a government request," I assured him.

Fareem was anything but convinced of this.

"It's Martine's farm, Fareem," I repeated by way of calming what seemed to me his unjustified dread. "In the end, she doesn't have to grow coffee if she doesn't want to."

He shrugged, still unconvinced. "I must go to her now," he said.

He walked out into the market, and after a time I rose, stepped over to the door, and looked out to where I could see them moving through the stalls, buying and bartering in the way they always had.

A few minutes earlier, I'd sent Seso out for a few supplies, and just as I was about to return to my work, I saw him come up to Martine and

Fareem and the three of them become a small, compact group within the general ebb and flow of the market.

It was a vision of them together in that market, together in the peace that had reigned in Lubanda at that time, which now, so many years later, struck me as quite poignant, a connection soon to be severed, a world soon to be consumed.

"What Martine did wasn't for herself alone," I said to Bill. "She wasn't just living for herself the way you said she was that day in the village."

"I know," Bill said softly. "Otherwise she wouldn't have done what she did. But unfortunately, that's not how she was painted." He shrugged. "White devils all look alike."

I released a breath made weary by old memories. "You know, Bill, in one way or another, we were both as naïve as Mr. Quayle in *Bleak House*," I said. "Convinced that Africa could be saved by teaching the natives to build pianoforte legs."

To my surprise, Bill offered no resistance, or even a counterargument, to this dark assessment. Instead, he took a sip from his coffee and looked out at the street, briefly but with great concentration, as if he were in the midst of a grave reevaluation. "Coffee," he said. "Why couldn't she just have grown coffee?"

The answer to that question was simple, and so I stated it.

"She didn't grow coffee because the nomads didn't drink it," I said. "They never took any stimulants, remember? You'd never have caught them chewing khat like Mafumi's thugs. Martine wouldn't have grown coffee any more than she would have grown opium. And even if she had, she couldn't have used it to trade with the Lutusi."

"The problem is that a society can't move forward on any kind of purely local exchange," Bill said in his most authoritative, think-tank voice.

"The trouble is that we always define 'forward' as moving in our direction," I said bleakly. "But not everyone can, and not everyone should."

Bill nodded. "Perhaps so," he admitted.

I shrugged. "Anyway, Martine had already set her course," I added, then told him about the first time the risk of defying the "big men" in Rupala became clear.

I could no longer remember why I'd come to her farm that afternoon, though it was probably because the feeling I had for her, a strange mixture of admiration and desire, had been steadily growing during my time in Lubanda. The reason for this attraction was the same as it had been at the beginning, when I'd first begun to visit her—the hard life she'd lived, the stronger elements of her character that I'd only recently grasped, the fact that she seemed satisfied by her meager lot and didn't in the least expect ever to have more than her hardscrabble farm. From time to time, she would pick up a little package from what amounted to the post office, always a book she'd bought with whatever tiny amount of discretionary income her farm provided. But other than these occasional packages, she received nothing from outside Lubanda, nor appeared in the slightest degree drawn toward any aspect of that outer world's allure.

Even so, it would be many years before I understood the strange power in those, like Martine, whose hopes are modest, whose struggle is to retain what they have and what they are rather than acquire what they do not have or become what they are not. It wouldn't be to mankind's advantage if all people were this way, of course, but it is distinctly to its advantage that some are. The tragedy for Martine was that this little nugget of understanding came to me too late, and was, in fact, a jewel purchased with her blood.

In any event, on that particular day, I wasn't Martine's only visitor. It was only a few minutes after I arrived that he showed up, the minister of President Dasai's newly formed Agricultural Commission. He came in a flashy new Land Cruiser, but was dressed in the humbler attire of a yellow dashiki somewhat similar to the president's.

"Ah, you must be Miss Martine Aubert," he said cheerfully as he came toward Martine, Fareem, and me where we sat beneath the scrawny little tree that gave the only shade to the front yard.

Martine glanced first at Fareem, then at me, and in that look I saw the first glimmer of real fear, her dread that a dark tide was approaching slowly but inexorably, and that at some point she would either have to resist it or get out of its way.

We all rose as he approached, a gesture of respect toward a man who did not seem in the least threatening.

"I am Farmer Gessee," he said as he thrust out his hand. "May I join you on this hot day?"

I was aware that all members of the Agricultural Commission had been given the title "Farmer," but I'd never heard anyone actually use it.

"Please do," Martine said, "Would you like a drink? You must be thirsty."

"No, thank you," Gessee said. "I will not stay long."

We resumed our seats as Gessee sat down opposite us. With a big smile, he swabbed his face and neck with a tricolor handkerchief—red, green, yellow, the symbolic colors of an idealized continental unity that has never in the least existed. "It is hot today," he repeated with an exaggerated amiability that appeared studied because it was. "And no place hotter, I suppose, than Tumasi, eh?"

"The hottest place in the country," Martine said amiably. "And the driest, too."

Gessee nodded as he eased back in his chair. "What a lovely farm. How long have you owned it, Miss Aubert?"

"My family has been here for over fifty years," Martine answered. This clearly surprised Gessee.

"Fifty years," he repeated. "And your father was from . . ."

"He was born in Congo."

"So you are . . . Belgian?"

"I am Lubandan."

Gessee smiled broadly. "Of course, of course. But a beautiful country, Belgium."

"I've never been there," Martine said.

Gessee's attention drifted over to the front window, into the interior of the house, his gaze focused on the one bed he could see. He released a slow breath, then looked at Fareem. "From what part of Lubanda do you come?"

Fareem grew visibly tense. "The north."

"There is some trouble up there," Gessee said. "Among the Visutu. Do you go often to that region of Lubanda?"

"My mother is old," Fareem said. "So, yes, I go home."

"A good son," Gessee said amiably. "My respects to you. It is important to respect the elders. That is one of our traditions in Lubanda." He turned to Martine. "So, you have owned this farm for a long time. Strange that there is no record of it in Rupala. No deed, I mean."

"A deed is not required," Martine told him. "Not if the owner has been in residence for more than fifty years."

"True, true," Gessee said with a big smile. "I see you know our laws."

Martine only nodded.

There was a brief silence, then Gessee said casually, as if to dismiss the point, "Anyway, the records are not so good in Rupala." He looked at me. "I fear that we Lubandans have not yet mastered the Western art of record-keeping." Now he glanced out into the bush. "And, of course, no records are kept on the Lutusi at all."

"Why should there be records of the Lutusi?" Martine asked in a perfectly polite tone.

Rather than answer, Gessee drew his attention to a small box filled with Martine's carved oyster shells. "What are these?" he asked as he picked one up and clicked it.

"I make them," Martine answered. "The Lutusi children use them for music."

Gessee clicked the shells again, then again, so that they sounded like snapping teeth. "You give them to the children, I suppose?"

"The Lutusi do not accept gifts," Martine informed him. "I sell them or trade them."

"Simple trade," Gessee said. "It is very rudimentary, the economy of Tumasi." He returned the shell to the box after a final set of rapid clicks. "Surely we can agree that Lubanda needs more than that," he added in a tone that remained quite polite.

Martine gave no indication of either agreement or disagreement with Gessee's remark.

"What do you think Lubanda needs, Farmer Gessee?" she asked.

Rather than answer, Gessee asked the same question in return. "What do you think Lubanda needs, Miss Aubert?"

"To remain itself," Martine answered.

Gessee looked at her doubtfully. "Backward? Primitive?"

"Those aren't Lubandan words . . . or judgments."

"Well, just what is Lubanda to you, Miss Aubert?"

"Lubanda is itself," Martine answered.

For the first time Gessee appeared both challenged and exasperated by Martine.

"Miss Aubert, as a Lubandan, you should know that Village Harmony requires that the nation's needs be considered," he said softly, but firmly, like an elder talking to a child. "It's not enough for any one person simply to exist on his—or her—own. A true villager must contribute to the life of the *whole* village."

"Forgive me, sir, but may I ask if these are your words or the words of others?"

"Others?" Gessee asked. "What others?"

Martine looked at him squarely. "The foreigners who want Luban-dans to change, to be as *they* are. Who want Lubandans to buy what they sell and to make what they, these 'others,' want to buy." Her tone was curiously plaintive, as if she were standing before the bar at some critical moment, standing nakedly before it, with nothing but her cause to plead. "Money is a chain, Farmer Gessee. Soon the ones with this money will say to you, 'We wlll give you money if you educate Lubanda's children.' And you will force our children into the sort of schools these 'others' wish you to have. And to fill these schools our children will be forced to walk miles and miles from their villages, and during this walk the work of the village will be neglected, and in the schools there will be no teachers of these foreign subjects and so the children will learn nothing." She stared at him resolutely. "But none of that will matter because only attendance will matter, numbers you can show to these 'others' who have the money." Her gaze remained as gently firm as her voice. "This has happened in our neighboring countries, Farmer Gessee, and it is only one of many ways that their people have once again become slaves."

"Slaves," Gessee yelped. He seemed genuinely shocked by the word. "Lubandans will never be slaves."

Martine's features did not change. She gazed without aggressive-ness, but without compromise, into Gessee's large brown eyes. "That is my wish," she told him.

Then, quite unexpectedly, she smiled. "Please, you should get to your point, sir," she said. "You're a busy man, and so I'm sure you didn't come all the way from Rupala to chat with a poor Lubandan farmer about Village Harmony."

"Actually, that's precisely why I came, Miss Aubert," Gessee replied. He drew in a long, obviously strained breath, but continued in a tone that was gently instructive. "In the Agricultural Ministry, there is some concern that your farm is unproductive."

"My farm isn't unproductive," Martine said. "I grow finger millet, fonio, teff, and a—"

"The old staples, I know," Gessee interrupted. "Subsistence farming. These are the crops of underdevelopment." He laughed. "Teff," he said scornfully.

"It is a good grain," Martine said like a mother defending her child. "There is much iron and calcium. And because the grain is small, it can be cooked with less fuel."

Again, Gessee laughed. "But please, my dear child, you must tell me, who eats teff?"

"I do," Martine said. "And Fareem does. And so do most of the people who live in this part of Lubanda, especially the Lutusi." She sat back and rested her hands in her lap. "It is what the people here have been eating for thousands of years," she added. "Do you know why? It is because they can grow it here. They can grow it in this heat, in this infertile ground."

Gessee had now quite clearly had enough of this discussion. He looked back and forth from Fareem to Martine, but carefully avoided a glance in my direction. "You are both farmers," he said, his tone now growing harder. "But you are also villagers in our great village of Lubanda. Do you really want your fellow villagers to subsist on teff, on millet, on—"

"Yes," Martine answered with great firmness.

"Why?" Gessee asked quite sincerely, as if Martine's position truly made no sense to him.

"Because we can," Martine answered. "With these crops, we will never starve. This has been true for as long as anyone can remember."

Martine paused, then drew in a deep breath. "The Lutusi have many stories, sir," she said respectfully. "They tell stories about being eaten by animals, about getting lost, about dying because of accidents or misjudgments. But there is one kind of death the Lutusi have no stories about."

"And what is that?" Gessee asked.

"Famine," Martine answered. "Because they have never experienced it."

Gessee faced her silently.

"Famine," Martine said quietly, but pointedly, "will come to them if we do not grow the crops we use. And when this famine happens, the great foreign stores of food will flow in, and they will remain awhile. But when they come no more, as they surely will come no more at some point, we will be left even more destitute than before because by then we will have lost the skills and patience needed to grow our native crops, the ones that sustained us. After that, the one skill we Lubandans will need, Farmer Gessee, will be the art of begging."

"I see," Gessee said quietly, then rose and once again offered his hand. "Well, thank you for receiving me with such kindness and generosity," he added, almost sweetly, as he shook first Fareem's hand, then mine. "A pleasure to have met you." He now offered his hand to Martine. "Please consider your obligations to our village, Miss Aubert," he said by way of a final word.

With that he attempted to draw his hand from Martine's, but she gripped it tightly.

"What obligation?" she asked.

Gessee glanced down at his hand, Martine's tightly curled fingers. "Please, Miss Aubert," he said softly.

"It is *ujamaa*," Martine said darkly.

The fire that flashed in Gessee's eyes could have torched a town. "That will not happen here," he said.

"It will if no one stands against it," Martine said. Then, as if turned with a key, her fingers opened, and Gessee jerked his hand from hers. "And that stand must be made at the beginning," she added, "when there is still time."

Gessee nodded curtly. "We will meet again," he said in a voice that made no attempt to conceal that he was a man to be reckoned with. Then he turned and headed back toward his Land Cruiser.

"What's *ujamaa?*" I asked once Gessee had climbed into it and headed back down Tumasi Road.

"It is a Swahili word," Martine answered. "It means 'familyhood,' but what it really means is that the private farms will be collectivized and the labor needed to work them will be forced." She watched the dust from Gessee's car drift out over the bush. "It will destroy Lubanda."

*Ujamaa.*

I'd suddenly said the word aloud, as if I were still in Lubanda, rather than in New York, facing Bill, who now looked at me worriedly.

"That's what Martine called Village Harmony," I explained.

Bill knew well what *ujamaa* was, of course, and that it had wrecked Tanzania, turned it into a military state ruled by one party, its agriculture collectivized, its schoolchildren dogmatized; that it was a system which had spiraled downward into economic collapse and finally war with neighboring Uganda.

Bill watched me silently for a moment, then hazarded a conclusion. "It's tragic, what it did to you, your time in Lubanda." He paused, then added. "What it is still doing to you."

I waved my hand dismissively. "In almost every way, I got away clean."

Bill looked at me pointedly. "In every way, except Martine." He waited for me to respond to this. When I didn't, he drained the last of his coffee and set the cup down firmly. "So, what now, Ray? As far as Seso is concerned."

I shrugged. "I either find out more, or I don't."

"Well, if it's any encouragement," Bill said, "I think he deserves for us to find out why he came here and what he brought with him." He smiled. "But I know you feel that way, too, and because of it you'll go the length for Seso, right?"

*Not for Seso, no*, I thought. *For Martine*.

On that thought, and even as I rose and said goodbye to Bill, I recalled how Fareem had retreated into the house not long after Gessee departed, leaving Martine and me on the porch.

"Come," she said after a moment, "I want to show you something."

We walked to the road, then across it and out into the wastes, where, after a time, we reached a small rise.

"He is up there," Martine said. "My father."

We walked up the gently sloping hill. At the top of it, there was a mound, clearly a grave. At its head there was a stone hand-etched with the name François Aubert.

"The wind and sand take away some of the letters every year," Martine said. "My father would have found that very funny, the way Lubanda never stops trying to erase him." She seemed to retreat into herself, remain briefly in that secret place, then return. "So I am going to be burned," she said. "If I am to disappear, it will be on my own terms." She knelt beside the stone and ran her fingers over her father's name. "He was as good as his own father was evil."

By then I'd read and returned the book she'd given me on the *Force Publique* about the outrages its members had committed against the people of the Congo: working them to death in the rubber forests, burning villages, torturing and murdering anyone who rebelled against this oppression. Her own grandfather, Emile Augustin Aubert, had been prominent among those who'd both ordered and participated in these atrocities.

All of this was still swirling about in my head when she rose and faced me. "My father would have liked you, Ray," she said, and took my arm. We headed back to the farm in this formation, looking for all the world like the lovers we were not, but which I hoped we would be in the future, a hope that suddenly returned me to an earlier conversation with Fareem.

"And what of Nadumu?" I asked. "Fareem mentioned him, but then stopped. Is he a secret?"

Martine smiled. "He was a young man I loved." She stopped and pointed to the north. "His village was there, beyond that hill. His father was the chief of this village. We played together as children, like the ones in your English book, Catherine and Heathcliff."

"Where is he now?"

"Paris," Martine answered. "He went to school there, and after this schooling he came back. He wanted me to return there with him. He said Lubanda was no good." She shrugged. "He looked down on everything here, and I think soon he would have looked down on me."

And so she had remained where she was and what she was, and this alone should have been enough to change the course I later took. But love erects a wall that reason cannot penetrate, nor experience, nor history, nor any force outside its own passionate demands, love still the arrow that pierces every shield.

# Eleven

Life is a story of lessons learned too late, of course, but even so I couldn't keep from dwelling on Martine at her father's grave, the feel of her arm in mine as we'd left it and headed back toward the farmhouse. With every step of that walk, I'd once again felt myself both enthralled and consumed by her absolute singularity, the fact that there was simply no one else like her, not in all the world. I would certainly one day leave Lubanda, as I'd always known, but it was increasingly difficult for me to imagine leaving Martine here as Nadumu had. For there really is a kind of love that you know will not come again. It has within it an element of desire, to be sure, but it is not carved from that alone. It is the recognition, fierce and abiding, that it is the core of this person that both summons and deserves your devotion, the utter and irreplaceable "herness" of her that holds you in the exact way the ancient oath proclaims, for richer or poorer, in sickness and in health, forsaking all others, a bond only death—and perhaps not even that—can break.

By the time I realized that such was my feeling for Martine, I was already on my way to failure in Lubanda. I'd abandoned my well-digging project, convinced by her argument that for all its good intentions, it would do a world of harm. But to remain near Martine, I had to remain in the country, and the only way I could do that was as an employee of Hope for Lubanda. For that reason I had to find something to do, and so during the weeks following that fateful arm-in-arm walk, I worked quite feverishly to find some other useful project. Nothing came to mind, however, so that it was with a distinct fear of being sent home that I returned to Rupala after having been summoned there by no less a figure than Malcolm Early, the second in command of Hope for Lubanda.

We met at one of the riverside villas the English had left behind, one that had since been converted into an entertainment center, complete with a movie theater, a billiard parlor, a large room stocked with pinball machines, and, of course, a bar. Only the bar still had the feel of the old regime. It had high windows that looked out over the river, and tables set far apart and covered with white tablecloths. The curtains, too, were white, and they'd swayed softly in the languid breeze like the lingering ghosts of an earlier colonialism.

Early greeted me warmly, with a firm handshake, then lit a cigarette and blew a wide column of smoke into the gently undulating air. "So, how are you finding Lubanda?" he asked in an accent that was softly Southern, and in that way elegant and genteel. He was both a creature and a practitioner of gentle persuasion, a man so smooth and softly polished he seemed carved from ivory.

"I find it a lovely country," I told him.

"Even Tumasi?" he asked with a wistful smile that was not at all doubtful so that he seemed almost to confess his own enchantment with such places.

"Especially Tumasi," I answered in a way that struck me as quite bold but one that gave no hint that its greatest charm—at least for me—was a woman.

"Why especially?"

"The people there," I answered, "particularly the nomads."

"Yes, the Lutusi are certainly impressive," Early said quite thoughtfully, which was surprising, since I'd expected him to be the sort of

NGO executive Bill had told me about, little different from corporate CEOs—ambitious, arrogant, and always hot to generate new and bigger projects for new and bigger fund-raising opportunities. In fact, I hadn't even expected Early to know the name of a nomadic tribe, much less be familiar with its customs, but he'd been very well-informed with regard to the ways of the Lutusi, particularly the various routes they took across the central savanna, which he compared with the "songlines" of the Australian aborigines. He talked about their marital customs, the "animism" that formed the basis of their religion, and even their rejection of any form of intoxication. He knew of the "bush schools" where the young were trained and initiated, and that the "devils" of the bush played shifting roles, sometimes malicious, sometime benevolent. As he talked, I began to think of him as the sort of intrepid man of the world so often encountered in the literature of foreign adventure, men who'd slept beneath star-dappled skies, waded swollen streams, faced imminent death in jungles or desert wastes, and who, in old age, compared their scars in the darkly paneled gentlemen's clubs of the world.

"By all measures, they are a very self-reliant people," he concluded after demonstrating his impressively thorough knowledge of the Lutusi.

I nodded.

Early took a sip from his glass, looked at me very solemnly, then said, "So, is it your opinion, Ray, that they are happy as they are?"

"Yes," I answered truthfully, since they certainly seemed so to me.

"Hmm," Early said. "You may be right, but it's a risky supposition, don't you think?"

"Risky for whom?"

"For the Lutusi," Early said. "And our conviction that they are happy may easily be a very convenient one for us." He looked at me pointedly. "And so when I hear talk of the poor in the underdeveloped world being happy or content or whatever soothes our consciences and relieves us of

131

responsibility, I'm reminded of my antebellum Virginia ancestor's opinion of a people he affectionately called 'darkies,' and whom he believed to be happy with their lot." He paused briefly to let his remark sink in, then added, "My point is that if you believe a people content with their misery, then you can be content with their remaining in it."

"I suppose that's true," I said, "but those "darkies" were slaves. The Lutusi are free."

"That's true," Early said. "But frankly, I doubt that it's possible for people like us to know if a people as different from ourselves as the Lutusi are actually happy or unhappy. Do you share that doubt, Ray?"

"Yes."

"Of course you do," Early said with a quick smile, "because any other view would be arrogant. The fact is, a man with water can never comprehend another's thirst. Wouldn't you agree?"

I nodded.

Early looked out the window and let his attention follow the drift of the river. "It is all a mystery," he said. For a moment, he continued to watch the river. Then, as if suddenly called back to his purpose, he turned to me.

"We are concerned about the Visutu in the north," he said. "Particularly Mafumi, because he is gaining power and calling for a Visutu takeover of Lubanda." He crushed his cigarette into the glass ashtray before him. "We fear that it has not sufficiently dawned on President Dasai that he has a real problem on his hands with this fellow." He sat back slightly, and folded one long, Lincolnesque leg over the other. "So tell me, Ray, what have you seen from your vantage point up there in Tumasi? Any dangerous activity?"

"A week or so ago I saw some government troops heading north," I told him. "And I know that people are being moved into the north of the country. Besai people. Truckloads of them."

"Resettled, yes," Early said. "The hope is to create settlements to hold against Mafumi. In my opinion, it's a doomed effort. Those people, unfortunately, are in Mafumi's path, and my guess is that they will be the first to feel the panga."

"And that can't be stopped?" I asked.

"I certainly hope so," Early said. "But the fact is, it will be hard for President Dasai to control the far northern part of the country if he cannot maintain his authority in Tumasi. It is Lubanda's central region, after all. If it falls to Mafumi, then Rupala will eventually fall as well. It may take one year or two, but it will fall." He let me ponder this disturbing prediction, then added, "All you have to do is look at the map, Ray. The savanna is the buffer between north and south Lubanda. Whoever has control of it will have a staging area in the heart of the country. That's why the savanna needs to be secure, developed, and contributing to the nation's economy." Early's attention now followed a military truck as it rumbled along the road that bordered the river. "We can't get projects approved without stability in Lubanda, Ray," he said. "And Lubanda cannot be stable without its central region being secure. We've made that clear to President Dasai." He smiled. "This is why I asked you to meet me here in Rupala. Because I need your help with regard to President Dasai's plans in that part of Lubanda." He leaned forward, and I could see that he was quite sincere in his concern. "I need your help because, frankly, there isn't a lot of wiggle room now."

With this assertion, Early's voice softened. "I wish things were simple, Ray, but they're not. It's not a choice between this government or that one in Lubanda. If Dasai falls, it will be at the hands of Mafumi, and we all know what will happen after that." He paused a moment and looked at me quite sympathetically. "Bill says you have developed a relationship with a woman in Tumasi."

"A friendship, yes," I said.

"We've been asked to intercede on the president's behalf," Early told me. "Hope for Lubanda has been asked, I mean. And by Hope for Lubanda, I mean you."

"Intercede in what way?"

Rather than answer, Early said, "This woman, she's a small farmer, I understand?"

"Yes."

"And, unfortunately, I'm told that she's acting rather foolishly."

"In what way?"

"Refusing to grow coffee," Early said starkly, though with the sense of truly having Martine's interests at heart. "Which would be better both for her and for Lubanda." Another pause while he watched this latest of his assertions gather force in my mind. "Bill says you can help her see this. He doesn't think anyone else can." He waited for me to respond, but I could think of nothing to say, so after a moment, he said, "I understand she has no deed to this farm of hers."

"She doesn't need one," I said. "Her family has owned that farm for over fifty years."

"And it is your opinion that this insures her against what?"

I stared at him silently.

"Against . . . pangas?" Early asked pointedly.

The stark nature of what he'd just said settled over me.

"Who would be wielding these pangas?" I asked.

The question clearly made Early uncomfortable, but he had no choice but to answer it. "There are people here. People in the capital, close to Dasai, who are very impatient. If Mafumi succeeds, they will be hacked to death on Independence Square, and they know this. We're not talking about their losing their posts. They will lose their lives, and the lives of their wives and children. The streets of Rupala will run red with their blood. At the moment that is politics Lubandan style."

It was a chilling assessment. A dark cloud was gathering over Lubanda, and everything and everyone was at risk.

"It's the critical nature of the situation that brings me here, Ray," Early added. "And it's why I want your help with this woman."

"Why is she so important?" I asked. "She's just a small farmer in a—"

"It's not that she won't grow coffee," Early interrupted. "One farmer, who cares? It's that she's a woman, and more important, a white woman, and she is defying a government of black men. She is making them look weak and helpless, and Mafumi can use this against Dasai. That is a fact that we must face. This is a sexist society, Ray, and there is no small element of racism as well. In such a society a man in government cannot be humiliated by a woman—especially a white woman—and expect to maintain his position. No matter how well-meaning, a nice, chuckling president cannot afford to lose face. Dasai knows that. And more important, the not-so-chuckling people around him know it, too, and believe me, they are in earnest."

"Gessee."

"Among others, yes," Early answered frankly. He leaned back slightly. "Your friend is taking a position that there is simply no time to indulge. By taking it and holding to it, she is making Dasai look weak. No. Worse than weak. Impotent. And this cannot be tolerated, Ray. Not with Mafumi daily building strength among his fellow Visutu in the north. The rest of Lubanda has to unite like the fingers of a hand. You can tell your friend that. You can put it in whatever persuasive way you wish. You can appeal to her patriotism. But, Ray, she has got to grow coffee."

"I'm not sure I can make her see it your way," I told him.

Early peered at me intently. "If she doesn't, she's taking a very grave risk." His eyes took on the darkness of the truth he stated. "I hate to sound so dire, but Lubanda has reached that point where, as we say, the pedal meets the metal, and in such circumstances, as everyone knows, people easily become ruthless."

We talked on for a few more minutes. I floundered about, using Martine's arguments, that the crops she grew were the ones the region required. A region had to be self-sustaining, I told him, it had to grow what its people needed, crops that would always be of value regardless of the fluctuations in world markets. What if the price of coffee suddenly plummeted? What would happen then? Didn't we already know? Tanzania had instituted *ujamaa,* and disaster had ensued.

During all of this, Early listened silently, but with no give in his eyes. At the end, when I'd sputtered to a close, he said, "It was nice meeting you, Ray, but I should tell you that you were brought here to generate projects, that you are an employee of Hope for Lubanda, and that as an employee, you are obligated to help us do what we need to do—in this case, to help President Dasai by making Tumasi less vulnerable to Mafumi, who is, I must remind you, the real nightmare in the wings. I need hardly add that your friend, or any of the other white people in Lubanda, would not fare well under his regime. If for that reason alone, she should cooperate with the Agricultural Ministry."

With that he stood up and offered his hand. "I hope you can see your way to doing the right thing, Ray," he said. "Because you're a good man, and I'd like to have you stay in Lubanda." He took an envelope from his jacket pocket and handed it to me. "This is for your friend."

I saw that the envelope bore the sunflower seal of President Dasai.

"Please give it to her with the president's respects," Early said, "and be there when she reads it."

"You want me to be there when she reads it?" I asked. "Why?"

"Because we need to know what's going on in her mind," Early said matter-of-factly. "You are our only source for that vital information."

"I see," I said quietly.

"Please forward weekly reports to Bill," Early said. He looked at me in deadly earnest. "We are the hope for Lubanda, Ray. You and me and Bill and the others who come all this way and do all this work."

With that, he placed his hand on my shoulder and gave it a friendly squeeze. "Have another drink. No need to rush." He took out his wallet, paid the check, then handed me a hundred-dollar bill. "Spend the whole weekend in Rupala. Get a hotel. Relax and think over our conversation."

He offered his hand and I shook it, then took advantage of his offer and ordered an American beer that was ice-cold and absolutely delicious, a pleasure I hadn't enjoyed for weeks and which I took time to savor. Beyond the window, I saw Early make his way to where a dark car waited for him. It had a sunflower on the door, and a driver in uniform behind the wheel, clear evidence that he was being picked up and chauffeured around by the president's office.

It was already late in the afternoon by the time I finished that chilled, refreshing beer. I'd never stayed anywhere that hadn't been arranged beforehand by Hope for Lubanda, so in a sense that night was the first I'd spent in the capital that wasn't supervised. I was on my own, but in that part of the city there were a few hotels, so I found lodging without much trouble. The place was called the Rupala Arms, its name the only thing about it that suggested a Western standard of accommodation. The room was decidedly African in the way they'd long been thought of by the rest of the world, with a thin mattresses covered with equally threadbare sheets, but the air-conditioning purred sweetly and the cool was luxurious.

The restaurant next door served two things: a saucy cassava paste for the locals and watery spaghetti for any foreigner who might wander in. I ordered the spaghetti, and as I ate, I thought about something Early had said, the question of whether I'd want this life—or the one in Tumasi—for myself or my children. My answer was decidedly no, and in giving it, it seemed to me that I'd joined the side of Malcolm Early, along with others who were bringing hope to Lubanda. Why should I— why should any of us, the fortunate ones, the ones from the West—be content with leaving Lubandans to a level of development we ourselves wouldn't want or tolerate or, truth be told, wish on our worst enemies?

I left Rupala the next morning, my dusty Land Cruiser having been washed early that morning. A teenaged boy had not bothered to ask me if I wanted it washed before washing it, but his hand was out for the expected tip. I gave him a few recently minted "sunflowers," crawled behind the wheel, and headed north for Tumasi.

"So, you came back," Martine said when I pulled into the dusty yard of her farm a few hours later.

"Of course I came back," I said.

"Most of the aid workers stay in the capital," she said with a joking smile. "In those villas along the river, drinking cold beer."

"You shouldn't be so hard on them, Martine," I told her. "They really are here to help." I handed her the letter Early had given me.

"What's this?" she asked.

"Something from the president," I said. "He gave it to my boss, who gave it to me." I smiled. "I'm just the messenger."

She opened the letter, read it, then returned it to the envelope.

"I'm being ordered to grow coffee," she said. "If I do, people will be sent out to teach me how to do it. Since we're low on water in this region, they say I must use the dry method for processing the beans. Everything required for that method will be supplied to me. All I have to do is use it."

"Coffee," I said quietly. "Well, next to oil, it's the most valuable commodity there is."

"To the West it is valuable," Martine said, "but not to me." She glanced out into the bush. "And not to the Lutusi or anyone else in Tumasi."

"How do you know it wouldn't be a good thing to grow coffee in this part of Lubanda?" I asked.

"Coffee has to be processed, Ray," Martine answered. "A lot of labor is required to plant, to harvest, to remove the cherry from the beans. All of it requires labor. Where do you think that labor will come from? It will come from the Lutusi, who will be forced to produce it." She shook the letter in the air. "This is the first step in their destruction," she said. "In the destruction of their world, which is also mine." She grabbed my hand and pressed the letter into it. "My answer is no."

Against the force of her determination, I could only stand silent.

"Fareem will want me to do it," she added, almost to herself. "He says that in the end, they will take my farm. And he may be right." She gazed out over her fields and for the first time, I saw terror in her eyes. Not apprehension. Not dread. But actual terror.

And so, with a hesitant, almost trembling hand, I touched her bare shoulder, then drew my fingers down and took her hand. She didn't respond, but she didn't pull away either, and so for a few luxurious seconds I savored this small intimacy.

Finally, she drew her hand from mine and turned toward me. "Come, let us go sit under the tree. It is cooler there."

And so we did, the two of us, alone, both more or less silent. I didn't know how to approach her, and I was afraid to make an argument against her. Caught in that web, I simply lingered for a time, talking of nothing in particular until, on the pretext of needing to write a report, I headed back to Tumasi.

It was the middle of the afternoon when I got back to the village. The market was in full swing, with a large group of nomads strolling among the stalls, buying cloth or jerry jars. The women sometimes folded a swath of brightly colored cotton over their arms or encircled their waists with it. The children played around them, chasing each other, sticks and stones the only toys they needed. The men moved slowly, and with great dignity, carrying their staffs like crosiers, hardly ever touching anything.

"How did it go in Rupala?"

I turned to find Fareem standing beside me.

"Martine will tell you," I answered.

"Then it's bad news," Fareem said.

"The government wants her to grow coffee, Fareem," I told him. "It's part of a larger plan, a way of stopping Mafumi."

"Nothing can stop Mafumi." His eyes endeavored to betray nothing, yet in their grim sparkle they betrayed the hopelessness he felt. Then he smiled, but with dark irony. "It's Lubandan Independence Day," he said. "There'll be dancing and a bonfire here in Tumasi. A big party. Martine is coming."

"She should have told me," I said. "I would have driven her into the village."

"She prefers to walk," Fareem said. "You must find that quite ridiculous, but it's the way she holds herself together. We all have to hold ourselves together, don't you think, Ray?"

I nodded. "Well, I have a little work to do," I said, and with that turned away and walked to my office.

I was still at my desk when night fell and the bonfire was lit. I could hear the drums, the chants, the singing, the general celebratory sounds of the village. After a time, I walked to my door and looked out. The air was pitch black so that the blaze of the fire seemed all the redder, a fierce, leaping flame. The people were dancing around it, and among them I saw Martine. She seemed entirely at home, her face radiant in the firelight, her long hair swinging back and forth, her white arms swaying palely in the dark air. She turned in a slow circle, her arms going up and down her body in the same dance as the women around her, sensuous and earthy, her expression at once joyful and serene. But beautiful as it was, it was not a vision I could enjoy without peril, because in order to stay in Lubanda, I had a job to do. And so I was soon back at my desk, writing my report, the one I would send to Bill in Rupala the next day, my work now very different from any I had ever imagined for myself. For without consciously realizing its consequences or calculating its awesome risks, I had become a spy.

# PART III

"The president certainly would not have kept you waiting, Mr. Campbell," the minister tells me as he gently takes my arm and turns me from the window.

"It's not his fault," I assure him. "I'm early. I know that our appointment is for noon, but when I landed in Rupala it was already after ten. I'd hoped to have time to go to my hotel, freshen up a bit, but with my late arrival, I had no time for that." I smile cordially. "I didn't want to be late for my appointment with the president."

The minister returns a smile as warm as my own. "I am sure he would have understood," he tells me. "He is, as his life has demonstrated, a very patient man."

And patient he has surely been, Lubanda's new, reformist president. Patient in exile, endlessly railing against Mafumi's madness, calling for regime change from podiums in London, Paris, Copenhagen. Patient as one after another of his exiled compatriots fell to Mafumi's assassins. Patient as he himself escaped numerous attempts on his life: stabbed in Lyon, shot at in Brussels, almost run over in Oslo, the last attack having left him with a slight limp. Everything about him suggests this unearthly patience. He is modest in his dress, and wears the scholarly gold-rimmed glasses that mark him as a thoughtful man, by all accounts fluent in English, German, and French, a moderate man whose inner compass shifts neither north nor south, but holds with impressive steadiness to his hope for Lubanda's future.

"It is only now that the president's work really begins, of course," the minister reminds me. "Lubanda was pillaged by Mafumi. He took everything and left us only"—he stops and nods toward the window, where the voices of the children can now be heard singing the new national anthem—"orphans."

This is a dreadful portrait of Lubanda's current situation, but on the road from the airport to the Presidential Palace I'd seen heartbreaking evidence for its accuracy. There'd been shantytowns as far as the eye could see, their dusty alleys filled with children. In addition, I'd passed a large tent city that looked like nothing so much as a vast field of tattered cloth flapping in the dry wind. And under each flap, of course, there'd been another gathering of destitute children.

"We would bring them all to the palace if we could," the minister informs me. "But as you know, our resources are limited."

I glance to the left, where a framed map of Lubanda is displayed. It is a paper map, dry and cracked with the years. A swath of brown traverses the map east to west and in that way designates the great savanna the Lutusi had once roamed. A black dot indicates the village of Tumasi, but there is nothing to designate Martine's farm, nor the dusty side of the road where Ufala had found Fareem so badly beaten, his first words to her spoken in delirium, *Martine, Martine.*

The minister clearly sees the distress that suddenly rises in me, though he could have no idea of its cause.

"I am told that it has been many years since you were in Lubanda," he says cautiously, perhaps in order to return me to some less troubling frame of mind. "And that you are now living in New York."

I turn from the map. "I came back ten years ago," I said. "And I came again a month ago."

The minister is clearly surprised to hear of this most recent trip. "You came to Lubanda a month ago? Why did you not tell us? We would have welcomed you and—"

"I came in secret," I inform him. "By way of Accra, then overland to the border. I crossed it at Gomoa. Without a visa."

"You entered our country illegally," the minister states without either alarm or accusation. "It is easy to do in the north." He looks at me quizzically. "But why did you come to Lubanda in such a way?"

"I was on a mission," I answer. "A secret mission. It had to do with a murder."

The word "murder" has always had a sobering effect, and I can see proof of that in the minister's eyes. It is as if simply hearing the word puts one at risk.

"Seso Alaya," I add.

The minister clearly does not recognize the name.

"He was a friend of mine," I inform the minister. "He was murdered in New York City three months ago."

The minister does not react in any way to this added information save with a quiet, "I'm sorry to hear of this."

He adds nothing to this expression of condolence. I do not press the matter, but instead let my attention drift back to the map. A slightly weaving line designates Tumasi Road, but no mark indicates the great wrong that occurred along its route. If life were kind, it would provide such markers, so that we could contemplate the risks, and thus be far more careful in terms of what we do. Halted in place, we would look ahead and judge whether hope or despair should guide us, vengeance, force, or mercy stay our hand.

But life is as it is, in all things as desperate and uncertain as the hope I have brought for Lubanda.

# New York City, Two Months Earlier

# Twelve

Because there seemed no way to pursue Seso's death, I'd more or less returned to my usual routine after showing Bill the photograph I'd bought from Dalumi. And yet, I continued to take it out and look at it from time to time. What could possibly have driven Seso to come so far? Hope has sometimes inspired such effort, I knew, but it has usually been driven forward by an even deeper fear.

*Fear.*

Another of risk management's simple formulations returned to me: *Fear freezes action.* I recognized that as a statement, this was, to say the least, a penetrating glimpse into the obvious, one so leaden, in fact, that it could only have taken wing in an academic wind tunnel, in my case a university classroom presided over by a forgettable professor who, to my surprise, had added a salient point to this otherwise quite unspectacular pronouncement. Standing behind a podium, he'd paused dramatically, stared solemnly at his captive audience, then added, "This is the simple truth that every schoolyard bully knows, along with every tyrant. Fear governs the human heart, and only the deepest and most passionate of purposes can overcome it."

I'd sat in the classroom that afternoon, surrounded by students far too naïve to grasp the cold reality of what the professor had just said, and thought again of the sweltering afternoon Seso had burst through the door of my house in Tumasi, breathless, terrorized. *You must come! You must come!*

Since returning from my last, ill-fated trip to Lubanda some ten years before, I'd avoided the memory of such fiercely unsettling moments. But now, by looking into Seso's murder, I'd ventured out of that risk-aversive cocoon, though only far enough to reach a dead end with regard to my little investigation. The odd thing was that despite reaching that dead end, I'd continued to feel uneasy and sometimes distracted, and at all times strangely empty. It was as if a small bird had briefly taken wing within the vast empty spaces of my soul, then, following its short flight, had settled back into a nest it no longer found comfortable.

Perhaps it was that deep discomfort, the unfilled hole within me, that once again returned me to my own little tribe, the classics. I thought of Venus, how she'd pleaded with Adonis to hunt only easy prey. In Tumasi, that male/female role had been reversed, I who'd urged Martine to be cautious, to weigh her actions, and finally to compromise, she who'd refused every avenue of escape.

We'd been standing beside my Land Cruiser the first night I'd pointed out the risks inherent in her position. By then I no longer had to make up reasons to drop in on her. I was a secret agent now, making contact with my target.

But why had I accepted my new mission as a spy?

The answer, of course, was simple. I wanted Martine to compromise, because I wanted her to be safe and I felt that her position was putting her at increasing risk. Malcolm Early's warning was continually ringing in my ears, each time more convincingly. Martine was a very conspicuous thorn in the side of Rupala's plan to develop Tumasi, and the big men in the capital would have to find a way to pull it out. It would be far better, it seemed to me, if Martine could see this as inevitable and any resistance to it as futile. If reporting her activities to Bill Hammond might serve that effort in some way, then spy I would.

But there was also this: I wanted to buy time for her to fall in love with me more deeply than she had for Nadumu, and I'd come to believe that perhaps she would. She was somewhat older now, after all, and certainly she no longer romanticized any aspect of life in Lubanda as perhaps she had some years before. In addition, there was evidence—for the possibility that her feelings for me were deepening. She'd begun to come to the market more often, and to invite me to her farm more often. We took long walks and talked of our pasts, she of her father's death when she was fifteen and her consequent struggle to keep the farm afloat in the wake of that loss, I of an easy Midwestern childhood, followed by my move to New York and my work in a school there. We'd talked about books as well, and it had become clear that she'd read considerably more English novels than just *Wuthering Heights*, the book she'd referenced the night she'd told me about Nadumu. She'd also talked in considerable detail about the terrible things her grandfather had done in Congo as a member of the *Force Publique*—the villages he'd torched, the prisoners he'd tortured, the massacres that had been carried out at his command—a bloody personal history that I thought might explain Martine's seemingly unbreakable commitment to Lubanda, an effort, as I suggested on that evening, a week or two after my meeting with Malcolm Early, at atonement.

"I am sorry," she said. "I have heard this word, but I do not know what you mean."

"That you feel guilty for what your grandfather did," I said. "And so you're trying to make up for it."

"Why do you say this, Ray?" she asked.

I realized that I'd reduced her to a stereotypically guilt-ridden liberal, but I saw no way out of the hole which I'd dug for myself. "I just mean that I know how much you want to help Lubanda." I shrugged. "The same way I do."

She shook her head. "Not at all like you," she said. She plucked one of her carved oyster shells from the basket beside her chair. "Here," she said as she offered it to me. "I want you to have this."

I put out my hand, but she didn't place the shell in it.

Instead she nodded toward my hand. "Look at your hand, Ray. The palm is up, but more important than this, your hand is under my hand. It is this way because the giver always has the upper hand." Her look was piercing. "The Bantu have a saying: '*The hand that gives, rules.*'"

She started to add something to this remark, but suddenly stopped cold, her gaze at first curious, then troubled, then darkly resigned as she stared out into her fields. "That is Farmer Gessee's latest move, by the way," she said.

I turned in the direction she indicated and saw eight or nine men walking, one behind the other. They were quite far away, but even so I could see that they were carrying pangas.

"They are walking my property line," Martine said. "They have been doing this every night for the last week." She watched them closely, like one following a serpent's slithering approach. "They will be careful not to cross it." Her eyes drifted over to me. "In Rupala they think I am selfish because I want to do as I wish with my property, but what will happen to Lubanda when none of us can do what we wish with our land? What power will be left but the one held by the big men in Rupala?" She shook her head. "Power is even more greedy than money, Ray, and because of that, we should fear it more."

Fareem came out of the farmhouse, his expression very grave as he stared at the distant line of men. "Gessee's people," he said. "We should go out there and tell them we know this."

Martine shook her head. "If we confront them, they will say we provoked them." She smiled in a way meant to ease Fareem's distress. "It is a beautiful evening. Quiet. Good for talk, so let us just talk."

And so we did, though even as we spoke of other things, we continued to watch the men as they slowly paced back and forth along the farm's property line. From time to time they would stop and face the farmhouse, hold in that position for a moment, then move again. They never raised their pangas and shook them in the air, nor made any other threatening gestures. It was their presence that threatened, the simple fact that they knew where Martine was and could come for her at any time.

There is nothing more forbidding than men awaiting orders. This was the truth I learned that night as the three of us watched darkness fall, the men still in the distance, parading back and forth, stopping to pose, then marching again, always in a straight line, as if to provide yet more grim evidence that they would do whatever they were told.

"How far do you think they might go to make you grow coffee?" I asked behind the mask of being on her side rather than one who listened, recorded, noted, and informed upon her. "Gessee and the others in Rupala?" When she didn't answer, I asked, "What are you thinking?"

She let her head loll backward and ran her fingers though her hair. "That I like the wild sounds. The animals and the insects." With that she rose and walked into the house, leaving Fareem and me alone beneath the tree.

"She's very afraid now," Fareem said after a moment. "She tries not to show it, but she's scared to death." A pause, then, "Last night she was talking about Patrice Lumumba, the way he was beaten over and over again before they killed him." For the first time, he seemed curiously defeated, like a man in a card game he knows is stacked against him. "It wasn't enough just to shoot him and throw him in a hole."

For a time we sat silently as the darkness deepened and thickened, turning the air into a solid brew.

"There's something I don't understand," Fareem said finally. He was still looking at the short column of men. "How do they know so well Martine's land line? There are no clear boundaries." He watched as the men continued to make their way single file along what appeared a straight line. "Martine walked them with you, didn't she, the boundaries of the farm?"

I stiffened a bit, at least inwardly, and wondered if he'd somehow gotten wind of the conversation I'd had with Early and now suspected that I'd even gone so far as to feed him technical information about Martine's farm.

"Yes, we walked them," I admitted casually, as if I sensed no suspicion in his voice.

Fareem abruptly turned toward me. "Have you ever thought of becoming Lubandan?" he asked.

Such a step had never once occurred to me.

"You'd have to renounce your American citizenship and pledge allegiance to our sunflower flag," he added quite seriously. "Which is the only way Lubanda's fate will ever really matter to you, Ray."

I don't know what my reaction would have been to this, but it didn't matter because Fareem suddenly spoke again. "Ah," he said solemnly, his gaze directed toward the far field. "The next step."

I stared out across the fields to where a low trail of fire began to move along the property line until all of Martine's farm was ringed in a necklace of flame.

"It's a traditional warning to a tribe that has intruded on another tribe's land," Fareem said as the fire quickly burned itself out and the fields were in darkness again. "They are saying that Martine is a squatter on their land. They are saying that she is like you, Ray, not Lubandan."

Had I been schooled in the principles that define my profession, I would have known that a fearful measure of risk had just been added to Martine's life.

"I was on a boat once," Fareem said. "In Kenya. We were drifting past a village. I heard a lot of noise, a lot of yelling, and when I looked over I saw a woman, maybe thirty years old. She was running toward the river. She was naked and lots of people were after her. Men, women, children. They were chasing her and throwing things at her and she was trying to get away from them. But there was no place for her to go but into the river. Someone on the boat said, 'She's a witch. They're going to skin her.' I don't know what happened after that. We had passed the village by the time the crowd was pulling her out of the river." He paused, then looked at me. "You cannot let that happen to Martine."

"I would never let anything like that happen to her," I assured him firmly, because I believed with all my heart that it was true.

Martine came out of the house just at that moment. She was watching the distant fires, but nothing about them appeared to surprise her. It was only the next step, and I could tell that she had anticipated it.

"Men," she said softly as she continued to stare out into the fields, where they were now jumping back and forth over the glowing embers, shouting, egging each other on, their display growing more and more crazed and violent as each worked to outdo the other. "They are such little boys."

# Thirteen

It was while still floating in the disturbing eddies of that memory, and perhaps urged forward by it, that I resolved to make one more effort in my investigation of Seso's murder, called Max Regal, and asked if he'd made any progress with regard to the case.

"It's pretty cold," Max said. "You talk to Dalumi?"

"Yes," I answered. "But he had nothing of value to say."

"I'm not surprised," Max said. "Okay, so the only new development since I talked to you is that we found where Seso got that tattoo. A parlor on Twenty-first Street. Other than that, we're at the same dead end we usually reach with these sorts of killings."

"So still no idea what Seso was doing here?" I asked.

"Nope. You?"

"Nothing."

Regal mentioned another case, a murder near the Shabazz market in Harlem. It had nothing to do with Seso, as far as I could tell, just another "African killing" that would go unsolved. I let him talk, then asked him to keep me in the loop with regard to Seso's death. He said he would, and that was the end of it.

Gail came into the office just as I hung up.

"You okay?" she asked.

"Yes, why?"

"Just that look on your face," she said.

That was enough to spur me forward. "Cancel my appointments for the rest of the day," I told her.

Gail said something in return, but by then I was far enough away that it didn't matter. I simply wanted to be out of the office and walking in the open air, beyond the awesome complexities, if we ever can be, of risk management. Certainly I had no destination in mind when I fled my office. I'd needed to think, that's all, to think, but more important, to *feel* Martine again, and by that very act, put something fearfully at risk. And a risk it surely was, particularly given the fact that in thinking of her I had to accept the awesome truth that I was doomed to live without she who had most warmed and informed me, whose presence had most lifted and enlightened me, and whose fulsome joys and sorrows had lent a fearful beauty to my life.

A path need not be a destiny, of course, and yet, as I closed in on the tattoo parlor Max Regal had mentioned, I felt myself following a trail that would perhaps lead me to a different place than the one I'd sought and found and accepted after leaving Lubanda. E. M. Forster had once written that the tragedy of unpreparedness is well-known; it is the tragedy of the well-prepared, of those who thought things through, made all the right decisions, and yet despite all their careful preparations came to ruin, that is the deepest one in life. Surely that had been Martine's tragedy, I thought, for she'd done everything she could to avoid the fate that overwhelmed her. Perhaps, in that way, she'd proved just how truly Lubandan she'd actually been.

It was the dark nature of that concluding supposition that had pressed itself deeper into my mind as I'd walked the streets that day. Some years before, a young female aid worker had been murdered in South Africa. Her parents had later forgiven their daughter's killer in a great display of Western "understanding" that Martine would have despised. That was what had made her unique, that she was genuinely a daughter of her country, without a trace of condescension toward her fellow Lubandans, and incapable of making excuses for them in the sickening way of Westerners, who, even as they make these excuses, seed them with the unspoken and unspeakable sense that, *Well, what do you expect? We're dealing with savages here.*

No one had known this aspect of Martine better than Seso, though during all the time we'd been together in Tumasi he'd actually had very little to do with her. Indeed, he'd seemed wary of having any connection to her at all. And yet, he'd told Dalumi that he'd been working for her.

But what work could this have been? Posing that question, I decided to pursue the only slim lead left to me with regard to Seso's activities in New York.

The shop had no name. The sign over the window simply said "Tattoos" and left it at that. Its front window hadn't been washed and so it was through a film of accumulated dust and grime that I looked at the various tattoos that were offered. There were the usual dragons and sea monsters and arrow-clutching eagles. A few vaguely Satanic offerings were also prominently displayed. Inside I could get rock band tattoos and musical instrument tattoos, along with a sketch of John Lennon's face.

I nodded when the tattoo artist came through the curtain and faced me from behind a small counter. He was small, but with the thick body of a former wrestler. His face had a battered look that reminded me of Rodin's famous sculpture of a pugilist at rest. He had the same cauliflower ears as that figure, and the same slightly flattened nose. But Rodin's statue had portrayed a man captured by a certain curiosity, if only to know if he'd been judged the winner of the fight. The man behind the counter had the dead eyes of one who no longer posed questions.

"I'd like a tattoo," I told him because nothing else occurred to me and it seemed too soon to launch directly into my purpose.

He laughed. "Bullshit."

When I said nothing, he looked me over doubtfully. "Where you want this tattoo?"

I couldn't tell if this was his actual question or code for a different one, so I said, "What are my options?"

He shrugged. "I can put it on your balls if that's where you want it."

"The chest will do," I said. "Right in the middle."

"The area will have to be shaved," the man told me, once again with an odd look, half conspiratorially, half uncertainly, as if we were partners in a dance whose steps neither of us knew. "Unless you're a waxer."

"I'm not."

"You got a design in mind?"

I decided that the moment had come. "An oyster shell," I answered pointedly. "You recently gave one to another customer, I believe."

I couldn't be sure that this was true. He might well not have been the man in the shop when Seso came here. For that reason, I added a chip to the pile. "He ended up dead."

Now something registered in the tattoo artist's eyes, and so I took the risk of capitalizing on the hint of recognition I saw in them.

"The tattoo was exactly like this one," I said as I drew the photograph of Seso from my jacket pocket and showed it to him. Quickly I added, "I'm not a cop. I'm sure the cops have already been here."

The tattoo artist's gaze settled upon me like the tip of a spear. "What you want from me?"

"I'm looking for whoever it was who killed this man," I said.

The tattoo artist said nothing, but I'd seen the look in his eyes before. It was part suspicion, but that wasn't the whole story. There was a force behind the suspicion, a hard-shelled capacity for taking what cops call a "trimming," meaning a very tough interrogation, and with every threat growing more determined to keep his mouth shut.

I returned the photograph to its now familiar place in my jacket. "The cops want to find out what happened to him because it's their job to do that," I said quietly. "I want to find out what happened because he was my friend." I offered my hand. "Ray Campbell."

I had hoped this would work, and I saw that it had when the man took my hand. "They call me Idi. They say I look like him, that crazy fucker. You know who I mean?"

If this was a simple test of my familiarity with modern African history, I was ready for it.

"I'd guess you mean Idi Amin," I said. "He's the only Idi I know."

"You think I look like him?" he asked.

"I can see the resemblance, yes," I answered.

"Because I am Kakwa," the man said. "Amin's tribe."

He did not say "African" or even "Ugandan," and here, in a nutshell, was one of life's grim truths, the simple, irreducible fact that we are all tribal.

"Maybe the only Kakwa in New York," he said.

Unhappiness sometimes provides a way into someone, and quite suddenly I saw this displaced Kakwa tribesman's unhappiness and sensed that it worked that way in him, that his wound, whatever it was, remained open, and thus was a door.

"The man's name was Seso," I said. "And if the cops told you he was a drug dealer or a thief or something low like that, then they told you wrong. Seso was a good man, a family man." I let this sink in before I added, "He came to New York for a reason. It took a lot of effort, and a lot of courage, and probably the last dime he had, and so I believe that the reason was important."

Idi watched me silently for a moment. He was obviously trying to make up his mind about me. In another face I might have seen fear or

162

some secret calculation of potential profit, but in this one I saw moral quandary, a soul working to do right, but unsure what that might be.

"Seso was Lutusi," I added. "He was probably the only one in New York."

Now this other lone tribesman stepped around the desk, walked to the door, and turned the "Open" sign around to "Closed." Then he returned behind the counter and parted the curtain that led to the back of the shop. "Back here," he said.

I followed Idi into the back room, where there was a bed and a chair, both of which matched the room's general squalor.

"Take off your shirt," Idi said in a tone of complete command, so that I began to imagine him as the real Idi Amin, the brutal tyrant who'd designated and equipped torture rooms in Kampala's most upscale hotel, rooms that had often been quickly mopped so that he could subsequently use them for assignations with his whores.

"I don't want a tattoo," I told him. "I'm sure you figured that out."

"Take off your shirt." Idi repeated sternly when I hesitated. "If the boss comes you say you was getting a tattoo, but you got scared and changed your mind." He looked at me as if I were a fellow conspirator. "I got to cover my ass, you know?"

I nodded "I understand."

I took off my jacket, folded it over the back of the chair, then removed my shirt and undershirt and folded them.

Idi nodded toward the bed. "On your back."

"Does it hurt, a tattoo?" I asked for little reason other than to keep the conversation going.

"The pain is worse for some than others," Idi answered in a matter-of-fact way that suggested he'd learned this in something other than a tattoo parlor.

I lay down on the bed, then noticed the mirror attached to the ceiling.

"Some people like to see the work as it goes along," Idi explained when he stepped over to the bed. He looked down at me, and under his gaze I felt entirely helpless. He was younger and stronger and although I might put up a fight, I knew it would be futile.

I suddenly imagined the grimmest of possibilities, that it was here, on this table, that Seso had been strapped down, a gag stuffed into his mouth, his shoes and socks removed, exposing the soles of his feet and their clusters of tender nerves; that it was here, in this back room, that his captors had applied the metal bars.

"To make it look real, I got to do some things," Idi said. "The boss is no fool, so it's gotta look real."

He stepped away and out of sight, though I knew he was at the little table I'd seen when I came into the room. It was located only a few feet beyond where I lay, so that I could hear the tiny, metallic sounds of what he was doing—sharpening the needles, assembling the tattooing gun. Shortly, I heard him open the door of the autoclave I'd also noticed, then the sound of a metal tray being placed inside it.

"It takes a little over twenty minutes to sterilize the needles," Idi said like a man giving a tour of his workplace. "Sometimes, when they are waiting, they are the most afraid."

It struck me that the psychology of the torture chamber didn't require much sophistication. There is the actual pain, but before that, there is the waiting, as the instruments are assembled, sharpened, heated according to their subsequent functions. Once, in Mexico City, I'd come across the strangest version of Christ's Crucifixion I'd ever seen, a wooden carving of the Son of Man not yet hung upon the Cross, but sitting on it, his feet nailed but not yet his hands, his lacerated back curled toward his bent knees, his head falling into the nest of his hands, his blood-matted hair in his fingers . . . waiting.

"I saw on TV, these two cons did their eyes," Idi said above the continual tinkling of metal. "Tattooed the whites, I mean. One did red. One did blue."

"Why would anybody want the whites of their eyes tattooed?" I asked.

"To be different, maybe," Idi answered.

"That's an easy way to be different," I said, "much easier than actually accomplishing something."

Idi shrugged. "The world's full of crazies, eh?"

I suddenly noticed that a Liberian flag hung from two thumbtacks on the wall.

"I thought you were Ugandan," I said.

"The guy who owns the place, it's his flag," Idi said indifferently.

"It's a terrible place," I said. "Boy soldiers wearing wedding dresses and female wigs while they hack people to death."

Idi said nothing.

"And then there was General Butt Naked," I added in my best old-chum voice, just a guy talking to a guy.

"Who's that?" Idi asked, though with little sense of actual interest.

"He was the leader of a wild Liberian soldier gang," I answered. "They thought being naked would protect them from bullets."

Idi glanced at the flag. "They were slavers, you know, those fucking Liberians."

I heard the door of the autoclave open, then more tinkling, and at last the sound of a small motor.

"So tell me, what else do you know about Africa besides this naked general?" Idi asked at one point.

"Not much, I'm afraid," I admitted starkly, now thinking both of my time in Lubanda and of all the years since I'd left it. "Not much at all."

I noticed Idi looking at me bleakly. Then, before I could ask my first question, he said, "There were two of them. They stood by while I did the tattoo."

"Africans?"

Idi nodded. "They wanted an oyster shell. Your man, he didn't say nothing at all. He was drugged, I think."

"Seso wasn't conscious?"

Idi shook his head. "His eyes opened and closed, but there was no light in them." He turned, walked over to the sink, and began to wash his hands, his back to me.

"So Seso never said anything to you?" I asked.

"Nothing," Idi answered. "It was just before I closed when they showed up. There were two of them, like I said. They told me the man, the one who ended up dead, they told me he was drunk. They made like it was all a big joke, getting a tattoo. They said he would wake up, see the tattoo, and be in big trouble with his wife, shit like that. It was all supposed to be just a couple of guys pulling a trick on another guy, you know?"

I smiled. "Men are such . . . little boys."

Idi nodded. "I didn't believe any of that shit, but I didn't have no choice."

From here, Idi narrated a tale of being forced to tattoo Seso. He'd refused at first, he said, but the men who'd brought Seso into his shop had made it clear that they would brook no objection.

"They did not say why they wanted this particular tattoo," Idi told me. "But they asked for it. The little one did. A shell, he said. So I did the tattoo he wanted and when I was finished, they took a picture of it. The smaller one, he had a phone, and he took a picture with the phone.

And I think he sent this picture to someone, because he fiddled a little with the phone, and then he said to the tall one, he said, 'Okay, it went.' But he didn't say it in English. That's what scared me even more. He said it in Ululu. You know what that is?"

As it happened, I did. "That's the Visutu dialect," I said, thinking how unlikely it would be to find it spoken anywhere but among that tribe, Mafumi's tribe. "How did you know it was Ululu?" I asked.

"I used go through the northern part of Lubanda," Idi answered. "The Visutu area. This was when Mafumi was in power. If you spoke English, or some other dialect other than Visutu when you were in the north, they cut out your tongue."

I knew that this was true, and that because of such extreme measures the Visutu had been thought of as the Khmer Rouge of Lubanda, bent upon ridding the country of every vestige of any culture but their own.

"So the men who had Seso, they were Visutu?" I asked.

Idi shrugged. "They spoke Ululu so I wouldn't understand them. And I didn't let on that I did."

For the first time I began to wonder if the new Lubandan government might have entrusted Seso with a secret mission that had, in turn, been thwarted by men still loyal to Mafumi. The new president had initiated a policy of reconciliation patterned after that of South Africa under Nelson Mandela. The risk of such a policy, of course, was that it allowed the criminals of the old regime to gather strength and with that strength seek once again to regain their lost power. Mafumi had been a cult figure, ardently worshipped. At his funeral, people had gathered in great throngs, weeping and fainting as his coffin passed through the streets of Rupala. The ghost of such a man—like his evil—lives after him, of course, and because of that, I thought it quite possible that members of Mafumi's ghost brigade had followed Seso across half the globe, beaten his feet, then strangled him, all in an effort to discover whatever it was he'd brought here.

But what could Seso have had that would have mattered to any of Mafumi's old guard?

"One more thing," I said quietly. "If anyone else comes here, those two or anyone else, people asking about Seso, I mean, be sure to tell them about me." I reached for my wallet, plucked out one of my business cards. "Tell anyone who shows up that I know what Seso brought with him," I added as I handed it to Idi, "then tell them where I am."

"That is very risky," Idi said, but he took the card.

Risky, yes, I thought, and thus an unusual step for me. And yet, the possible gain seemed worth it. For although we may get a second chance to make back the money we squandered, we rarely get the chance, however inadequately, to address a wrong, much less one done long ago, in a distant land, to one who never knew we did it, nor would ever know.

# Fourteen

Not long after moving to New York, I came to realize that a city of dreams can only grow from soil enriched by broken ones, and that by that measure, New York has the richest soil on earth. You see the still breathing corpses of these old dead dreams everywhere: crowding the bars, walking the side streets, sitting idly in the park. It was impossible for me to imagine Seso as ever being such a person, however, and for that reason I felt certain that he'd not come as a refugee from Mafumi's tyranny, nor ever planned to stay here.

So why had he come?

And what had he brought with him?

There are mysteries in science, and mysteries in art, but the greatest mystery has always been another person's deepest motivation.

So what was Seso's motivation in making so long a journey?

He'd told Dalumi he worked for Martine, which clearly suggested that his coming to New York, along with whatever he'd brought with him, had had something to do with her. In addition, there was the matter of the shell tattoo, equally an image from the past.

To this I could add only that Seso had felt protective of Martine, at least to the extent that on one particular morning he'd warned me, and expected me to warn her, that she should get the hell out of Lubanda. We'd been driving across the savanna when he'd issued this warning, its great expanse suggestive of a limitlessness that was purely fictional. "If she decided to leave now, there would be time," he said. "She could return to her country."

I shook my head. "Martine was born in Lubanda. She is the same as you, Seso."

Seso shook his head. "She is not the same."

Seso made no further elaboration on this statement, but I should have known from the gravity of his expression that for him the truth of life was this: a tribe need not welcome you simply because you claim to be a member of it, and so is it also with countries.

"She will never willingly leave Lubanda," I added darkly, and with that recognition, as I would later realize, a fatal shift began.

By then I'd written several reports to Bill, all of which had painted an increasingly intransigent Martine. *If Gessee sent those men to walk her property line and set that fire, then he should have known better,* I'd written a week or so before Seso offered his warning, *because nothing of that sort will ever make Martine grow coffee.*

*Nothing of that sort.*

It was only months later, when I'd been obsessively revisiting my final weeks in Lubanda, that I'd realized just how ambiguous those words were and how differently they could be read—in one way as a suggestion that nothing could change Martine's mind with regard to growing coffee, in the other that somewhat harsher methods of intimidation now had to be considered. In Lubanda, as I should have known, the second reading would have been the more likely.

And so it had been, as events quickly proved.

It was an old woman named Ufala who brought the news. She and Seso had become friendly, and so he'd gone out to greet her that morning, and perhaps buy some small amount of whatever she had to sell. Ufala had walked down Tumasi Road a day or so before, he told me, once again with that grave expression on his face. Her route had taken her past Martine's farm, where she'd noticed Martine taking down a doll she'd found hanging from the front gate. It had a white face, and bright red hair, she told Seso, and it dangled from a cord that had been wrapped around the doll's neck.

"Ufala says there is talk," Seso added after he'd told me this story. "Bad talk. They say the white woman is a witch."

In certain cultures certain words may be used frivolously, while in others they are uttered only in dead earnest. Seso's tone was grave.

"They say she is a witch with men," he added, "and that this is why Fareem stays with her."

"Martine's father found Fareem on the road," I told Seso. "He'd been captured in the north, then abandoned. He was eight years old, the same as Martine." I looked at Seso sternly. "So, please tell me what anything about Fareem's living and working on Martine's farm has to do with witchcraft?"

Seso said nothing, but I could read the answer in his eyes: *it is not the truth that matters; it is the untruth that is nonetheless believed.*

"Seso?" I said more firmly. "You don't believe such nonsense, do you? That Martine's a witch?"

"She should be careful, this is what I know," Seso said in an oddly plaintive voice. "This talk makes it dangerous for her here."

"Who's talking, exactly?" I asked him.

Seso shrugged. "Ufala says it is in the wind. It is everywhere, this bad talk. They say she is a foreigner."

I offered no response to this, because, in the most fundamental sense, I believed that it was true, that white and black racism were equally alive and well in the world, and that for that reason Martine lived in a garden in which she was and would always remain the invasive species.

"Martine is NOT a witch," I said.

171

Seso said nothing in reply, but simply stood before me, unable to argue the point further because I was his boss. Even so, I knew that his fear for Martine was now being fueled by rumor, Martine's peril made even more clear and frightening by a white-faced, red-haired doll that had been hung from the gate of her isolated farm.

And yet, when I saw Martine a few hours later, she made no mention of this latest attempt at intimidation. She was in the field behind the house, hoeing at the dirt, wet with sweat, her arms smeared with grime. There was also a line of dust across her forehead, though I didn't see it until she removed the straw hat she used to shield her eyes from the sun.

"Hello, Ray," she said warmly as I approached. Her tone was as bright and welcoming as always, so that I wondered if my alarm was unjustified, Seso's story just one of the many rumors that often swept the village.

"I just wanted to make sure you were okay," I told her.

"Why wouldn't I be?" Her hair was a nest of wet tangles, and its very disarray, the fact that it was moistened by her body, sent a charge through me.

"One of Seso's friends told him that you've had a problem," I said. "A doll. A red-haired doll. You weren't going to tell me?"

She returned the hat to her head. "No."

"Why not? If you are in danger I need to—"

"Because it is not your fight," she answered.

She lifted her hand to cut me off. "It is not your fight, Ray. It is not Fareem's either. It is my fight." Her voice was firm, but it was the firmness of a woman who had begun to realize how hard the road ahead would be and how resolved she would have to remain in order to walk it. "Who told you about the doll?"

"Seso," I said. "He's afraid for your safety. He says there's talk. Bad talk, he calls it."

When Martine offered no response to this, I said, "Seso says there are rumors. People think that you're a witch. They think you've cast some sort of spell over Fareem."

"And what does Seso think I should do about these rumors?" Martine asked.

"I don't think he believes that there's anything you *can* do about them."

"Except leave Lubanda, yes?" Martine asked. "Not simply that I should obey the big men in Rupala and grow coffee. So it's not what I grow, it's what I am."

"I suppose he sees it that way, yes," I answered candidly. "That you're a foreigner, Martine. I know you don't think of yourself that way but—"

"And how better to prove that I am a foreigner than by leaving this country?" Martine asked. Something deep inside her, perhaps some core belief, or if not that, the substance of a long illusion, seemed to crack. "Why can people not see that I am nothing other than Lubandan?"

In that instant I suddenly recognized that the loneliest of us, life's true exiles, are not those without a country, but those who are at odds with the country they love.

I might have spoken to this sudden revelation, but Martine turned away and began to dig in short, violent strokes.

Then she abruptly stopped and stared at me.

"A few days ago I was walking on Tumasi Road," she said. "There were lots of people around, just people walking the way we do here. Then, as you say, 'out of the blue,' this Land Cruiser is coming up the road. I could see its cloud of dust a mile before it got to where I was. It went by me, then stopped, and the guy behind the wheel, he drives back to where I am still walking along with the rest of the people. 'You need a ride?' he asked me. I refused, and so he drove on without me. But he had marked me, Ray. He had marked me. Because he had stopped for me, and no one else. And why had he stopped? Because I was white. And this was seen by all the others on the road."

She paused, her gaze burning into me.

"Don't you see?" she asked in a tone that was fiercely plaintive, a voice crying in the wilderness. "It is what *you* do that makes me a witch. You and the other foreigners who have come to Lubanda. It is what *you* do that marks me, not what *I* do."

She saw that this last remark had pierced me, and immediately worked to calm herself, even adding for good measure a tone intended to soothe me.

"It was just a doll, Ray," she said with a soft shrug. "You should not have come all this way." She cast her gaze over the broad expanses through which cut the red swath of Tumasi Road. "My mother left Lubanda when I was ten years old. She was afraid of going mad if she stayed here. She told me this and I think it is true. She was a frail person. Like a bird, always looking around, afraid. She was never Lubandan. Fear was always with her here." She appeared to seek some other way to describe her mother. "Her mind did not have deep roots," she added finally. She turned to face me. "She wanted to take me with her, back to Belgium, to Liège, which was her home. She told me about the canals. How beautiful they were. All that water."

"What did your father say to all this?" I asked.

"He said that I should go if I thought it would make for me a better life," Martine answered. "But, Ray, how could I have a better life if I never felt at home?"

"You would have adjusted after a while," I told her. "Everyone does."

She shook her head. "No," she said, then looked again out over the arid distance. "This is my only home."

This was hard for me to believe because I could not imagine Martine living out her life in Lubanda any more than I could imagine myself doing so. In fact, I could not imagine anyone really wanting to live on a small, hardscrabble farm, with no running water, to die in this spare land, be buried in its arid soil? Did not everyone doomed to such a life dream of escaping it? Was not this, of necessity, Martine's dream as well?

I was ashamed to admit any of this to Martine, of course. And so I simply glanced about.

"Where's Fareem?" I asked.

She looked at me quizzically. "He is on his way to Tumasi."

"Really? I didn't see him on the road."

She looked at me worriedly. "You didn't?"

"No."

She suddenly gripped the handle of the hoe more tightly, and although she said nothing, I saw the fear in her eyes.

"Do you want to go look for him?" I asked with a nod toward my Land Cruiser.

I half-expected her to hold to her rule of only walking, but she immediately cast all that aside. "Yes," she said quickly.

We headed for the Land Cruiser and within a few minutes we were moving as rapidly down Tumasi Road as its condition would allow. The savanna swept out limitlessly on both sides, and as we drove we sometimes saw deer, and once an elephant, but there was no sign of Fareem.

Neither of us actually spoke the dread that was in our minds, the fear that the same men who'd hung a redheaded doll from her gate now had their hands on Fareem. We knew just how easy it would be for such men to fall upon him. There were countless places along the road where they could lie in wait, silent and unseen, behind the tall grasses or towering termite mounds.

That Martine said nothing about any of this as we drove down Tumasi Road later struck me as a willful refusal on her part to face the growing menace.

As I drove, I sometimes glanced over at her. She was sitting stiffly, facing straight ahead. Her blowing hair seemed the only thing that moved. There was dust in her face and dirt on her hands, and her lips were sun-parched from her long days in the field. A triangle of sunburn was visible beneath the open collar of her shirt, and a swath of grime crossed her forehead where she had no doubt wiped sweat from her brow with soiled fingers.

Several times I started to say something, but some quality in her face, some stillness in her eyes, completely silenced me.

And so I only stole glances, and with each one, I felt an inexplicable pang both of loss and the fear of loss. Not just the pain of longing, nor even the agony of desire, but a sense of irrecoverable loss and floating peril that could mean only one thing: Martine was at risk, and the thought of her being harmed was as unbearable to me as the notion that she would one day disappear from my life, that I would return to America, marry a different woman, embrace a life that would never know again the passion I knew now.

"Stop," she cried suddenly.

It had been one of those moments in which my gaze had briefly lingered on her, so that I hadn't seen a figure walking out of the bush.

"Fareem," Martine breathed as her relief at seeing him flooded over her. "It is Fareem."

He was alone as he came back onto the road, but in the distance, I saw two men moving in the opposite direction, farther out into the bush.

By then, Martine had bounded out of the Land Cruiser and was rushing toward Fareem.

"Ray had not seen you on his way to the farm," she told him, almost frantically. "I was afraid that . . ."

"I know," Fareem said quietly, then pointed to the two retreating figures. "They're from the north," he said. "They say that Mafumi now has camps inside Lubanda." He looked at me. "They say he has many men in Tumasi now. They say that these men are preparing the way for him to invade Lubanda from across the border."

All of this was exactly what Malcolm Early had both feared and predicted, but I said nothing of this and instead concentrated on my task of gathering intelligence.

"Did these men say how many of Mafumi's agents are now in Tumasi?" I asked.

"No," Fareem answered in a way that seemed abruptly guarded, as if my question had alerted him to the sinister presence of a different kind of peril. He said nothing about his suspicion, however, and instead turned to Martine. "I was not in danger," he assured her with one of his wide smiles. "The president will protect me." He laughed contemptuously. "As he does all his children."

Fareem had never spoken of President Dasai so disparagingly, so that it was now evident that any faith he'd ever had in the government in Rupala was broken. I knew that with its breaking, he was now at one with Martine, the two of them equally determined to stand firm against the whole broad scheme of Village Harmony, a hardening I duly reported later that same night, sitting at my desk in Tumasi, writing in the yellow glow of a candle whose grotesque underdevelopment I found so furiously exasperating that I felt nothing but resentment toward Lubanda, a country that seemed purposely to stand against me, as if both the place and its people were malevolently determined to thwart my most fundamental hopes.

# Fifteen

Of course, devoted white liberal that I was, I'd fiercely chastised myself in the wake of these brutally hostile feelings toward Lubanda. Who was I, after all, to judge it in the harsh light of my own expectations and by a standard I had myself imposed.

And so, as I continued to follow the ever-diminishing clues to Seso's murder, I felt the tightening noose of my old guilt, as well as the awareness that it was precisely my need to confront it that had urged me to take the risk of setting Seso's killers on my trail. I'd known that the chances were slight that anything would come of this, however, so it actually surprised me when my office phone rang a few days later, and I heard Idi's voice.

"You didn't expect those guys to come back, did you?" he asked without reminding me of who he was. "The ones who killed . . . what was his name?"

"Seso. And no, I didn't expect them to come back. Why would they?"

"Well, you were right, they didn't come back," Idi said. "But someone else did."

Idi's voice was relaxed, so quite obviously this person had posed no threat to him, and would probably pose none to me.

"A black man," he added, "Dressed in a suit. Glasses."

"What did he say?"

"He showed me pictures of two men. He asked if they were the ones who brought your friend to me."

"Were the men in the picture the same ones you saw with Seso?" I asked.

"Yes," Idi said.

"Where are these men now?"

"The man didn't say. He just gave me twenty dollars, and that was it."

"Did you tell him about me?" I asked.

"You said for me to do it, so I did."

"And you gave him my address?"

"That was our deal, eh?"

"Good," I said quietly, then paused before adding, "So, I guess I should expect a visit."

"Maybe so," Idi answered. "You ready for him?"

"He doesn't sound very dangerous."

"You never know, he could be a bad guy," Idi reminded me. "You sure you are willing to risk that for your . . . friend?"

He seemed certain that I wasn't, that any display of real feeling or loyalty from someone like me for someone like Seso was an empty show. He had no doubt seen too many people rush for the plane to have any faith in foreign avowals of love and loyalty. Abandonment in the face of danger, rather than steadfastness in confronting it, was one of history's dark lessons, and Idi had quite obviously learned it well.

"Someone I knew in Lubanda also never trusted foreigners," I told him. The old pain struck again. "And she was right."

If I'd expected this heartfelt admission to penetrate Idi's firmly established view of me, I was quite mistaken.

"You paid me to tell you," he said matter-of-factly, our transaction now complete, and our need to be connected over, "so I did."

179

And with that, he hung up.

Not that I'd expected him to do anything else. He had more immediate concerns, and so did I. Chiefly the question of whom this latest visitor to the tattoo parlor actually was.

I thought of a Lubandan proverb: *The elephant makes bigger tracks than the viper.* It was typically Lubandan in its back-to-the-puckerbrush sense of the basic. The viper was betrayal, and the proverb simply meant that by its very nature betrayal is a secretive thing, a slithering thing, which, at its most successful, leaves a false trail by which the betrayed remains forever unaware of either the treachery or the traitor.

I was still considering the twisting nature of deceit when Gail's voice sounded from the outer office.

"Going out for a smoke," she called.

"Okay," I said. "Do I have anyone this afternoon?"

"The Patroness." Gail answered as she peeped her head into my office.

Indeed, she was just that. Lauren Mayes had inherited a fortune and had spent most of her life dispersing large amounts of it. She funded hospital wings and theaters and museums. Her name was always listed among the five-star benefactors. Over the last few years she'd taken an interest in the undeveloped world, particularly West Africa, so that she'd come to remind me of Dickens' Mrs. Jellyby in *Bleak House,* a comically classic do-gooder forever engrossed in the affairs of Borrioboola-Gha. I knew that this association was unfair, however. Mrs. Mayes was a heartfelt giver, an honest, decent person, though one who probably had no idea where her money actually went, or to whom, or that the sums that flowed from her many charitable trusts might as often provide warlords with AK-47s as they did clean water to a distant village. For the fact remained that an impenetrable veil had fallen over the whole altruistic enterprise even before Martine wrote her *Open Letter,* and little since her wilderness cry had changed.

Perhaps it was my complete acceptance of the fact that nothing had changed over the twenty years since I'd left Lubanda that caused me to stop dead and once again consider what had happened there and the part I'd played in it.

"Take the rest of the day off," I told Gail. "But first, cancel all my appointments."

"Again?" Gail's expression grew more deeply troubled. "Are you sure?"

I nodded. "Beginning with the one this afternoon with Mrs. Mayes," I said. "I need time alone, here in the office, to catch up."

She didn't believe this, and I knew it. The look in her eyes told me she suspected that I must be having an affair with a married woman or committing some other such indiscretion.

"You can take tomorrow off, too," I told her. "As a matter of fact, I'll call you when I've gotten caught up."

This surprised Gail even more, but by the clock, it was time for a cigarette, so it didn't surprise me when she responded with a hasty "Whatever you say" and left it at that.

During the next couple of minutes I listened as Gail canceled my appointments, then, no doubt desperate for a cigarette at that point, quickly gathered up her things and rushed out of the office with a quick "Bye."

I didn't know when or if the gentleman to whom Idi had given my business card would show up, but I calculated that the risk of this confrontation's being violent was very low, and so I simply waited in my office for the rest of the day. I didn't work at confirming, denying, or ameliorating any of my clients' risks, however. Instead, I found myself sitting with my hands on my desk, my computer screen idly displaying a series of floating abstract images, my mind not so much thinking as receiving images and sensations, almost all of which came from my time in Lubanda. I remembered the taste of the bread Martine baked, unleavened, the grainy taste of teff, as well as the honeyed flavor of her homebrew. And then there were the many dinners I'd enjoyed at the outdoor table or on her ragged screened porch. Like other Lubandans, she'd flavored cassava paste with various spices brought to her by the Lutusi, for which she exchanged her own homemade products, mostly from her harvest, but occasionally something she'd made—a woven basket, a wooden bowl, an old-style African broom.

I recalled that Ufala had been unable to adapt to the long-handled broom, preferring the whisk broom, with its short handle, a style little changed from its ancient prototype, the Old English *besma,* meaning "bundle of twigs." She'd had to stoop low during the whole process of sweeping, a backbreaking labor, it had seemed to me, though each time I'd pointed out the sleek new broom I'd brought from Rupala, she'd shaken her head and refused it. Once, when I'd mentioned this to Martine, she'd smiled and said, "The hardest thing in life, Ray, is to understand those you cannot understand."

At one point that afternoon, I reached for the atlas I kept in a bookshelf filled with other reference books, thumbed my way to Lubanda, and stared at the map for a long time, my gaze tracing the route that led from Rupala to Tumasi and which still bore the simple name "Tumasi Road." A few black dots designated the larger villages that had huddled along the road, places I knew well and which I could see quite vividly in my mind, a collection of round mud huts with vaguely conical roofs, a shape that reminded me of the tepees of the Plains Indians, though fashioned from wood rather than skins. But then, there'd been no need to protect Lubandan villagers from the biting cold that had lashed the American plains. In Lubanda, the need had been for cool and ventilation, a roof of sticks perfectly designed to allow heat to rise and air to circulate. This, too, had been one of Martine's many illustrations of the ways in which Lubandans managed their lives, dealt with their environment, and generally, in a thousand ways invisible to foreigners, held to their own ways.

She'd made her position most emphatically clear to Theodore Calley, the head of Helping Hand, yet another of the American charities bringing aid to Lubanda at that time. He'd arrived with Farmer Gessee and his entourage, and together they'd strolled through the market, no doubt in order for Gessee to point out its backward reliance upon local products. It was clear from the sour look on Gessee's face the moment he glimpsed Martine among the market throng that he took no pleasure in finding her in Tumasi that day.

But Gessee was Gessee, an actor first and foremost, and so, rather than change the day's itinerary or hustle Calley back into his Land Cruiser, he launched himself into the crowd, shaking hands and patting backs, the consummate politician.

I saw all this from my little concrete stoop, Seso standing beside me, the two of us watching Gessee move from stall to stall, talking confidently of the richness of the savanna, the large amount of coffee it could produce if only there were enough fertilizer, irrigation, and the like, all of which cost a regrettably large amount of money.

He'd at last come to a halt near the center of the market, and there he'd hoisted himself onto a platform. The people had crowded in around him, Seso and I now among them. At one point, Gessee noticed my white face among all those black ones and gave me a quick, friendly nod. Then he introduced Calley as "a great friend of Lubanda." Calley waved broadly, as if he were riding in a motorcade, and mouthed "Hi" and "Hello" and "Wonderful to be here." He was young and he looked energetic, and I had little doubt that his intentions were good, a fact that made his subsequent exchange with Martine all the more

awkward, but also curiously poignant, at least in memory, with Calley looking strangely perplexed by what Martine said, but not angry,
and with no hint of the flaming disapproval I'd glimpsed in Gessee's
darkly sparking eyes.

That it happened at all surprised me because just as Gessee was
about to speak, I saw Martine still standing near one of the market stalls.
She was holding a small bowl, turning it over in her hand and paying
no attention at all to the show that was going on a few yards away. Her
indifference seemed completely natural, rather than a display. She had
heard Gessee's pitch before, and expected to hear nothing new in this
latest one. The bowl was more important to her, and after she turned it
over in her hand, she checked her basket quite thoroughly, as if looking
for something she might offer in exchange for it. By then Gessee had
mounted the platform and was addressing the crowd, first introduc-
ing Calley, then giving his standard speech about the future of central
Lubanda, how much it could contribute to Village Harmony.

Martine appeared not at all to be listening to any of this. She had
obviously found nothing in her basket and was—at the moment when
the word was spoken—well on her way out of the market, where she
would have swung to the left and made her way toward home, all of
which I fully expected her to do.

But the word stopped her in her tracks, Gessee by that time glori-
ously elaborating on the word that had halted Martine's return to her
farm, frozen her in place like an invisible hand, then drawn her around
to face the market, the crowd, Farmer Gessee.

The word was "love."

"It is love my dear friend, Mr. Calley, is offering the people of
Lubanda," Gessee told the villagers of Tumasi. "And we are to be the
grateful receivers of his love."

"Not good," Seso whispered darkly as he watched Martine head back toward the crowd, her head cocked slightly to the right, as if questioning whether she'd actually heard Gessee correctly.

She moved unhurriedly forward, and once, perhaps twice, she slowed or stopped, as if briefly undecided as to whether she should do what she was planning to.

At a certain point, she caught Gessee's eye, but he continued speaking, giving her approach no notice, though I could see he was well aware that she was moving toward him, glancing at her quickly and almost surreptitiously, as one might regard an unlikely yet potential assassin.

He'd finished his remarks by the time she reached the outer perimeter of the crowd and raised her hand to ask a question, as if she were a student in his class. Gessee looked away and started to step down from the stool. He clearly had no intention of acknowledging her. But Calley was an American, and thus very familiar with the custom of public officials taking questions from the crowd, and so, with a broad smile, he said, "Yes, you have a question or a comment, ma'am?"

"A comment," Martine said. "A comment about Farmer Gessee's mention of love, your love, the world's love for Lubanda. I have a comment on that, yes."

With Calley in full happy-warrior mode, Gessee had no choice but to say, "Of course, my child." The big smile beamed. "So, what is your comment?"

"My comment is that charity is not the same as love," Martine said.

Gessee had nothing to say to this, but Calley did.

"And what is that difference?" he asked.

"The difference is that charity asks people to give," Martine answered. "Love might ask them not to."

Something in Gessee's eyes hardened, but he didn't speak.

Calley, young, naïve, with no more than a few days in Lubanda, was not unexpectedly perplexed. And yet, rather than offer some off-the-cuff response to this, he said, "I'm not sure I understand."

"Then I shall put it this way," Martine said in that measured way of hers. "There is sometimes more love in not giving than in giving."

"How so?" Calley asked quietly.

"Because if you have more than you need and you give to me from this extra that you have and which I do not have, then you must be superior to me, yes?" She looked at Calley with all the force of her character, that great, commanding stillness in her eyes. "And if I take from you and take from you, and more and more I take from you, then in the end I will become like a person long in bed. My muscles will wither, and I will not be able to get up, and so I will remain an invalid forever, one who cannot walk, cannot clean or feed himself, yes?"

At that point, Gessee, smiling sweetly because he had no choice, stepped toward her. "Mr. Calley is trying, Miss Aubert, to help Lubanda."

Martine's voice held its firmness. "I am sure he is," she said, "which makes it all the harder for Lubandans to refuse his gifts."

Gessee continued to offer his fatherly smile, but I saw something register in Calley's eyes, a sudden awareness that he was perhaps not as ready for his post as he'd thought himself.

Martine glanced at Calley, but only for an instant, before returning her gaze to Gessee, where she held it briefly before she turned and headed back toward the road.

She was still faintly visible, a lone figure, moving slowly away from me, by the time Gessee and Calley had climbed back into Gessee's car. I noticed that while Gessee was expansively waving to the crowd, Calley was gazing up the road, to where Martine's withdrawing figure could be seen, though only blurrily, behind a wavy veil of heat.

Here this story might have ended had I not noticed and later recalled that a third man had been seated in the back of Gessee's car as it pulled out of Tumasi that afternoon, a small, bespectacled man, well dressed in a tailored suit, and whom I'd never once thought of until, nearly twenty years after leaving Lubanda, and three days after Idi's call, he walked into my office, nodded silently, then said, "I know what Seso Alaya had."

# Sixteen

Think of Beria, Stalin's infamous enforcer, with his round face and little rodent eyes. Add black skin and small, distinctively shaped ears that curl in upon themselves like tiny, limbless embryos. Give him hands a bit too large for his body and a shiny nose that looks polished. Include a dollop of courtliness, but with a rough edge, as if he'd been sent to some bush finishing school, and you'd have the man who introduced himself to me that afternoon.

"Nullu Beyani," he said.

He put out his hand and I took it.

I offered him a seat, and he settled into one of the two chairs that faced my desk.

"My apologies for entering your office unannounced, but I didn't see a receptionist."

"She's not here today," I said. "What about Seso?"

He smiled. "You are quick to come to the point, I see," he said. "All right, I'll get, as you say, down to business. You've been looking into this fellow's murder, I understand."

"Yes," I answered.

"For a client, I was told," Beyani said. "Something that Mr. Alaya wanted to show a client?"

Before I could answer, he smiled knowingly and a little cleverly, a man clearly accustomed to reading other men with great precision, perhaps because his own life had from time to time been determined by knowing the right card to play.

"It's obvious that you wanted me to know this," he added. "One does not leave so broad a trail if one does not expect it to be followed."

"I wanted someone to know it, yes," I admitted, now playing my own card as a trump to his. "What brought you to my friend, the tattoo artist?"

"That one is no friend of yours," Beyani said. "Nor anyone else. The Kakwa do not walk, they slither." When I offered no encouragement to this comment, he continued. "As to your question, it happened this way: once Mr. Alaya was identified by the police, Rupala was notified that one of our citizens had been murdered. That is, of course, only standard procedure in such a case."

This was probably true, though I couldn't be sure, and so recorded it in my mind as an unproved assertion.

"Like you, Mr. Campbell, I am investigating this murder." His smile was razor-thin. "But I am here in a manner that is not to be made public. That is why I did not go to the police, but instead to Mr. Alaya's hotel, which led me to—"

"Herman Dalumi," I interrupted in order to demonstrate that I was probably one step ahead of him in almost everything.

But if this ploy had an effect, Beyani was actor enough not to show it.

"A colorful fellow," he said. "He'd seen a picture of Seso, and noticed a tattoo. I surmised that Seso might have gotten this tattoo near his residence, so I walked around a bit. This led me to the Kakwa, who led me to you." He seemed pleased by his gumshoe skills. "May I ask how you became involved in the case?"

"The police found my client's name and phone number in Seso's room."

"Who is your client?"

"That's confidential."

Beyani did not press the issue. Instead, he drew a wallet from his pocket, pulled out a card, and handed it to me.

I took the card and read it: *Nullu Beyani, Lubandan Security Police.*

"Did you have this same position under Mafumi?" I asked.

Beyani ignored my question, which was answer enough.

"Concerning this 'something' Mr. Alaya claimed to have," he said. "The Kakwa seemed more than happy to inform me that you know what it is." He smiled like one guessing a punch line before it is delivered. "Or claim to know."

"'Claim' is right," I admitted. "Because it was just a hook to reel you in." I countered Beyani's smile with one as direct as his own. "I figured that if you were after Seso because you wanted to know what this mysterious thing was, you'd come to me, and now you have."

Beyani's smile was a sliver of ice. "You took quite a chance in putting me on to your investigation," he said. "Since I might have been Mr. Alaya's killer."

"That's true," I said. "But it did bring you to me, and I had no other die to cast." I sat back and looked at him doubtfully, as if I thought myself the object of some scam. "So, tell me, why did Seso come so far to bring this information?"

Beyani ran his fingers down the length of his bright green tie. "As we say in Lubanda, 'Fear speeds the plow.'"

"What was he afraid of?"

"What we all fear: that our crime will be discovered and that we will be punished for it." He took off his glasses, wiped them with a white handkerchief, and with that small task completed, returned them to their place. "Did you know that Mr. Alaya worked in the archive under Mafumi?" he asked.

"Yes."

"Our new president decided to allow him to keep his job," Beyani said. "Many such people have been allowed to keep their posts. It is part of the president's policy of reconciliation. But this does not mean that all earlier crimes will be forgiven." Something behind his eyes abruptly darkened. "For example, the Tumasi Road Incident."

I gave no hint of the inward shudder that went through me at that moment, but instead maintained what I hoped would seem a wholly professional demeanor.

"You are familiar with this tragic episode in Lubandan history, I believe," Beyani said.

The word "incident" struck me as a political choice, proof enough that even after all these years, this crime was still reverberating through the governmental halls of Rupala.

"An outrage like that," Beyani said, "it gives a terrible impression. That we Lubandans are animals. Especially when the victim is a foreigner."

"Martine Aubert was not a foreigner," I told him.

Beyani shrugged. "Anyway . . . white."

"What could Seso have had to do with what happened on Tumasi Road?" I asked. "He was nowhere near the place where it happened."

"This is so," Beyani said. "Alaya did not, as we say, draw blood. His role was to provide information." He watched me closely for a moment before he added, "Seso Alaya was a spy."

*Spy.* The word itself seemed to darken the air around us.

"His job was to inform on the white woman," Beyani added.

"To whom?" I asked.

"Mafumi's people, of course," Beyani said. "The ones who had already infiltrated various villages in Tumasi. And for his work, he was later given a position in the archive."

"Why would Mafumi have needed someone to spy on Martine?" I asked in as clinical a tone as I could manage.

"Because he needed to prove that he was an enemy of white rule."

"Martine didn't rule anything," I told him. "She was just a farmer."

"She was white—that was enough," Beyani said. "To do such a thing to a white woman, it gave Mafumi—what is the phrase here?— 'street creds.'" He shrugged. "Besides, as you know, he immediately took credit for it."

"He also took credit for the moon landing, which, by the way, happened before he was born," I reminded Beyani.

Beyani laughed. "Mafumi had a somewhat exaggerated sense of himself, as we all know. But in the case of what happened on Tumasi Road, it was indeed Mafumi's men who did this harm."

"I thought it was Gessee's men," I admitted. "He hated Martine, after all, and he'd tried lots of things to intimidate her."

I recalled the steps by which Gessee's intimidation had grown ever more threatening, as well as the consequences of Martine's refusal to give in to it, memories too painful to think about, as Beyani clearly saw.

"Gessee had nothing to do with what happened on Tumasi Road," he said with a dismissive wave of his hand. "He was a schoolteacher before he became agricultural minister. He would never have been capable of such savagery." His gaze hardened. "What happened to that woman was . . . uncivilized." He watched me for a moment, then said, "I am aware that Miss Aubert was a friend of yours, and that it is hard for you to hear of such things, to have them returned to you in this way."

When I said nothing, Beyani peered at me coolly, but with some effort, like a man trying to read a book in a language he only partially understood.

"Seso Alaya fled Lubanda because he knew we were closing in on him," he said. "But he knew he would need a bargaining chip to stay here. Something that would buy him safe harbor. This is what he had for your client."

Again I remained silent, the ploy that almost always works to keep someone talking.

"The names," Beyani said starkly. "The names of the men responsible for the attack on Tumasi Road."

I labored to absorb this in the calm, unflappable way of a seasoned risk analyst, the greatest risk always being that you uncover your own error. For surely, I felt, my name, by any reckoning of responsibility, should appear among those other names, perhaps at the head of the list.

The terror of that judgment must have glittered in my eyes, because I saw a certain hint of unexpected sympathy come into Beyani's.

"I know that this is a difficult matter for you to discuss," he said, "and I also know that it is difficult for you to believe what I have told you about Mr. Alaya. It is always hard to admit that one has been betrayed." There was that ever-changing smile again, a little jagged this time, and not quite a match for the look in his eyes. "Especially by a servant."

"He was a friend," I corrected.

"No, he was not," Beyani responded firmly. "He was a spy who gave information that led directly to the Tumasi Road Incident, and had he not fled here, he would almost certainly have been arrested in Lubanda."

"Do you know who killed him?" I asked. "You had a picture, I believe."

"The men in that photograph killed Mr. Alaya to silence him, as well as any others who might be tempted to expose them," Beyani said. "But in doing this thing, they only confirmed what we already suspected." He sat back haughtily, a little man puffed up by this recent accomplishment. "They are now in Lubanda, as I told the Kakwa. We will soon find them, and when we do, they will be brought to justice." A dark irony glittered in his eyes. "And at that point, thanks to Mr. Alaya's many treacheries, the case opened by the Tumasi Road Incident can, at last, be closed."

Suspicion is a spade that never tires of digging, and so I suddenly found myself recalling all the times Seso had found it convenient to straighten my desk, where my letters to Bill Hammond lay open and available to his eyes. The last one had been short. He could have read it at a glance: *M.A. to Rupala, via TR,* and by which he would have known that Martine was on her way to Rupala by means of Tumasi Road.

"I would never have suspected Seso of working for Mafumi," I admitted. "And certainly never of betraying either me or Martine Aubert."

"Yes, well, you should keep in mind that Mr. Alaya was Lutusi," Beyani said by way of explaining Seso's treachery. "They are a rootless people, wanderers who live by trade, and, as we know, traders are by nature deceivers." He seemed suddenly to see the two of us as old comrades in arms, equally shaped by the dark forces of Lubanda. "Stay safe," he said, as he rose and offered his hand.

I shook it like one sealing a friendship. "Thank you."

He turned and left my office as quietly as he'd entered it, leaving me alone to sit and think. There was a lot to absorb in what he'd told me, a lot to consider and put into order, a procedure in which I was well trained. *Return to first principles,* I reminded myself. *The devil is, indeed, in the details, so examine them carefully.*

The process that followed took only a few minutes, but at the end of it I felt sure I'd covered the ground and come to a reasonable conclusion.

Point one was that Beyani had given a credible account of both himself and Seso. The motive he'd given for Seso's being in league with

Mafumi, for example, was entirely believable. Men had betrayed others for far less cause, after all. What was it that Zhivago's brother says? That he has killed men far better than himself with a small pistol. Surely it was possible that Seso, anticipating that Mafumi might well take charge in Lubanda, had been enticed into providing information to his local agents. He had probably had no idea that such harm might flow from his betrayal of Martine. He had simply passed information on to a higher source, which was no different—at least at the beginning—from what I had done. Later, with Beyani closing in, he'd tried to make a deal with the only real power he knew, Bill Hammond. The names had been his last chips in a desperate game, and he'd gambled that Bill would not pay dearly for them.

Such were the salient details of Beyani's story, and as I reviewed the risks of believing it, I could find only one false note. It had sounded at the very end of our meeting, and yet its faint echo had continued to ring in my ear:

*The Lutusi are by nature deceitful.*

*Seso was Lutusi.*

*Therefore Seso was deceitful.*

The problem was that the truth of the third, concluding proposition could not be inferred, because the first one was false.

I knew this because of a chance encounter I'd had while traveling north of Tumasi. By then I'd given up the idea of a well, and was now exploring the notion of creating "nomadic schools," as my later proposal called it, to be manned by a troupe of traveling teachers. It was an absurd idea, patterned on my romantic understanding of the way medieval actors had roamed from village to village, put on their shows, then departed for the next village. It could not have been more ridiculous, as Seso must have known, and yet he'd given no hint of how he felt as he'd traveled with me on this occasion, translating my proposal to a group of Lutusi elders.

The elders had listened silently, then asked what they should give in return, and when I'd replied, "Nothing," they'd briefly talked among themselves, then walked away.

It was one of the few times Seso had shuffled off the gloom that usually surrounded him and broke into a smile. "They think the school you offer is worthless," he said.

"Why?" I asked.

"Because you ask for nothing in return," Seso explained. "It is only nothing that is worth nothing in return, so they think you are dishonest in what you offer them, that you are a deceiver, and they will not associate with such people."

That is why the Beyani syllogism did not hold. The Lutusi were traders, but they were not deceivers. Beyani had constructed a flawed syllogism. Therefore, I could not believe him.

But where did this doubt leave me?

I didn't know, save that Beyani could not be trusted, might not be at all what he purported to be, might, in fact, be one of those very men he claimed to hunt, himself one of those who'd clicked the shells on Tumasi Road.

And if this was true, how might I find evidence of it sufficient to warn the current leader of Lubanda that there was a viper in the grass, and not a defanged one by any means, but a member of his own security force.

I had no answer for this question, and so was left with no more lucid thought than how strange it was that after so many years, Tumasi's shadow had once again crossed my path. I considered the little string of time that had run from my first arrival in Rupala, where I'd met Seso, then driven with him to where I'd intended to live more or less indefinitely, how on the very day I'd arrived in the village I'd found Martine fiddling with her basket, Fareem at her side, a first encounter whose grave risks I could not have guessed.

For a moment I found it all too large to analyze. For it was a risk whose perils were still with me, the present now as fraught with danger as the past, so that for an instant I felt myself swirling in the fearful jeopardy of the moment and thus unable to grasp how the winding way of Tumasi Road had finally curled into this fatal noose, with Martine doomed long ago, Seso recently murdered, myself a scrupulous manager of risk, and now Nullu Beyani added to this fateful mix, a Cassius who might well conceal a dagger in his gown, one aimed squarely at brave, risk-taking Fareem, the merciful and perhaps imperiled new president of Lubanda.

# PART IV

He is in his middle forties now, and time has added its layer of thickness, as well as the lines that spread from the corners of his eyes when he smiles. They are still eyes that glitter with intelligence and a keen sense of man's capacity for evil. I would have recognized him immediately even if I had not followed his rise within the ranks of those who'd fled Lubanda, then opposed Mafumi's tyranny from afar, a risky business if ever there was one.

"Ray," Fareem says as he rises, comes from behind his quite modest desk, and offers his hand in the warm way of those long-lost days. His handshake is no less firm than of old and there is something confident and reassuring in the force of his grip. Here is a man who does not fear being in charge, facing his enemies, doing what must be done.

"So good to have you back in Lubanda," he tells me. He tilts his head slightly to the right, and with this motion, more glints of silver sparkle in the black nest of his hair. For a moment he seems as weary as his history. Exile has added depth to his eyes, and struggle a layer of gravity to their expression. He was never frivolous, but now he seems a vessel carved from care. I had expected to see vigor, but instead I see fatigue. It gives him the air of a great statue that has been exposed to the harshest of elements, long exposed, perhaps fatally exposed, so that he seems at the beginning of a long decline.

201

"Hello, Mr. President."

"Mr. President?"

He laughs, but his is different from President Dasai's laugh. It is thinner, and there is no hint of the jolly and naïve Black Santa with his fatherly chuckle. Fareem has been through too much to have so rich a laugh. He has known flight, exile, poverty, along with the awesome peril of his political responsibility. He has been stabbed, shot at, and run down by a speeding car. A limp provides the evidence for just how narrow was his escape.

"Never call me Mr. President," he says after a soft cough. "We've known each other too long for that."

"In good times," I add pointedly, "and in bad."

"We parted angrily, yes," Fareem admits. His voice has the tenor of a reed gently blown. "I apologize for the dreadful things I said to you. After all, none of it was your fault." He shakes his head as if to free his mind of memories. "It was a bad time for Lubanda."

"For some it was worse than others," I remind him.

He makes no pretense that he doesn't understand that this reference is to Martine.

"My white skin was a blinding light, Fareem," I add. "I couldn't see her for it." When Fareem remains silent, I continue, "And the black skins of Lubanda's people were just as impenetrable, so they couldn't see her either."

Something behind Fareem's eyes darkens and I see that Martine's fate still casts a shadow over him. "I think of her often," he tells me.

"I think of her every day," I confess.

"Of course you do," Fareem says gently and sympathetically. "But times have changed, so the point now is to do the right thing."

"The right thing?"

"For Lubanda."

"Indeed," I agree. "But it isn't always easy to know what the right thing is."

"True," Fareem says. "If it were, then nothing would ever be at risk."

He is tall, but no longer muscular. In fact, he is slightly stooped. There was a time when he could run and jump, when he toiled over modest crops in arid fields. He could do none of that now. Struggle and hardship age a man, but Fareem seems almost crippled by the hardships he has endured, chief among them the rigors of his own effort to return to Lubanda. He has not farmed for the past twenty years, and those decades spent in the West have altered his accent and given him a sense of gentlemanliness and sophistication, but at a considerable price. He is like a man dangling between two voids. He has neither the false grandfatherly manner of Dasai nor the psychopathic egotism of Mafumi. In that way, he appears almost to embody the moderate political policies by means of which he has pledged to lead Lubanda into the future. Even so, his smile remains fixed in sadness, making him seem very much the product of a long and painful enlightenment.

I glance about. "Mafumi spent a great deal of money on this place."

"He did, yes," Fareem tells me. "He called it his palace but I have renamed it the Presidential Residence." He smiles that melancholy smile. "Even so, I do not live here."

"Where do you live, Fareem?"

"In a small house on the outskirts of Rupala," Fareem informs me. "Lubanda is poor, and it did not seem fitting that I live in luxury. I am not a chief, and I do not intend to behave like one." Now his smile is so delicate it seems barely on his lips at all, and in it I can see how relieved he is that the tragedy we shared in Lubanda has not built a wall between us.

"Normally, I would invite you to sit down," he says. "But I thought you above all might want to see the future that is now possible for

Lubanda." His gaze is full of sympathy. "Your experience here was dark," he adds, "and I would prefer you leave us this time with some of those shadows removed."

"It wasn't all dark," I remind him.

"No, not all," he agrees. "There were those dinners on the farm, sitting beneath that pathetic little tree, all those many talks. All these things I remember fondly. What do you remember fondly, Ray?"

"The way she danced in the village that night. By the fire with the other women of the village. The way she swayed and turned and lifted her arms. She was happy then, because she still had a homeland and felt certain that she would always have one."

Fareem appears to see this memory playing like a film in my mind.

"I remember that evening well," he says. "It was an Independence Day celebration and there was something that seemed immortal in the way Martine danced so slowly, as you say, with her arms lifted . . . like wings."

Before leaving New York, it had been hard for me to imagine Fareem as the president of Lubanda, a country still adrift in the wake of Mafumi's death, reeling from the desolation he left behind, a country divided into factions, with so many old wounds still open. Such a man must have countless enemies, and to rule well he must make many more. I can hardly calculate how many of his fellow countrymen must be at this very moment plotting his fall, licking their lips at the prospect of all that can be done to him before they finally kill him. I have no doubt that Fareem has envisioned himself skinned, burned alive, hung by his heels, and filleted with box cutters.

And yet he does not seem to be concerned that the fate of President Dasai might one day be his own. Clearly he expects to fare better than any of Lubanda's previous leaders, avoid their mistakes, rule more wisely, and perhaps by this means ultimately become Lubanda's version of Nelson Mandela, the true father of that very country that made an orphan of Martine.

"Do you leave Rupala very often?" I ask him as my mind turns to the time we'd gone north with President Dasai, the attempt on that supremely naïve president's life, that chuckling president's obliviousness to the risks that surrounded him.

"Quite often, yes," Fareem answers. He buttons the jacket of his suit, then runs his fingers down his lapels. "You must find it odd to see me dressed this way. Like a Western man of business. It is not my normal attire, of course, but Westerners prefer to see African heads of state dressed 'appropriately,' as one might say, in business attire. It makes us seem less strange, less dangerous." He shrugs. "Otherwise, one can be perceived as something of a clown. Mobutu in his leopard skin cap and Mafumi in his red toga. And so I am a suit-and-tie man now."

His demeanor is gracious and trusting, very different from that of the ever-vigilant young man he'd been all those years ago, forever patrolling the edges of the farm, certain that Gessee's men were out there. There'd been a catlike watchfulness about him then. Now he seems like one who has already glimpsed his future and, with more certainty than human life allows, considers it his destiny.

"This way, my friend," he says as he directs me toward the door. "I have something to show you."

I do not move. I have something to say to him as a preamble to what I have come to do. "We all grow old, Fareem," I tell him. "We all weaken and grow ill." I pause as if at a precipice, then deliver a yet harder truth. "And at one point or another, we all lose our bearings and in that state, we make dreadful errors." I gaze at him poignantly. "I know I did."

Though he cannot possibly know what else I might say, or why I have come to say it, he looks at me with an expression of fierce inquisitiveness as to where this stark declaration is leading, allowing me to see that which is truly great about him: his tremendous capacity for risk.

"But given the dark nature of our shared fate," I continue, "it's the luckiest of us who love our country, our parents, love our wives and children, love our friends." I pause briefly before I add, "As I know you loved Martine."

His hand on my shoulder is almost as light as Martine's was on that final evening.

"I did, yes," he says. "I did love Martine." He smiles, his hand now gently urging me forward. "Come with me, Ray," he summons me gently, "into the new Lubanda."

I know instantly that Martine would have wanted me to come back to her country, especially now. And, oh, Martine, how I would have loved for you to be with me here today, the two of us observing Fareem as he leads us out of the Presidential Residence, the soft nods and warm smiles he offers to the doorkeepers, the cleaning women, the old man who prunes the garden and the young woman who sweeps the pathway with her old, frayed *besma*. Would we not listen as Fareem tells us of his dream for your country—your country, Martine, not mine; though as I walk beside him, with you the ghostly third party to this moment, I feel my briefcase grow light in my hand, perhaps as winged as you yourself had seemed on the night of your languid dance, dreaming, as I know you must have been at that moment, and as I am dreaming now, that there might yet be hope for Lubanda.

# New York City, One Month Earlier

# Seventeen

Few "truths" are objectively true. Most are a matter of perception and so it is perception that must be closely considered in risk management. If the perception of the source of information cannot be trusted, then, of course, neither can the information. Both the fear of loss and the anticipation of gain distort "truth," for example. But truth's opposite does not reside in such understandable and to some extent calculable variables. The opposite of truth is disinformation, the fabricated used to conceal the actual. For these reasons, in risk management, a "truth" may or may not actually be true, but a lie is a deliberate act of deception, and therefore must be thoroughly investigated.

"So, who do you think is the liar in this case, Ray?" Bill asked. "Beyani or Seso?"

We were in Bill's office at the Mansfield Trust, Bill sitting royally behind his massive desk, leaning back in a chair that was the leather version of a throne, the view of Manhattan that filled his window yet more regal. I'd just given him a detailed report on my conversation with Beyani that had left him in the same uncertainty as it had left me the day before.

"I don't know who Beyani really is," I admitted. "But if his story about Seso is a lie, then he must be lying for a reason."

"And what might that reason be?"

"I can't be sure," I admitted. "But he claims that Seso was involved in what happened to Martine on Tumasi Road. If that's a lie, then perhaps Beyani is the one who was involved in it."

"And so he had Seso murdered to protect himself?"

I nodded. "Or others, perhaps. But in either case, he isn't who he claims to be."

"Or who Fareem thinks he is," Bill added, "since he hasn't removed him from the government."

I looked at Bill pointedly. "Which means that Fareem could be very much at risk."

"And you want to help Fareem," Bill said. "You don't want to take the risk that he might end up like Dasai, hanging upside down in Independence Square."

"It's just that simple, yes," I admitted.

I knew that the moral logic was no less elementary. I hadn't saved Martine, and so saving Fareem—if, indeed, he was at risk—was as close as I could get to making amends for the terrible consequences of my error. She had loved him, after all. But more than that, they'd shared the same dream for Lubanda. And so saving him, it seemed to me, was like saving some small part of that dream.

"The problem is how to warn Fareem," I said. "I know I could just write him a letter, tell him about Seso's murder and my talk with Beyani."

"Then why not do that?" Bill asked.

"The problem is that I'm not sure he'd take me seriously or even give a damn about what I had to tell him," I answered. "Don't forget, he despised me. The last time we were together, he said so to my face. I have no idea if he still feels the same, but even if he doesn't, he might find a warning from me—sounded from such a safe quarter and perhaps with some ulterior motive—somewhat less than urgent."

"Okay, but what's the alternative?"

"A face-to-face meeting."

"In Lubanda?" Bill asked with a hint of worry.

"Yes."

"Things are still very unstable there," Bill reminded me.

"True, but Fareem has taken great risks in his life," I said. "For that reason, he might only respect other men who do the same."

Bill looked at me quite sympathetically. "We don't have many opportunities to do the right thing, do we, Ray?" he said, as if turning over a few of his own failed chances.

"Actually, we have plenty of opportunities to do the right thing," I said. "It's taking back the wrong thing we can't do."

Bill eased his ample weight back in his even more ample chair. "How can I help?"

"You can make me an emissary of the Mansfield Trust," I answered. "There's no way Fareem would refuse to see me if I were clothed in that golden mantle."

Bill nodded thoughtfully. "Okay, I can do that," he said. "Let me know whatever papers you need." He smiled. "I'll even supply the briefcase." With that, he rose and offered his hand. "Good luck," he said. "For Fareem's sake."

A few days later I arrived at the Lubandan Consulate to fill out the forms necessary to obtain a visa. The man at the reception desk was dressed in a white shirt and dark pants. He gave me the forms, then indicated a row of empty chairs. "Your name will be called," he said.

And it was, by a tall woman of around forty, dressed in what passed for "African dress": a dashiki with a matching headdress. "I am Sinasu Vinu. I review visa applications. Will you come with me, please?"

I followed her down a short corridor into a tiny office.

"Please be seated," Ms. Vinu said.

I sat down in the metal chair that rested in front of her desk. As an office, it had the same modest furnishings I remembered from government offices in the capital during President Dasaï's rule. In those days, a portrait of the rotund and beaming president in his yellow dashiki would have adorned the wall, but the photograph behind Ms. Vinu was of Fareem, standing beside the new Lubandan flag, dressed in a far from stylish gray suit. There was a large poster next to the presidential photograph. It showed a map of Lubanda over which the word *ufufuo* was inscribed in letters of different colors.

When Ms. Vinu noticed me looking at the poster, she said, "It's Swahili."

"But Lubandans don't speak Swahili," I said.

"I know," Ms. Vinu said. "And we are always saying 'Africa is not a country' to remind foreigners that there are many different nations on our continent. Unfortunately, this is still a difficult lesson, and so the president decided to use a Swahili word because that is the language Westerners associate with Africa."

"What does it mean?"

"It is a beautiful word," Ms. Vinu said. "It means 'recovery,' or perhaps even 'resurrection.'"

"Your new president's hope for Lubanda," I said with a heightened sense of the mission I had set myself with regard to Fareem, remembering all he'd suffered at the hands of Mafumi's agents before leaving Lubanda, then the equal pain of his long exile, the many risks he had taken while I had lived safely in New York, calculating ones that were nowhere near as great.

"It is, yes." She smiled cheerfully, then asked me for my identification, my itinerary, proof that I'd had the necessary inoculations—the usual information required for a visa. I gave her what she needed, and she immediately began filling out the forms she'd assembled on her desk.

"It will not take long," she assured me.

"I'm patient," I told her.

My attention returned to the picture of Fareem, and inevitably I considered the increasing pressure to which he and Martine had been subjected during the last three months I'd been in Lubanda.

By then, she'd endured increasingly threatening attacks posted on trees or village message boards. But since literacy was not widespread in Tumasi, they'd more often been crude drawings that even the least educated minds could understand. During those last months, they'd steadily escalated in both the nature of their accusations and the crudeness of their content.

When Martine had found them on her property she'd ripped them down. But typical of her, rather than destroy them, as I discovered one evening when I arrived for my weekly dinner at the farm, she'd taped her entire collection to the living room wall.

"Martine says that if she were president of Lubanda, she'd use one of them for her presidential seal," Fareem told me when he showed me the display. The first showed a redheaded white woman distributing money to various "enemies" of Lubanda, mostly countries on Lubanda's border or tribes against which the peoples of the central region had been in either recent or ancient conflict. A second showed the same woman outside a polling location grandly tossing cash to a crowd of destitute Lubandans, obviously buying their votes. A third had Martine shopping near a crudely drawn Eiffel Tower while standing on a mound of dead Lubandans raggedly draped in the sunflower flag. There were others of this sort. The last, however, was quite different, and I noticed Fareem's expression tense when he saw that I had reached it.

"I found it nailed to one of the fence posts out front," he told me. "When I saw it, I ripped it off the post, but Martine had seen me do this, and so I had to show it to her."

In the final drawing, a naked Martine is on her hands and knees, surrounded by several shirtless, spectacularly muscled black men, one of whom is placing a noose around her neck while another beats her bare feet with an iron bar.

"What did Martine say when she saw this?" I asked.

"What she always says, that men are simple," Fareem said. "Then she just added it to the wall."

I hesitated to ask the question, but decided that I had to do it. "Fareem, does Martine ever think about leaving here?"

Fareem shook his head like a man confronted with an insurmountable object. "Never."

This, too, would have to be reported to Bill Hammond, I decided on the spot, as it was further proof of Martine's determination to stay the course.

I looked at that last of the drawings, noted the lethal threat it portrayed.

"This sort of thing is not a joke," I said.

Fareem nodded. "I know."

"So what's Martine going to do about it?"

"Nothing," Fareem answered.

"But she should report it," I said.

He was quite surprised by this response, as well as by the urgency I'd been unable to conceal.

"To whom?" he asked.

"The authorities," I answered. "I mean, look at this thing. When men start fantasizing things like this, they sometimes end up actually doing them."

My mind filled with the ugliest images, all of them real-life versions of the hideous drawing on Martine's wall.

Fareem saw my distress and moved to calm it. "Martine doesn't think anyone can do anything about these things," he told me. "We don't even know who's hanging them around."

I turned back toward the drawings, the obscene lies they conveyed. "Who do you *think* is doing it?"

"My guess is that it's Mafumi's people," Fareem answered. "They're all weak in Rupala. They wouldn't have the guts to print something like that."

"They may not be as weak as you think," I warned.

For the first time Fareem seemed off balance and uncertain, as if suddenly undermined by a grave suspicion.

"How do you know that, Ray?" he asked.

He was staring at me very intently, like a man trying to read a coded message in dim light.

"Politicians never are," I said quickly, covering any direct knowledge under a blanket of generalized opinion. "They're all alike, aren't they? If they're really challenged, who knows what they might do."

Fareem was still peering at me oddly when Martine came in from the kitchen, a steaming bowl in her hands. "Dinner," she said.

We discussed the usual subjects as we ate: the state of the farm, the fact that a group devoted to "the greening of Lubanda" had planted the wrong trees along the river in Rupala, all of which had promptly died. As always, there was little discussion of the world outside the country, and none at all of movies, music, the celebrities whose wayward lives dominated the culture of the West. It was not that Martine felt hostile toward these things, or that she thought life in Lubanda somehow superior to it; she had lived here too long to romanticize the life she and most other Lubandans lived. On the other hand, she gave off not the slightest hint of ever having considered the possibility of living anywhere else.

It was as if she were a plant, and this the only soil that nourished her, or even allowed her to live. And yet, for the past several months, as I'd spent time in her spare surroundings, listened to her talk of fonio and teff, observed the labor of the planting and the harvest, the smoking of meat, the carving of shells, I'd often thought that regardless of whether she knuckled under to Gessee's big plans for Tumasi or not, her life was wasted here, a round of changeless days that would inevitably lead, as poets say, to dusty death.

After dinner, we all washed the dishes together, and Fareem, who had no doubt long ago sensed my feeling for Martine, discreetly went to his corner of the house and drew the curtain.

"He seems to think that I want to be alone with you," I whispered.

"Yes, he does."

"And he's right, of course," I told her. "So, come, let's go for a walk."

We walked out to the road, then turned right, toward Tumasi. It was a cloudless night, so we walked in the darkness beneath a wild array of stars and a faintly glowing crescent moon.

"So quiet," Martine said after a moment.

"Yes, it is."

"Is it ever quiet in New York?" she asked.

"Not really, no," I answered.

"Is it ever dark?"

"Sure," I said. "In some neighborhoods. But not like here."

She smiled softly. "The darkness here is . . . old."

She said this simply as a fact. The darkness of Lubanda was old because it had not changed since the dawn of time, it was a world frozen not in amber, whose shadows might be altered, but in a thick primordial tar.

Even so, I suddenly wondered if Martine might actually be comparing this ancient Lubandan night with the brightly teeming world beyond it, the great cities with their towers of light and streaming traffic and ceaselessly reverberating sounds. Could it be that my tales of New York, the little stories I'd related over the last nine months, had had the desired effect of piquing her curiosity? If I could just once get her out of Lubanda, I told myself, she would never want to go back.

"A place with big lights," she said as if she were answering a question she had secretly asked herself. "That is the best place for you, Ray. You would never be happy here."

So was it possible that from time to time she'd actually imagined us together in Lubanda? I asked myself in that charged instant. Had she lain awake as I had, thinking that we might share all the joys and burdens of a life lived together? Had she entertained the notion that we might one day plow the fields and harvest the grains on her small farm, and only now, in this darkness, come to realize that it could never be, that I would not only come to despise Lubanda, and all that living here entailed, but that I would finally come to despise Martine herself, and rue the day I'd joined my life with hers?

"You are the same as Nadumu," she told me. "And so, like him, you must understand what I would be in some other place."

"And what is that?"

"An orphan."

"Did he ever think of stayng with you?" I asked. "Here in Lubanda?"

She shook her head. "No. To live here, to be Lubandan, this was to him the same as being nothing, and he was afraid of being nothing."

"What are you afraid of, Martine?" I asked.

She drew in a long, curiously troubled breath before she answered.

"I am afraid that all Lubandans will come to feel the same as Nadumu felt when he came back here," she answered. "That to live here, to be what we are, is to be small, worthless, a failure. It does not bother me when outsiders feel this way about us." She looked at me pointedly. "But at all costs, Ray, we Lubandans must not feel this bad way about ourselves."

I knew that Martine was justified in having these thoughts. I also knew that I was one of those outsiders who'd come to think of Lubanda in precisely that "bad way."

Such was the hard truth that glittered in my eyes, and which she recognized immediately.

And so she gave no quarter to the reality that stood between us. "I will never leave Lubanda." She reached up and pressed her hand against my face. "And your home could never be here."

She was right, of course, and she knew that she was right. In some fit of love for her, I might pledge my undying devotion to Lubanda, but she would not believe it and because of that we could never be together, since she would never allow me to live with her in Lubanda and she would never leave it. Back home, my rival in matters of love had always been another man. With Martine, the only woman I had ever loved, it was a country.

My memory of this moment of excruciating clarity was suddenly interrupted by the sound of Ms. Vinu stamping my visa.

"Enjoy your time in Lubanda," she said as she handed it to me.

"Thank you."

I put the visa in my pocket, left her office, turned right, and headed back toward the reception area. Several photographs lined the walls of the corridor, men and women in native dress, all of them officials in the consulate office. They were smiling brightly, their eyes sparkling cheerfully, full of welcome. There were other pictures as well, of these same officials greeting various dignitaries or sitting at conference tables, looking busy. None of them drew my attention in a way that was more than passing until I reached the last one. It, too, was an ordinary photograph, nothing dramatic, and it was only the presence of a familiar face that caught my eye. It was Nullu Beyani with a group of Lubandans, a delegation of ten, Beyani by no means the central figure, but simply one of the men who'd gathered together for a group photo, all of them in an impressive office, with an impressive view of Manhattan in the background, beaming happily as they posed with Bill Hammond.

# Eighteen

You need not be a classicist to know that Dante placed traitors at the hottest spot in Hell. Of course, from the photo I'd seen at the Lubandan Consulate, I couldn't tell who the traitor was in the current situation, or even if there was one. There was no indication that Bill had ever actually been introduced to Beyani, after all, and even if he had, there was no reason he should have remembered him. As head of the Mansfield Trust, he'd no doubt received scores of such delegations.

As for Beyani, I had only the feeling I'd gotten in his presence. Some men give off violent vibrations, and he'd been one of that dreadful fraternity. I'd felt it in his shape-changing smile and in the steely look of his eyes even when they showed sympathy, which itself might have been no more than the work of a polished actor.

In the end, it seemed to me that only one thing connected these two men in a way that was relevant to the risks Fareem might well be facing: both of them would know that I was headed for Lubanda, Bill because I'd told him so, and Beyani because quite obviously he really was some sort of official in the current government, a fact of which I could not have been certain before I'd seen the picture. For that reason, if for no other, it now seemed better for me to enter Lubanda in secret, by way of Ghana. I could fly into Accra, hire a driver, and head northeast. There would no doubt be many places where I could cross the border into Lubanda without a record being kept of my entering the country. The border stations along its sparsely populated northern border were rarely manned, and even if they were, any official word of my crossing into the country would take weeks to arrive in Rupala, if it ever arrived at all. More than likely, my name would be scribbled onto a piece of paper that would later be used as kindling or for some other, equally rudimentary purpose.

Swift action seemed the least risky approach as well, and so within a few days I'd gotten a Ghanaian visa and was on a plane bound for Accra.

During that flight, I recalled how I'd flown out of Lubanda nearly ten years before. Prior to takeoff, the plane had been thoroughly sprayed with some chemical aerosol. This had never happened on a flight in the States or in Europe and so it had seemed perfectly symbolic of our alien presence on the continent, Lubanda not a country but a collective carrier of agents with which Westerners were unfamiliar and from whose unpredictable effects they had to be protected.

I'd been one of a crowd of Westerners who'd been leaving Lubanda that day, all of them quite happy to be doing so. They'd laughed and joked and repeated the by then well-worn conclusion that Lubanda, along with the rest of Africa, was beyond hope, Mafumi's insane antics being merely the latest of a slew of continental disasters. The man seated next to me had ordered first one celebratory scotch, then another, and after a moment unleashed a boozy attack on Lubanda and Lubandans that had ended in a drunken reference to "that crazy woman who walked down Tumasi Road." His red-rimmed eyes blinked slowly. "Do you recall that incident?" he asked me. "When was it now?"

"Ten years ago," I answered softly. "Her name was Martine Aubert."

"She was French?"

"She was Lubandan."

Lubandan, yes, I thought now, Lubandan in a way she'd known I could never be, an intuition that had proved lethally correct.

And so nothing could have seemed less subject to the rules of risk management than that I was now returning to that country.

It was a late-night flight and, with my usual transatlantic Ambien, I arrived in London quite refreshed, transferred to the British Airways terminal, and waited an hour for the plane to Accra.

The young woman who sat beside me was Danish, an aid worker headed for Kumasi, Ghana's second-largest city. It was her first trip to the country, and she was going there to administer the distribution of a food product that, she said, was a "miracle" in treating infant malnutrition.

"Is there a lot of infant malnutrition in Ghana?" I asked, simply by way of making conversation.

She looked at me blankly, the soft sparkle of her youthful idealism resting upon her like a dew. "I suppose so," she said, as if perplexed by the question. "So, what do you do in Accra?"

"Nothing," I answered. "I am going to Rupala."

"Is that a city in the north?"

"No, it's in another country," I informed her. "Lubanda."

"You have business there?" she asked sweetly.

"Memories," I answered.

As if brought to attention by the weight of that word, I imagined Martine not as she had been, but as she would be now if she'd been allowed to live out her life on her farm, a woman in her forties, sitting on her porch, reading or listening to that scratchy old gramophone, or perhaps simply peering out into the reaches of her beloved country.

"Sir?"

It was the young woman's voice, and when I turned to her, she was staring at me worriedly.

"Sir, are you all right?"

When I looked at her quizzically, she nodded toward my hands, which, as I saw immediately, were trembling.

"Are you afraid of flying?" she asked.

I shook my head. "No," I said truthfully, then even more truthfully added, "Other things."

I tried not to think of those unnamed other things for the rest of the flight, but despite that effort, I found myself assaulted by ever more disturbing memories of Lubanda, particularly the last few weeks of my life there. It was as if I were moving backward in time as I was moving forward in space, a curious turn of mind, and, as I recognized, a danger unanticipated by the standard rules of risk management.

But memory is the judge who at last must face the facts, and because my mind was clear, and I knew those facts well, I couldn't stop myself from recalling Martine in a hundred different ways: walking with a basket on her head; hoeing her fields; harvesting honey with a homemade bee suit. These were images of her that rose into my mind, lingered a moment, then faded as other images emerged, first in *pentimento,* then with a vivid fullness, to take their place. They came and departed without context, as if I were flipping through a scrapbook, but each new vision drew me closer to her, until I finally came to the evening when I'd found her sitting on her small porch, reading in the twilight.

She struck me as remarkably unruffled, given the increasing pressures of the last few weeks: the men who'd walked her property line and lit a fire around it, the intimidating visits by various officials from the Agricultural Ministry, the increasingly threatening letters from Rupala, and, latest of all, the crude drawings that were still appearing, and whose images had grown more violent over the last few days, her red-haired effigy assaulted by every imaginable savagery. The latest examples of crudity had been so viciously graphic—Martine eviscerated, beheaded, her body parts fed to pigs—she'd not added them to the collection on her wall, but simply plucked them from wherever she found them and tossed them into her cooking fire.

"Checking on me, Ray?" she said as I got out of the Land Cruiser.

"I guess you could say that," I told her.

It had been more than three weeks since my last visit, time I'd used to come to terms with our last encounter. In the wake of that disappointment, I'd begun to prepare for my departure from Lubanda. I'd remained dutifully committed to completing the few small projects I'd started, but the wind was no longer at my back. I might still have had hope for Lubanda, but I had none whatsoever that my love for Martine was anything but doomed.

"Where's Fareem?"

"Up north to visit his family," she answered. "He'll be gone for the next few weeks."

"He should be careful up there," I said. "Mafumi's people are gaining power in that part of Lubanda."

She looked at me as if she'd just spotted an unexpected figure in the distance. "How do you know that, Ray?" she asked.

"Bill Hammond keeps me informed."

She stared at me somewhat quizzically. "And do you keep him informed as well?"

It was a clear suggestion that Fareem had mentioned our earlier conversation to her, how I'd seemed to be quite in the know as to what the men in Rupala might be wiling to do. If they gave me such information, was it not reasonable to suspect that I gave them information in return?

"Yes," I answered.

"About me?" Martine asked. "Do you keep him informed about me?"

I shook my head. "No," I lied.

I couldn't tell if she accepted my denial, but she said nothing more on the subject. Instead, she glanced toward the road in the direction of

Rupala. "And then there's Farmer Gessee," she said. "He's now threatening to put a special tax on my crops. Taxes on *teff*, can you imagine?
A luxury tax." She laughed, but it was a sharp, almost jarring laugh,
seeded with dread. "He wants to take my land because he knows that
when you take someone's land, someone's property, you don't just take
that person's right to oppose you; you take his *power* to oppose you."

She said nothing more in reaction to this transparent scheme on
the part of the Agricultural Ministry, and so, in the casual manner of a
spy, I asked, "What do you plan to do?"

She looked out across the broad expanse of the savanna, twilight
only now beginning to color the air.

"My father loved this time of day," she said. She appeared almost to
return to that lost time, be a little girl again, safely cradled in her father's
arms. Suddenly she looked at me. "So do I."

I'd had the usual number of high school and college romances,
but at that instant, I felt certain once again that I had never loved, nor
ever would love, anyone the way I loved Martine. That this love was
unrequited, and likely to remain so, made it all the more fierce. Her
foreignness no doubt deepened her allure. But what made my desire
for her almost uncontrollable at that instant was her settledness, the fact
that while I was still in the process of taking shape, she was fully formed
and completely finished. There is nothing stronger than the gravitational
attraction that draws a boy, which is what I was, to a woman, which is
what Martine was. Such was the force that simultaneously crushed and
lifted me at that moment, and which I could control only by battening
down every hatch and by sheer will hold back my devouring need to
reach for her, pull her to me, and yes, yes, as if I were the half-crazed
suitor in some cheap romantic novel, smother her with passionate kisses.

She returned her gaze to the distant fields for a moment, while
I sat, a romantically boiling mass, beside her. Then she looked at me

again, and something in her eyes changed, so that I knew that she'd glimpsed the ardent love I could not get rid of and which she had willed herself never to return.

"I'll get you a beer," she said quickly, then rose just as quickly and went into the house.

She stayed inside longer than necessary. I heard her clinking glasses in the kitchen, then the sound of water being poured into a basin. When she at last returned, her expression had changed. She seemed less at ease with me, and her tone struck me as more formal.

"Your drink," she said.

She handed me the glass, but let go of it the second I grasped it, as if even so casual a nearness was perilous.

"Thanks."

Rather than sit down in the chair next to me, she walked all the way to the other side of the porch and leaned against one of its supporting posts.

"You must be looking forward to getting back to your real life," she said.

I put on a stolid front. "Yes, I am," I answered with an unexpectedly sudden display of my disappointment at the little I'd accomplished here. "I'd hoped to help shape Lubanda's future." I released a bitter little laugh. "Shape its people."

She took an edgy sip from her glass. "The line between shaping people and distorting them is very thin, Ray."

"No doubt," I said with a shrug, then finished the last of my drink and all but leaped to my feet. "Well, I'd better be going."

She didn't offer her hand in farewell as she always had in the past, and I knew that this was because she feared even so glancing a touch might convey too much.

"Well, see you soon," I said casually, my eyes at that instant no longer able to meet hers.

"Of course, Ray," she said tenderly. "Anytime."

I made my escape with quick steps and a leap into the Land Cruiser, though I was very careful to ease back onto the road rather than churn up an angry cloud of gravel like some spurned teenager.

Even so, I couldn't help but glance into my rearview mirror as I pulled onto Tumasi Road. Through the haze of its dust-coated glass, I saw Martine return to her chair and her book, turning the pages until she found her place, so beautifully self-contained in the soft glow of the lantern that I knew absolutely that I would never know such painful loss again, nor ever again open myself up to so dire a risk.

Seso was sitting outside chatting with Ufala when I arrived back in Tumasi. He nodded as I strode toward the house. I gave back only a crisp wave in return, then silently swept past him, dashed to my desk, and drew out the pad and pencil I used to make my reports to Bill Hammond.

As I wrote, I imagined Martine back at her farmhouse, sitting in her chair, immersed in her book, a vision of her that suddenly turned my hurt into a steadily building anger.

It was the sort of male rage that I might have quelled by pumping iron or swimming laps. But there was no gym in poor, dismal Tumasi, no pool, and so I took up my pen instead.

*Dear Bill:*

*This evening I once again spoke to Martine about the situation with regard to her farm. I am even more convinced that she will not under any condition concede to growing coffee, or anything else she doesn't want to grow.*

All true so far, and none of it different from what I'd written in earlier reports. But like one suddenly carried to an unexpected shore by an unexpected wave, I crossed the line from spy to advisor.

*It is, of course, possible that Martine derives a sense of power from remaining a determined obstacle to the big men in Rupala. If this is so, then their only hope is to render her as powerless as possible.*

How Martine might be rendered powerless by "the big men in Rupala" was not a question I posed, or even considered. Instead, I simply took the note, put it in an envelope, walked out into the night, and handed it to Seso. "To be mailed," I said.

He saw something in my eyes, but seemed only confused by it.

"All right," he said as he took the letter.

He said nothing else, nor did I. Rather, I simply walked back into the house, turned out the light, crawled into my bed, pressed my face into my pillow so that Seso wouldn't hear me, and, overwhelmed at last, began to cry not for some beloved country, as Martine must surely have done at some point during the days to come, but for a woman whose love for Lubanda I could neither change nor transfer to myself.

# Nineteen

It was late in the afternoon when my plane touched down in Accra. Customs was slow, but I avoided the chaos of baggage claim by carefully packing everything I needed into a bag small enough to fit in the overhead compartment.

The spare nature of my luggage came as no surprise to the man I'd chosen to drive me to the Lubanda border. His name was Dolvo, or at least that is what he had always called himself. He was one of those shady types known to everyone who seriously assesses Third World risks—a procurer, and probably a pimp, a man long accustomed to living on the edge.

"I've decided that Gomoa is the best place to cross the border into Lubanda," I said to him.

Dolvo did not seem in the least concerned that this was a three-day journey, much of it through very rough country and along roads designed to destroy both life and limb.

"Okay," he said. "You have a hotel in Accra for tonight?"

"I don't want to stay in Accra," I told him. "I want to drive to Elmina."

Dolvo looked puzzled. "But it is late. You should stay in Accra. We can leave tomorrow morning."

"No, I want to get out of Accra tonight because I know what the traffic will be like in the morning," I explained. "If I'm already in Elmina, it'll cut several hours out of the drive north."

Dolvo nodded. "Okay." He pointed to the left. "The car is this way."

The heat of the airport was nothing compared with the heat outside it, a wall of heat that gave the air a thickness made yet thicker by the exhaust fumes of the waiting taxis and the slightly sweet smell of smoking meats. I had not been on the continent for nearly two years, but once again it struck me that there is nothing like Africa. It greets you at the airport and spills out from there on, a fierce "itselfness" that works like a shredder on the best-laid plans of anyone outside it.

A blue twilight swam in upon us almost immediately. The sprawling clay-dirt parking lot was unlighted, so that darkness suddenly closed in like a mob. Scores of cars and vans of all description were scattered over the vast undulating terrain, a labyrinth of battered metal, many of the vehicles without doors or windows.

"Which hotel in Elmina?" Dolvo asked as he pulled himself in behind the wheel of a battered Volvo station wagon.

"The Oceanside," I said.

Dolvo jerked the car into gear. "I know that one," he said.

Over the next few hours we made our way out of Accra, passing through its dimly lighted neighborhoods and onto the pocked, half-clay/half-broken-asphalt road that followed the winding coastline to where, in the distance, I finally saw the ghostly white walls of Elmina Castle. By then we'd threaded our way through a continual throng of humanity, most everyone selling an inexplicable sameness of goods—bottled water, wooden bowls, carved figures—heaps of identical wares hawked from roadside stands or carried on vendors' heads.

The hotel in Elmina was not unlike the one I'd stayed in twenty years before when I'd spent my one vaguely luxurious night in Rupala.

And yet, despite the chaos of the parking lot and the sweltering crawl through the outer reaches of Accra, I found myself thinking not of these hardships, but of Martine, how happy she'd been as a farmer, how at home in Tumasi, the way she'd written about "the pleasure in what others see as lethargy, but which is actually little more than the unhurriedness that comes from our acceptance of a pace that is our own."

It was the unhurriedness I'd noticed in Ufala as she swept the small concrete porch outside my door, and in Seso as he folded my laundry, and which I'd seen in the Lutusi as they rested on their haunches, patiently waiting as their herds grazed.

Surely nothing had more fully confirmed Martine's claim to be Lubandan, I thought now, than the unhurriedness she'd embraced, and which I'd seen her abandon only once.

It had been a terrible scene, one I'd observed from my door only a week after I'd penned my report to Bill, then crushed my face into my pillow and, like a little boy denied his heart's desire, sobbed myself to sleep.

Gessee had arrived in the village toward the middle of the day, his two uniformed bodyguards at his side, a sure sign that he expected trouble.

"Miss Aubert," he said coldly when he reached the stall where Martine had come to buy her weekly supplies.

Martine turned to him. "'Farmer Gessee," she said evenly.

"I was headed to your farm when I saw that you were here in the market," Gessee said. He reached into the pouch that hung from his shoulder and drew out an envelope that bore the president's seal. "I have something for you."

Martine stared at the envelope, but didn't take it.

"What is it?" she asked.

"Just read it," Gessee said with a vaguely gloating look.

231

Martine took the envelope, opened it, read it. There was only a hint of surprise in her expression when she looked up from the paper and stared into Gessee's motionless brown eyes.

"You're saying I do not own my farm?" she asked him. "But my father bought this farm when he was a young man. I was born there. It has been in our family for well over fifty years." She thrust the paper toward Gessee. "You can take this back to Rupala, because it does not apply to me or to my land."

Gessee did not move to take the paper from her. "You are a squatter on national land, Miss Aubert," he told her. "The land you live on belongs to the people of Lubanda. This is an order to vacate the property within one month."

"I can read," Martine said.

"You read, but you do not understand."

"Believe me, I understand."

"Then you will vacate?"

Martine continued to press the paper toward him. "No, I will not," she said.

Gessee now took the paper and with exaggerated calm neatly folded it. "Then you are defying the government's order."

"I am not defying anything," Martine replied. "That order does not apply to me because in Lubanda, occupancy for over fifty years constitutes ownership. That is the law in our country, sir."

Gessee's smile had a note of triumph. "I am well schooled in Lubanda's laws, Miss Aubert," he said. "And, yes, occupancy for fifty years does constitute ownership." The smile broadened with his sense of victory. "But it only applies to native Lubandans."

"I am a native Lubandan," Martine said.

"No, you are not," Gessee said. "At least not according to the government's newly adopted definition of that term."

"Newly adopted?" Martine asked.

"Three days ago," Gessee said. "On Wednesday at two thirty-five in the afternoon to be exact. The Lubandan Cultural Authentication Act."

Gessee's eyes swept over to me and in their collusive sparkle I saw just how well he had read my little report, and with what speed and ruthlessness they have acted to take from Martine any vestige of power.

"I have not heard of this new law," Martine said.

Gessee shrugged. "That is hardly my responsibility, Miss Aubert."

"What does it say?"

Gessee drew in a long, vaguely weary breath, as if he found it quite tiresome to deal with Martine any longer. "With regard to the matter at hand, it means that fifty years of occupancy confers owner-ship only to native Lubandans, and by native Lubandans it means 'culturally native.'" He smiled the smile of one who knew he had, at last, gained the upper hand. "It isn't just a matter of birth," he added. "It is a matter of—"

"Being black," Martine interrupted.

"Being of Lubandan cultural origin," Gessee said. "I think we both know that you do not fit that category, Miss Aubert."

For a moment, Martine stared at Gessee from the depths of what seemed a profound sadness. Then, as if the slow fuse of the last few weeks had suddenly reached the powder keg, she drew the paper from Gessee's hands, lifted it to his face, and ripped it in two.

"This is nothing but racism," she said. "And you are a racist."

And I thought, *No, Martine, no,* and rushed toward where they stood, still facing each other. But I was too far away to interfere with what happened next, and probably would have failed in that attempt. A red wave had taken Martine, the pent-up response to those increasingly threatening letters from Rupala, those hideous drawings, and now this transparently racist attempt to take her land.

"You are also a thief," she said to Gessee. "You and the other men in Rupala are no different from common burglars because the only thing you work to get—actually work to get—is something that doesn't belong to you."

Gessee's tone hardened. "You should watch your mouth, Miss Aubert," he said. "You are talking about our president."

"*Our* president?" Martine cried. "How is Dasai *our* president, if I am not Lubandan?"

Gessee glanced about, clearly aware that the people in the market had gathered around him, and now quite obviously playing to them. "Quite right," he said with a nod to the crowd. "He is *our* president, Miss Aubert, not yours."

For a moment, Martine held her tongue. She was obviously trying to control herself. But as the seconds passed, the lava heated, slowly but inexorably, then spilled over once again.

"You and all the rest of you in Rupala," she said vehemently. "You are like a bad chief, one who lays all the work on his people, mostly the women."

"Mostly the women," Gessee repeated, and glanced meaningfully at the surrounding men.

"Yes, mostly the women," Martine said flatly. "Only with you, it is the foreigners you expect to work for you. People in countries thousands of miles away. You expect them to work and pay their taxes so that this money can be given to you."

Gessee only watched her silently, like the villagers who had gathered ever more thickly around them. Then he said, "You insult our chiefs, Miss Aubert." He shook his head as if ashamed for her. "No Lubandan would do that."

For a moment he stared at her as if he were sorry for this alien who did not belong, and never would belong, in his country. Then he knelt down, picked up the pieces of the presidential letter, and with a great show of reverence returned them to his pocket.

"I will report your response to the president," he said once he'd risen to face Martine once again. With that, he turned and walked away, nodding to the crowd and shaking hands as he made his way to his car.

Within seconds he was gone, but the tone of the market had changed. A low murmur rippled through it, and I noticed a few hostile glances.

I had made it to within a few feet of where Martine had exploded, then stopped and waited in the aftershocks of that explosion. For a moment, Martine stood in place, her head unmoving, her eyes very still, breathing slowly, with nothing but the nervous energy of her hands to suggest the gravity of what had just happened.

"Martine?" I asked, when I finally moved toward her.

"I should have kept quiet," she said worriedly as she turned toward me. "I should have just read the letter and kept quiet."

More than ever before, she seemed isolated and under siege. She'd thought that being born in Lubanda had assured her acceptance, made her truly Lubandan. But the murmur and the glances told a far different and more perilous story.

"Let me walk you to the road," I said.

She nodded, but said nothing.

Together we moved through the market, a sea of either hostile or averted eyes. Martine kept her head up and walked at a measured pace, but something had broken in her, and she was in the midst of trying to put it back together again.

At the road she stopped and turned toward the village. By then, the market had resumed its usual life, and for a moment she gazed at it with a look of dark nostalgia, as if it were something already in the distant past, a backward glimpse in time.

"I knew they would try to take my farm," she said softly, as if only to herself. She was silent for a moment before she turned to me and added, "Will you help me keep it, Ray?"

I'd never expected Martine to ask me to intervene on her behalf, but this was exactly what was being asked, and so my lover's chest swelled with exhilaration.

"Of course I will," I assured her. "I'll leave for Rupala tonight. I'll talk to Bill in the morning. He has some influence, I'm sure."

She placed the basket on her head, turned and moved up the road a few paces, then stopped suddenly, as if by a thought, and faced me. "Let me know what happens."

"Okay," I said. "And I hope I have good news."

"So do I," Martine said, though it was clear she had no such expectation, so that as she turned and moved away from me again, it struck me that I'd never known a person more helpless than she was now. The big men in Rupala were poised to take her farm. Gessee had provoked her into a reaction that had turned the village—or at least its men—against her. Fareem was visiting his family in the north, leaving her alone at the far end of Tumasi Road.

For all those dire reasons, and surely as a last resort, she'd been forced to turn to me as her final hope for remaining in Lubanda—me, Ray Campbell, this pathetic, love-struck foreigner whose soul, though drying quickly, had not yet quite turned to dust.

# Twenty

There is an old, half-comic but somewhat serious maxim among more intrepid travelers: *Never trust border guards who are wearing only parts of their uniforms.* Had I applied that rule at the Lubandan border, I would have told Dolvo to stop before we reached it, then, as inconspicuously as possible, turned around and returned immediately to Accra. For even in the distance, I could see that one of the guards was wearing a cap at least two sizes too big, while the one who stood beside him was wearing striped uniform pants that fell over his shoes and rested in the dust. My guess was that a larger man, long fattened on bribery, had grown yet more greedy, and as a consequence had died here, these various uniform parts now all that remained of him.

"Visutu," Dolvo said as he eyed the border crossing some fifty yards ahead. "You should have a gun."

He'd offered to provide me with one shortly before we'd left Accra, but I'd known that it was just something he wanted to sell, and that the price would be ridiculously high.

"It would be risky, having a gun," I said now by way of refusing his offer once again.

Dolvo nodded toward the border. "These ones in the north, they fly the new flag, but they are still Mafumi's tribe," he said.

And indeed this was true. Up ahead, at the little concrete border station, I could see Lubanda's most recent flag as it waved limply in the sweltering air: against a green and gold background two hands clutching each other in the middle, the skin of the hand at the right growing steadily darker from the wrist, while the other took the opposite direction. As an immediately comprehensible design, it effectively captured Fareem's much-stated hope of a fully integrated, fully cooperative Lubanda. As a policy, it was certainly less utopian than Village Harmony, but my fear was that it might be no less indicative of Fareem's peril. If Mafumi's old guard was still in charge of border stations such as this one, then it was surely possible that some were in Rupala as well, and that they were determined to replace Fareem with a kinsman whose brutality was more to their liking. For after all, though Visutu, Fareem had stood against Mafumi, his own fellow tribesman, and thus must surely be counted a traitor to those who still mourned the loss of their favored tyrant.

"The new president is trying reconciliation," I told Dolvo, though at the moment I said it, I imagined Fareem the victim of a plot, soon to be assassinated, or worse. Anything was possible. I knew that after the Janetta Massacre, Mafumi's men had sliced off the penises of the village's men and boys and strung them in dangling groups on fishing lines, where they'd hung like the catch of the day. Reconciliation with such men? What policy could be more charged with peril? I had never been convinced that reconciliation, despite the new president's devotion to it, was not, as he'd put it, "the way out of Hell." For how are men ever made better by ignoring what they do?

"They are devils," Dolvo said. "Even armed it is dangerous in this part of Lubanda."

This was true, and for a moment I did honestly revisit my decision to return to this country, as well as my reason for doing so. But just at that instant, a gust of wind suddenly lifted Lubandan's struggling flag and curled it toward me beckoningly, like a finger. Risk assessment pays no heed to paranormal signs, of course. It doesn't follow the movements on a Ouija board or derive its information from the tea leaves at the bottom of a cup. And yet, the sudden movement of that flag abruptly stiffened my resolve to help Fareem if I could.

"Drive on," I said.

The man in the oversized cap strolled over to the car as it drew to a halt before a makeshift blockade made of strips of rust-streaked, corrugated tin.

"Out of the car," he said.

We did as we were told, and were escorted into the little concrete shed by the other guard, the one in the long pants. A man in civilian clothes sat behind an old TV tray that had the picture of a young woman drinking from a classic Coca-Cola bottle. Such relics of the fifties could still be found in American bric-a-brac shops, but I'd never seen one in actual use.

"Name," the man said.

We gave our names, but there was no attempt to record them. Rather, the man behind the desk simply stared at us for a moment, then said, "No foreign currency is allowed in Lubanda."

This was nonsense, of course. There was no such policy. But extortion at the border was nothing new, and so I understood that dollars would now be "exchanged" for an internationally worthless Lubandan currency according to whatever rate the man behind the Coca-Cola TV tray decided.

"You have to buy Lubandan money with the money you got," the man explained. His eyes flitted over to Dolvo. "Him too."

"I'm the only one crossing the border," I told him, firmly, because I'd learned long ago that firmness was something—perhaps the only thing—that all bullies understand. "My driver is going back to Accra."

The man smiled. "There is a charge for crossing the border without a driver."

Never mind that only a few yards away I could see a steady stream of local people crossing the border on foot, making it clear that this charge applied only to whites. This double standard was also nothing new. At Kinshasa airport, I'd watched luggage handlers riffle through incoming baggage, then sell their contents back to their rightful owners with an unruffled sense of criminal entitlement that would have stunned Al Capone.

I looked the head of this border station directly in the eye. "Look," I said flatly, "I know this border station has nothing to do with the government in Rupala. It has nothing to do with border security or immigration, or the control of contraband or anything else. This is a place to rob foreigners, and you are thief, but I don't care because I need to get into Lubanda. So just stop the bullshit and come up with a fee for you and your friends that will leave me enough money to continue my journey."

The man did not seem in the least offended by this outburst. He was a thief, and knew it, and now he knew that I knew it, too, so the matter was pretty much settled.

"I sell you fifty dollars' worth of Lubandan currency," he said. "You can use it when you cross. Another fifty for crossing without a driver."

He looked at my single piece of baggage, and so I acted quickly. "And another fifty for keeping my luggage?"

A smile crawled onto his face. "You are not new to this country," he said as he put out his hand.

I took out my wallet, plucked the agreed-upon amount of cash from it, and gave it to him.

By then the two other guards had joined us, both of them eyeing the cash as I handed it over.

"You can go," the man behind the TV tray said to Dolvo, and with no word of farewell, my driver turned and left the room. Seconds later, still standing in place, I heard the engine of his car fire, then the sound of wheels on gravel as it pulled away.

"You are alone now," the man behind the TV tray said. His smile returned. "But you are safe." He laughed. "Lubanda, it is one big family now." He leaned back slightly and folded his arms over his chest. "There are not many villages out this way. Where do you plan to stop tonight?"

"Janetta," I said.

Perhaps he saw something in my eyes at that moment, the shadow of some old, remembered crime that needed no words to convey it. People had perhaps seen that same shadow in them before, though none could have suspected the nature of that inward injury, nor that there might be acts of love so fraught with error as to make the deepest hatreds blink.

"Good luck," he said. Something drew the lingering smile from his lips and curled them downward. "I think you're going to need it."

I turned and left, glancing back only once to where the man sat intently thumbing the bills.

I was on my way to Rupala, of course, hoping to warn Fareem before it was too late. And yet, as I moved deeper into Lubanda, I found that I hardly thought of him. All my thoughts were of Martine, and the night she'd asked me to help her save her farm, the long ride to Rupala, which I'd not reached until early morning. It was a memory that worked upon my soul like a barbed whip upon the body, vicious, unrelenting, every recollection drawing blood.

Bill had been quite obviously surprised to see me standing outside his office door that morning.

"You look road-weary," he said.

"I drove all night."

He turned and unlocked the door to his office. "I've actually been surprised by how rarely you've come to Rupala," he said cheerfully. "But then, I'm sure Tumasi has its charms."

The lascivious nature of his smile told me everything. He thought that Martine and I were lovers, a supposition based upon the simple fact that in isolated Tumasi we were the only man and woman of the same tribe.

"Come in," Bill said as he ushered me into his office.

It was very plain and decidedly functional, with nothing but a metal desk and a few filing cabinets. Its only adornment was an enlargement of the photograph of President Dasai I'd taken with Fareem's broken camera, its starburst crack neatly cropped out so that the president stood quite magisterially before a Lubandan sunset, fists at his waist, the man of the hour.

"That was a good day," I said almost to myself, my memory of those events now entirely romanticized, for it had been early in my time in Lubanda, my love for Martine only beginning. We had shared a moment of grave risk, and had later made light of it upon returning to Tumasi. What could have been more thrilling?

Bill laughed. "A good day? You were shot at. You could have been killed." He nodded toward one of the room's metal chairs. "Have a seat."

I sat down, and waited for Bill to do the same.

"So, what's on your mind, Ray?" he said.

"I've come about Martine," I told him.

Bill made a nest of his fingers and placed it firmly on his desk. "What about her?"

"Gessee is trying to take her farm," I said. "He's been doing it for quite a while. That tax on teff, for example was just a way of doing that, but since then it's gotten worse."

Bill made no argument against this.

"Now he's saying she's not 'culturally' Lubandan," I continued. "And for that reason, her land can be confiscated by the state."

"That's the new law, yes," Bill said.

"It means that Martine, because she isn't black, will lose her farm," I said. "It's pure racism."

Bill laughed, "And the fact that blacks can be racists surprises you, Ray?"

"No, but an outright racist policy does," I fired back. "Especially when it's aimed at a woman like Martine . . . a woman who is—"

"Good God," Bill interrupted. "You've fallen in love with her."

I nodded. "Yes," I admitted.

"And so now you're playing her knight-errant," Bill said, neither with approval nor disapproval, but merely as a clear statement of the case.

"I want to help her, yes," I conceded. "You've read my reports. You know what's been going on in Tumasi. Those men at the edge of her property. Those horrible drawings."

"Which have evidently had no effect on Martine," Bill said gravely.

For a moment, he remained silent, his expression unreadable, making me feel like a man working with an instrument whose interworkings he didn't understand.

Finally, he said, "Ray, if you've come because you think I can somehow change what the government intends to do, you've wasted your time, because there's nothing you can do and there's nothing I can do to help Martine keep her farm." He opened his hands as if to show how empty of power they were. "I'm sorry, but that's the way it is." He suddenly looked as if he now had to get on with things he could do something about, the matter of Martine keeping her land decidedly not among them. "So," he said wearily. "Anything else?"

I knew that I was being dismissed, but I had failed so dismally to help Martine that the prospect of returning to her and admitting that failure was more than either my love for her or my pride in myself could bear.

"So, what do Gessee and the others think Martine will do once they've taken her farm?" I asked.

Bill leaned back, and for the first time he seemed uncomfortable with his helplessness. "I don't know," he answered. "Her farm will be taken by the state and they'll grow coffee on it. What Martine does after that is of no concern to anyone in Rupala." He glanced toward the window, where a new building was going up. "I suppose she can come here. She speaks English and French. She should be able to find some kind of work." He looked at me, and a sad little smiled crawled onto his lips. "Can she type?"

"There has to be another way for her," I answered sharply.

Bill suddenly looked as if he'd been drawn into a conspiracy whose direction and possible consequences he didn't like. "Do you have a suggestion?"

It was precisely at that moment that the idea came to me, in a movement I could only describe as a dry rustling in my mind. I said nothing as the plot took shape, a pause sufficiently brief to suggest the risk ahead, but not long enough to deter me from taking it.

"More pressure," I said at last. "The government could put more pressure on Martine."

"Pressure to do what?"

"Leave Lubanda."

"They've already taken her farm, Ray," Bill reminded me. "What else can they take?"

"Her citizenship," I answered.

The idea had come to me because I'd done as Bill had asked—read Lubanda's Constitution very carefully—though it had never occurred to me that I might use that knowledge against Martine.

"Her Lubandan citizenship could be taken from her," I repeated, this time more emphatically.

Bill looked as if he were turning a kaleidoscope, trying to bring its disparate elements into crystal clarity. "What are you talking about? Martine was born in Lubanda."

"That's true," I told him, "but she can still be stripped of her Lubandan citizenship."

Bill watched me darkly. "How?"

"Remember when I first came here, you gave me a copy of the Lubandan Constitution," I said. "Well, I read it, just like you said I should. And there is a section in it that says that citizenship can be denied to any person *or their descendants*, who entered the country illegally or gave false information, or who—and this is the part that applies to Martine—'who committed acts against Negritude.'"

"Acts against Negritude," Bill repeated. "What does that have to do with Martine?"

"Martine's grandfather was a member of the *Force Publique*," I said. "She told me this herself. She also gave me a book about it. Her grandfather's in it." I leaned forward. "His name was Emile Aubert and he slaughtered God knows how many Congolese. Tortured people, burned villages. If he doesn't qualify as a man who has committed acts against Negritude, then no one does." I eased back in my chair. "Just by using the Constitution, Gessee could denationalize Martine. She'd be a stateless person. They could even refuse to give her a work permit. They could do anything really. She would have no rights whatsoever. She would be completely helpless."

"And you feel that at that point, Martine would leave Lubanda?" Bill asked.

I nodded. "And when you get down to brass tacks, isn't that really what Gessee and the others want . . . a black Lubanda?"

Bill was silent for a moment, clearly reluctant to admit this stark truth of Lubandan politics, but at last unable to deny it. "But where would she go?" he asked. "She isn't a citizen of any country but Lubanda."

"She could go to the States," I said.

"With you?" Bill asked. "You mean as your—"

"Yes," I interrupted.

Bill smiled knowingly. "It's like that old Bible story, isn't it? The one about David and Bathsheba. How David sent her husband, Uriah, to the forefront of the battle in order to kill him."

"I'm not killing anyone," I said. "I just know that Martine has to leave Lubanda . . . whether she wants to or not."

At that moment we were two men in collusion with regard to a woman whose best interest we were convinced we knew better than she knew it, a woman whose future we were conspiring to shape without regard to the risk we ran of distorting it.

"So, I take it you want me to tell Gessee about Martine's grand-father," Bill said.

"Yes."

Bill's gaze was unearthly still, and in that stillness I saw our collusion grow darker as he became steadily more convinced that we were of the same tribe, he and I, and for that reason we should naturally join forces to rescue a third member of our pale clan from a life we had decided she had no right to choose.

At last, he nodded. "All right," was all he said.

On the ride back to Tumasi, I knew exactly what Bill was going to do. He was going to call Gessee and give him the power he needed to deal with Martine with a finality that would surely appeal to him, and which could be provided to him via a mechanism enshrined in the Lubandan Constitution rather than any further resort to transparently phony last-minute laws. As a treacherous scheme, it was perfect, because Martine herself would never know what I'd done.

She was on her dusty little porch when I got to her farm that evening.

"How did it go in Rupala?" she asked tensely, as if her life depended upon whatever news I had for her, a fact far more certain than she knew.

I sat down and released a dramatic sigh. "I'm sorry, Martine." I told her. "There's nothing anyone can do."

She drew a small piece of wood from the pile beside her chair and began to whittle it with her father's pocketknife. "I did not think there would be."

I hesitated long enough to take a breath, then delivered far graver news. "And they're going to take away your Lubandan citizenship."

She looked darkly amazed that such a thing could even be contemplated.

"But I was born here," she said.

"I know, but there's something in the Constitution," I told her. "It's about the descendants of people who committed acts against Negritude. Acts against blacks at any place or any time. Like the ones done by your grandfather in—"

"That provision has never been applied to anyone," Martine interrupted in a way that suggested her complete dismissal of this ploy. "It was just part of the anticolonial rhetoric back when Lubanda became independent. Some racist fringe group wanted it, and Dasai caved in to get the Constitution ratified. It was never meant to—"

"Yes, but it's there, Martine," I said. "It's there in black and white and they're going to apply it to you."

She stared at me silently, as if numbed by an unexpected blow.

And so I waited, as she sat, very still, like someone in a daze. It was surely sinking in, I thought, the desperate nature of her situation, the fact that there was no way out of it. She would lose her land and her citizenship. She would be declared an alien, and anything might happen after that. She would be a woman alone, a woman without resources, in a country that had cast her out.

"You have to leave Lubanda, Martine," I said. "With your citizenship revoked, you wouldn't even be entitled to work here. You wouldn't just be landless, you'd be . . . homeless."

Her eyes glistened. "An orphan."

It was but one level of the depth of my error that I'd expected her finally to accept the unforgiving and irrevocable fact that she was not and never would be Lubandan. I was certain that from the ruins of this newly enforced orphanhood, she would begin to fashion another life in another place. After all, as I had so carefully calculated, no other choice remained to her. I had set her adrift in the bulrushes, utterly confident that I could also pluck her from them.

But instead of accepting the dire fact I had just presented to her, Martine suddenly gave a defiant jerk of the knife, then rose quickly and fiercely and stood, staring down at me, her hair falling in a red curtain to her shoulders, the blade of her knife glinting in the candlelight. "How can I repay you, Ray?" she asked in a tone so ambivalent I wondered if she'd guessed my treason, and now intended to repay me by cutting my throat.

She didn't wait for an answer, but as if in response to some inner signal, she turned and walked into the house. I remained on the porch, unsure of what to do, listening as she moved about inside. I heard drawers opened and closed, papers shuffled.

When she returned to the porch she was carrying a large cloth bag. "It's cured goat," she said as she held it before me. "I wish I had something of more value," she added with a thin smile, "But I am only a poor Lubandan farmer."

Since there seemed nothing else to do, I took the bag. "Thank you," I said, and started to rise.

"Don't go," she said. "Have a drink with me." Something deep within her seemed to tremble. "I don't want to be alone right now."

I nodded.

She was a long time returning with our drinks, and once, glancing toward the house, I saw her standing in the kitchen, her back to me, her head down, her hands gripping the edge of the sink as if to keep herself upright. A few minutes later I heard her crank the gramophone, then the melancholy strains of a cello.

"What are we listening to?" I asked as she returned to the porch and handed me a glass of that familiar homebrew.

"Elgar," Martine answered. "He wrote it after World War One. He was in mourning for a world he had lost." Then, to my stark amazement, she faced me with an expression that looked carved of granite. "But I'm not going to lose mine."

"But Martine, you—"

"I'm going to tell the world about what's happening here," she said firmly. "I'm going to write some sort of paper. I'm going to take it to Rupala. I'm going to take it on foot, and give it to anyone who will read it. Reporters. Anyone. They're going to have to do more than take away my right to be Lubandan. I will never leave Lubanda. They will have to kill me first."

Within that fiercely voiced assurance, I saw the adamantine nature of Martine's will. She would never relent, never take any route of escape. I had offered her a way out of Lubanda. With every other door closed, I had hoped she would take it. But now that hope seemed not just tragically misplaced, but deeply and fundamentally in error.

And so later that night, now once again in Tumasi, I hastily sent a note to Bill, telling him that my little plot had failed and that he should keep secret what I'd told him about Martine's grandfather. The two-word note he returned to me two days later could not have made the nature of my error more obvious: *Too late.*

Martine's determined voice returned to me: *They will have to kill me first.*

And I thought, *What have I done?*

# PART V

"Where are we going?" I ask as Fareem opens the door of the old black Mercedes that brought me from the airport.

"You will see," he tells me. "Please, get in before the heat makes both our shirts wet."

Once inside the car, I glance at the mirror in the front seat and notice that this is not the same driver as the one who met me at the airport. The current man behind the wheel has eyes that sparkle less jovially, and his face is leaner. Perhaps he is one of Beyani's men. I calculate the risk that my earlier visit to Lubanda has been discovered, along with the dreadful thing I found there. In reponse, I am careful to hold tightly to my briefcase.

"It is good to see you again, Ray," Fareem says as he settles in beside me, his lean body barely causing a crinkle in the car's old cracked leather. He glances about the once plush interior, his gaze completely unconcerned by the motionless eyes of the driver. "We are selling Mafumi's fleet of luxury cars," he casually informs me, his tone without apprehension that those who once enjoyed the pleasures of this fleet might resist the loss of such luxury. "A consortium in Brussels is taking them all." He slaps his hands together. "All of them gone, just like dust from the hands."

"But these cars must have belonged to Mafumi's old guard," I say cautiously.

"Of course they did," Fareem says.

"Won't they feel deprived of them?"

"Perhaps so, but they will get used to it."

"I've found that those who once had much rarely adapt well to having less," I tell him.

Fareem offers a look of great sympathy. "Your vision of life has grown much darker since you left Lubanda," he says.

"Reality has a way of summoning the shadows," I tell him.

Fareem laughs his worldly laugh. "Is that the view of some Greek oracle?"

"More the simple lesson of experience."

"Perhaps, so," Fareem says. "But the lesson of my own experience tells me that men do not need luxury cars as a prerogative of government service." He smiles. "Besides, such luxury separates them from the people."

"So what will be the president's car?" I ask lightly.

"I think perhaps it will be a hybrid," Fareem answers. "Lubanda has little superstructure at the moment, and so it stands to reason that the president should have a small carbon footprint."

I glance out the window, Rupala baking in the heat, everything increasing that heat: the packed clay of the ground, the ripple of corrugated metal, the stacks of cement blocks, even the steel rods that jut up from the capital's many unfinished buildings, structures begun with donor money, then abandoned when the money was withdrawn.

"There is so much left to do in Lubanda," Fareem says solemnly when he sees me peering out the window.

"Yes," I agree, thinking now of my mission, uncertain though it is, a shot, as they say, in the dark. "Yes, there is much for Lubandans to do."

We are now on the wide boulevard that once led from the Agricultural Ministry to Embassy Row, the one street in Rupala that has been repaved and provisioned with traffic signals.

"This is to be Lubanda's Champs-Élysées," Fareem tells me. "A proud avenue that will open onto Independence Square." He shrugs. "At least that is my dream."

I look at him. "What was Martine's dream?"

Fareem visibly saddens at the mention of her name. "I don't know," he says, then shrugs softly. "A complicated person, Martine."

"Actually, I think she was quite simple," I tell him. "And so was her dream."

I start to tell him what Martine's dream had been, and of how recklessly I had betrayed her, of the fact that here, in Rupala, twenty years before, I had rolled the dice for a woman who was not even present at the table, and how on the outcome of that toss, a braver and more knowing heart than mine had been forfeited. I want to tell him all of that, expose the full measure of my error, but the car suddenly slows and Fareem points straight ahead. "Our national square has taken on a vital function," he says.

The square is large, and years before it had served the people of Rupala mostly as a park. There were areas of grass and shady walkways. None of this is now visible, however, for what opens before me is a tent city teeming with children.

"This is the tragic legacy of Mafumi," Fareem tells me as our driver wheels the car over to the curb and brings it to a halt at the southern perimeter of what had once been Independence Square.

"Over there is where they murdered President Dasai," Fareem says. He nods to the right, where there is nothing but more children. "And there is where his entire cabinet was executed. Their bodies were so riddled with bullets there was nothing to cut down from the post but bloody hunks of flesh." He shakes his head at the inexplicable savagery of this. "They just kept shooting and shooting." He looks at me. "There is much evil done in this world."

"There is, yes," I tell him, "but almost all of it is done in the name of something good."

Fareem chooses not to engage my little philosophical remark, but instead, indicates a far corner of the square. "And that is where Farmer Gessee met his end."

"Yes, I saw it on the Internet," I tell him. "All the executions. A whole day of them. The 'White-Out.' The assault on the zoo."

Fareem is clearly surprised to hear this. "So you have been following the descent of Lubanda?" he asks.

I nod. "All the way to the bottom."

He smiles appreciatively. "And now the ascent can begin, I hope." He glances toward where the new Lubandan flag waves above the square, no doubt daily saluted by its throng of orphans.

"Perhaps our flag should bear a phoenix," Fareem says cheerfully. "A symbol for new hope."

"But that's a Western symbol," I remind him. "Not in the least Lubandan."

"Western, yes," Fareem says. "But perhaps only a suggestion of our shared hopes for this country." He glances at my briefcase. "Have you brought hope for Lubanda, Ray?"

I nod. "Yes," I assure him, though I know that what I have brought to this beleaguered land is profoundly risky. Still, all else seems so profoundly to have failed.

I smile sadly, then add. "It is the only hope I have."

# Janetta, Lubanda, Three Weeks Earlier

# Twenty-one

*What have I done?*

The question was again ringing in my ears as I made my way south, the vegetation growing more sparse with each step.

And so Bill had been right—it was atonement I sought in coming back to Lubanda, an effort to save Fareem because I'd failed to save Martine by assuming that what I wanted for her should be what she also wanted for herself, an error that had set in motion a chain of events that had quickly spun out of control.

No part of what my error had wrought could now be changed, however, and so my present task was to reach Rupala as quickly as possible, meet with Fareem, alert him to the risk I'd discovered, and hope that he would take my warning seriously.

I'd made it to Janetta within two days of crossing the border, encountering very few people on the way. The ones I met had seen few whites since Mafumi had taken power, and so I was a curiosity to them, but little more than that. I offered them nothing and they owed me nothing, and so they had the luxury of ignoring me or not, according to their own will, which was generally to look up, perhaps wave or smile, then return to the labors and relaxations that were deeply and abidingly their own.

The walk itself was long, and swarms of tsetse flies sometimes attacked me so fiercely I broke into a full run to get away from them. Still, it was the heat that most drained me. It beat down relentlessly, the sun at times so bright I felt that I was staring directly into it. The few villages I passed were baked by it, and everywhere, everywhere, people crouched beneath whatever shade could be found, motionless even as I passed, save for the near-naked children who sometimes rushed toward me, followed me a few yards, then gave up the chase and retreated back into the sheltering shade, movements of engagement and nonengagement that were, for them, as natural as the tides.

Janetta had been the village to which Fareem had fled in the wake of the Tumasi Road Incident. It had sheltered him for several weeks, and for that reason, Mafumi had decreed that its people suffer a terrible retaliation for Fareem's later activities in Europe, particularly his creation of a Lubandan government-in-exile.

Mafumi's revenge upon the people of Janetta had been characteristically savage—infants, toddlers, and small children sandwiched between strips of plywood and rolled over by trucks, women nailed to trees, men and boys hacked to death—an outrage that had even penetrated the cloud of mindless celebrity noise that generally engulfs the West. From Paris, Fareem had issued a grave condemnation of these events. I could still remember him standing erect and with great dignity quoting Voltaire to the effect that as long as men believe absurdities, they will commit atrocities.

A few villagers still lived in Janetta, and all of the ones to whom I spoke remembered the visit Fareem had made some months before to lay a wreath beside the large tree at the center of the village.

"It was the tree where they nailed the women," one of them told me, an old man, clearly one of the village elders. "The president got down on his knees. His shoulders were shaking." He shrugged. "But he did not stay long. He was on his way to another village."

"Which one?" I asked, thinking that I might retrace Fareem's return to Rupala.

"Tumasi. It is all the way across the savanna. I don't know why he was going there."

I knew, however, and it seemed typical of Fareem that he would have connected these two towns, each so dark a stain on Lubandan history.

"I know Tumasi," I told the old man. "I lived there twenty or so years ago."

"You lived in Tumasi?" he asked, quite surprised to hear this.

"I came there to help Lubanda," I said with a shrug, "but I didn't."

The old man nodded, but I could see that he'd lost interest in the subject. What did he care if some foreigner had once come to help a place far away from his own village.

For that reason I might have dropped the subject, but the day had been long, and the tree above me gave some relieving shade, and so I risked further boring this old man by taking out the one photograph I'd brought with me, as a kind of amulet, a way of reminding me of that lost time, of what I had been, and what they had been, and what had happened to each of us. It showed the key players in my life at that time, all of us standing in front of my house, Seso a little off to my right, Fareem and Martine to my left.

"I lived here," I said as I offered him the picture. "In that little house."

The old man took the picture from my fingers, the same weary look in his eyes until a stark recognition suddenly came into them. "He was here," he said. He pointed to the picture, his finger trembling over Seso's figure. "He was here that day."

"What day?"

"The day the president came to Janetta," the old man said. "I noticed him. We all did. Because he was Lutusi and we do not see many Lutusi here." His expression showed the oddity of what he'd seen. "Especially alone. The Lutusi are never alone."

"What was he doing?"

"Just standing," the old man answered. He pointed to the tree that stood in the distance, the one he'd pointed out before, where the women of the village had suffered such grievous outrage. "All alone," he added. "Just standing there. The Lutusi do that when there is danger near. A lion or a snake. They stand and don't move."

"And he stood just that way the whole time?" I asked.

The old man nodded slowly. "It was *sidumo*," he said.

*Sidumo* was a Lutusi word. It meant "warning," and I suspected that the old man had used it as a way of determining if I'd ever really lived in Tumasi.

"Did the president see this warning?" I asked.

The old man shrugged. "I don't know."

"Did the Lutusi go up to the president, or talk to him?"

The old man shrugged. "I don't know."

"When did the president come here?" I asked.

"It was in the summer," the old man answered. "Very hot."

This meant that Seso had left Lubanda almost immediately after coming to Janetta. Three months had passed since then, so the "very near" danger about which he'd tried to warn Fareem now had to be very near indeed.

I felt a renewed energy and got to my feet, now determined to reach Rupala as fast as I possibly could.

I reached Kumuli two days later. It was a dismal collection of stalls and small shops huddled at the edges of a nearly impassable road. A few old cars crawled through its labyrinth of alleys like gigantic metal insects, but otherwise everyone was on foot, the women carrying their burdens of wet clothes and bundles of cassava on their heads.

Typical of such places, there were small enclaves of aid workers who, with the death of Mafumi and the rise of Fareem, had already begun to trickle in. As I discovered, they'd taken over a line of tumbledown structures along the river. I knew that they would have access to the Internet, and that was what I needed most at the moment.

The first building I came to sported a large sign out front. A map of Lubanda had been painted on the board, and superimposed over the map, the large-eyed face of a child quite clearly in need of help. There weren't any flies in the child's face, but there was enough supplication in those pleading eyes to give a sense of how bad things were here.

The door was open, and so I walked inside. A young man greeted me with a quick "May I help you?" His name was Pearson, he said, and he was the "chief in-country officer" of an NGO called Children First. He was quite enthusiastic, and in many ways he reminded me of myself when I'd first come to Lubanda all those many years ago. There was the same energy, along with the same sense of rising expectations, of personal adventure melded with goodness, the whole intoxicating brew.

"The main problem in Lubanda," he said, "is displaced children. There are thousands of them. The army's out trying to find them so they can be taken to Rupala." He paused as if expecting a question at this point, but I didn't have one and so he continued. "Of course, the hope is that these children can be taken out of the capital eventually. But that will take a lot of money, so we are hoping to help raise the necessary funds." He smiled as I once had, proud of the hope he was bringing to Lubanda. "That's why we're here. We want to be in a good position to start repatriation projects once the funding arrives." He was on a good-intentions roll, and I could do nothing but recall how much I must have been like him on the day I'd met Martine.

It was what he said next that surprised me.

263

"Basically, we're waiting for the Mansfield Trust to get on board," he told me. "It's the key to everything."

"Everything?"

"The flow of aid."

"I see."

He appeared to think he'd gone on about all this for too long, and so he changed the subject. "So, what brings you to Kumuli?"

"I'm on my way to Rupala."

"Really? Are you a . . ." Any possibility of guessing what I was seemed suddenly to escape him.

"I do risk assessment," I told him helpfully.

"What kind of risk?" Pearson asked.

"All kinds," I answered, and added nothing else on the subject. "Actually, I was wondering if you have an Internet connection, and if so, I was hoping I could go online for a few minutes. Check my mail, that sort of thing."

"Sure," Pearson said. "Come with me."

He led me to an office where I took a seat at the computer. "Thanks," I said to Pearson, who was lingering at the door.

"Oh, right," he said, now aware that I wanted a little privacy. "I'll be on the porch when you're done."

He closed the door behind him, and I set to work writing a combination of words into the search engine: *Janetta, Lubanda, Presidential Visit*.

The search engine's first result took me to the home page of Lubanda, its flag festooned on an otherwise blank background. I scrolled down a list of possibilities until I came to *Janetta Commemoration*. When I clicked on the link, Fareem appeared in a color photograph. He was standing solemnly before the tree that had come to represent the massacre. In other pictures, he was seen at the village well or sitting cross-legged with the chief. In all these pictures the impression was that Fareem had come alone to Janetta. But in the last of the photographs, taken as he is about to get into his car, he stands with a group of men in suits and uniforms, several tall, a few rather squat, but only one of them somewhere in between. The man is well dressed, and he stands just at the edge of the group, his hands folded before him in an attitude of great patience, his little Beria eyes peering through the lenses of his gold-rimmed glasses.

*Beyani.*

Could it be, I wondered, that it was of a danger this lethally near that Seso had hoped to warn Fareem? I could think of only one person who might be able to tell me.

"Thank you for letting me use your computer," I told Pearson when I joined him on the shaded porch of the bungalow.

"Where are you headed?" he asked.

"Sura," I answered. "It's a small village about fifteen miles from here."

"I could drive you there, if you want," Pearson said. His smile was open, winning. "I won't have much to do until the money comes in."

"There aren't any drivable roads to Sura," I said.

Person looked genuinely puzzled. "Then how do you plan to get there?" he asked.

"I'll walk," I said, then gazed out across the savanna, an area of the country I still remembered quite well since I'd repeatedly explored it while looking for the perfect place to dig my well.

"Sounds a little dangerous," Pearson said.

To one who knew nothing of Lubanda, such a walk would look dangerous indeed, I thought, but it was actually quite safe. I had plenty of food and I knew where water could be found. My command of the Lutusi dialect was slight, but I had carefully calculated that it would be sufficient for me to trade a few items in my bag for some sheep stew.

"Well, good luck," I said to Pearson.

"You too," he said with a smile as bright as his good intentions. I walked to the road, then across it into the savanna.

It was the very land the Lutusi had wandered, and which I'd assumed them still to roam. I knew that Dasai had been killed before he could make farmers out of them, and Mafumi had barely seemed to notice them. I'd expected that, sheltered by this indifference, they would be living as they always had, but instead, as I moved deeper into their old territory, I was surprised that I didn't encounter a single one of them. It was as if they had disappeared from the land in which they'd once so freely roamed. I knew the places where they'd always camped as they moved across the savanna, a route that had not changed in recorded memory. But rather than tribesmen, I found cold fire pits that had not been used for weeks.

And so I walked alone, through one abandoned camp after another, until I reached the outskirts of Sura.

The town itself was little more than a gathering of aid-funded structures, buildings that would have long ago been completed had not construction abruptly stopped after Mafumi took power, leaving whole blocks as little more than concrete facades sprouting steel support rods like iron antennae. These would have been churches and missions and NGO offices and aid-worker housing. Left unfinished, they had sprouted into small open-air markets where the local products—grains, smoked meat, goat's milk, baskets, and the like—were sold or bartered in the immemorial way of the savanna. Other than the occasional T-shirt or baseball cap, there were few items from the West, an absence that brought to mind Martine's belief that if there was Lubandan gold, as she'd written in her *Open Letter*, it should remain in its veins, and that if there were Lubandan diamonds, they should remain in the rough, and that by a similar understanding of the ageless way of things in this quiet country, coffee need not be grown among a people who did not drink it.

It didn't take long to find Bisara. I had gone to his house with Seso on a number of occasions. He had not moved, but in every other way it was clear that he had changed a great deal over the preceding twenty years. His hair had grown gray and his features were far more deeply etched. Even from a distance, he appeared weathered by the hard years under Mafumi. Fear freezes a man, but terror shrinks him, and Bisara gave every evidence of that shrinkage. He was thinner than before, and frailer, as if his bones were little more than splinters. When he rose, he seemed barely able to support his weight and for that reason gave off the same sense of imminent collapse as the tumbledown shanties that now composed the village.

But for all of his obvious decline, Bisara recognized me immediately. Unlike before, however, he didn't rise or put out his hand, or smile broadly as I approached, as he had of old, and in that diminished capacity for surprise I saw one of the common effects of extreme misrule, that it deflates life and drains it of some vital energy. By the end of Mafumi's terror, Lubanda had barely had a pulse.

"Hello, Bisara," I said quietly.

He looked at me distantly, suspiciously. "What are you doing here?" he asked darkly.

"I've come because of Seso," I told him. "He was murdered in New York City about three months ago."

Bisara didn't appear surprised, since he had long lived in a nation whose life was a fabric stitched with murder.

"I'm looking for the men who did it," I added. I knew that this was not actually my mission, but it hardly seemed the time to complicate matters.

Bisara nodded, but said nothing, a demeanor far different from that of the jovial man I'd met so often during my time in Lubanda.

"The people who killed him put a pair of crossed pangas in his mouth," I said.

He looked away, like a man calculating the odds of making a huge mistake. Then, after a moment, his attention swept back to me. "Some men came here. They were looking for Seso."

"When did they come?"

"After Seso left," Bisara answered.

"Why were they looking for him?" I asked.

Bisara looked away again, a gesture I'd seen before in people accustomed to being terrorized, beaten into submission, made to betray family and friends because they simply couldn't take the pain any longer.

"They tortured you," I said softly.

He glanced down. "My feet."

"Did you tell them where Seso was?"

Without looking at me, Bisara nodded, his gaze now on the ground. "Yes." A cloud of shame settled over him. "I did not think they would go so far to find him."

"Is that all they wanted from you?" I asked. "Just to know where Seso was?"

He shook his head. "They were looking for something Seso had. They thought perhaps he had given it to me, or maybe I knew where it was, but this I did not know."

And so the torture must have been prolonged, I thought.

"In New York, a man told me that Seso had evidence against certain men, and for that reason, he was murdered," I said.

Bisara thought this through a moment, then said, "Can you trust this man who told you these things?"

"No," I admitted. "His name is Nullu Beyani. Have you ever heard of him?"

Bisara shook his head.

"Beyani said that Seso had evidence against the men who attacked Martine Aubert on Tumasi Road," I said. "He said he found it among the documents in the archive where he worked."

This clearly puzzled Bisara.

"Seso worked in the archive, this is true," he told me. "But not with documents. It was only pictures." He appeared briefly afraid to say more, but then, quite suddenly, he stoked his courage and continued. "Mafumi was a big collector of pictures, Seso told me. Dirty pictures sometimes. Sometimes pictures of murders and people being tortured. This is what he liked to see."

His voice remained soft as he told me all this, barely above a whisper, and he often averted his eyes when he spoke. Under torture, he had betrayed his friend, told his murderers where to find him, and the shame of this act rested upon his shoulders like an iron yoke.

As if they were unspooling from a roll of film, I saw images of myself on those nights when I'd hunched over my desk, penning reports to Bill Hammond, letters Seso had probably read, so that he'd long observed the steadily deepening nature of my life as a spy.

"I know how you feel, Bisara," I said, and placed a hand on his shoulder. "Believe me, I know."

Bisara's eyes turned toward me. "The pain," he said. "I did not want to tell them."

I knelt down beside him. "I've come back to Lubanda to save a man who I think is in serious peril. Your president, as a matter of fact. Seso knew him well. I think he is in danger, and I think Seso may have come to America for that reason. I think this because he called a mutual friend and told him that he had something to show him. He was murdered before he could do it."

Bisara took all this in, but said nothing.

269

"Seso came to Janetta when the president was there," I added. "He stood all alone, staring at the president. The man who saw Seso at Janetta used the word '*sidumo*' to describe what he was doing."

"*Sidumo*," Bisara repeated. "Yes, that is the Lutusi word for 'warning.'" He looked at me gravely. "But it also is the word for 'accusation.'"

Years before, Martine had warned me that I knew nothing about Lubanda. Now, it seemed to me, I knew even less, so that the nuances within the Lutusi dialect, a pared-down language of no more than a few thousand words, were still unknown to me.

"Accusation," I repeated softly as I recalled the old man's description of Seso, the way he'd stood so stiffly and symbolically. Whether this had been a gesture of warning or accusation, or some other nuance of a word I didn't even know, the situation remained the same: Fareem was at risk.

As if summoned by my sense that time was running out, a memory suddenly returned to me in the way of a gift and took me back to my third or fourth day in the village, Martine standing with an old Lutusi, the two of them obviously in the midst of a trade. I remembered the way she'd agreed to whatever the Lutusi had offered even though he'd stood empty-handed before her, apparently offering nothing, illustrating the fact, as Martine had later explained, that when the Lutusi have something of great value, they do not show it, but give it to someone they trust for safekeeping until the trade is made. To this memory I now added the fact that Seso had been welcomed back to his tribe, though only on condition that he rigorously and unswervingly follow to the letter each of its customs.

Pondering all this, I now wondered if it applied to whatever Seso had had for Bill Hammond. The supposition that came into my mind remained unproven, and yet I found it compelling, for it did seem possible that strictly following Lutusi custom, Seso might not have brought whatever he had for Bill to New York. Rather, he might have left it in Lubanda. Left it with someone he trusted.

I looked at Bisara.

"This thing Seso had," I said. "Who would he have left it with?"

For a moment, Bisara didn't answer, but I could see that he was going through a dark risk assessment, calculating the danger of telling me whatever else he knew.

"Someone he trusted," he said finally. "But someone they wouldn't suspect, the men who were after him. That is why he did not leave it with me. Because they would have guessed that he might do this." He shrugged. "I am sorry. I do not know where this thing is. A Lutusi does not reveal the name of the one who has such things to anyone."

"Do you know where Seso went after leaving Sura?" I asked.

"Tumasi," Bisara said.

"Tumasi," I repeated, and instantly felt life's ever-tightening noose grow tighter, squeezing out every illusion until I was left with the bare truth that whether inadvertent or not, or done with the best of intentions or not, the world is at last the misbegotten creature we make with our mistakes.

# Twenty-two

There are gravely transformative moments in life, moments when the air abruptly shudders and a darkness falls over you, and you feel that you've suddenly awakened in a much more dangerous part of town. Such was my feeling as I thanked Bisara, shook his hand, then turned and headed toward Tumasi.

It was a journey of nearly forty miles, and on the way I let myself open to a flood of memories that detailed my final days in Lubanda, the most vivid of which was of the last time I'd seen Martine.

She'd walked into my office carrying a basket she'd stuffed with supplies.

"I've finished my *Open Letter*," she said.

"*Open Letter?*" I asked.

"That's what I've decided to call it," she said. "*An Open Letter to Foreign Friends.*"

Her tone was measured, resolved, with something classically fatalistic about it; she seemed to me like a soldier moving up the line toward a battle whose dreadful perils she had already calculated and accepted.

"I was going to address it to President Dasai," she added, "but I've decided to write to all of you instead." Her smile struck me as deathly pale, a cold, dead smile that made it clear to what degree she had considered the dangers she faced. This was not some naïve foreigner foolishly trusting in the kindness of strangers. This was a Lubandan who well understood the perils of her country. For that reason, she reminded me of that carved wooden Christ I'd seen in Mexico, simply, fatally . . . waiting. "To Lubanda's foreign friends, I mean."

"I see," I said, though I no longer considered myself a friend of her country. It had thwarted me in too many ways by then.

"Friends because most of you really are friends of Lubanda," Martine said. "Some of you are here for bad reasons, but most of you are not." She looked at me quite sincerely. "I do know that, Ray."

For the first time since I'd met her, Martine seemed fragile, and yet at the same time, unbreakable by any outside force. Her features had deepened in some inexpressible way and her gaze had the steadiness of one at peace with the choice she'd made.

"I really do know the good you want to do," she told me.

I stared at her silently. What could I say to her, after all, save offer a full confession of my many errors, the latest having been the deepest of them all.

"I've written several copies of this letter and I am taking them to Rupala," she added. "I'm going to give them to the charities there, the NGOs, and to any journalists I can find."

"What are you telling them in your . . . open letter?" I asked.

"That they should all go home."

She saw how absurd, perhaps even cruel, I found her position.

"Look, Ray, the fact is this," she said. "Others came and took things out of Lubanda, and in the process, they did a lot of damage. Now these same people are bringing things into Lubanda, and in the process, they are doing damage once again."

"I'm not going to argue the point," I told her. "Others will do that for the next hundred years. But, Martine, you know they're out there. Mafumi's people. Gessee's people, too. You're caught between them."

"So is Lubanda," Martine said.

"Lubanda is a country," I reminded her. "Not a woman alone, with enemies on both sides."

She was silent for a moment before she said, "Do you not love your country, Ray?"

"Of course I do."

"Then why can you not understand that I love mine, too?" Martine asked.

I searched desperately for an answer to this question, but the only one that came to me put me in Geesee's quarter, and Mafumi's. Unhappily, I realized that my conviction that Martine was not truly Lubandan was no less fervent and unbending than theirs.

"I really have nothing more to say about all this, Martine," I told her by way of sidestepping the question.

She stared at me silently for a moment before she said, "Fareem believes you're a spy. He told me this before he left." She looked at me piercingly. "Are you?"

At last I told the truth. "Yes," I said, "but I haven't reported anything that wasn't meant to help you."

"Help me what?" Martine asked.

"Survive," I said helplessly, because it was the only answer that occurred to me—one, of course, which left out the fact that I had equated her survival with leaving Lubanda and marrying me.

For a moment, Martine said nothing; she simply stared at me. I feared that this silence might end in an explosion, a lashing out at me in the same way she'd lashed out at Gessee. But instead she seemed suddenly more interested in the spy network of which I had been a part. "Who do you report to, Ray?"

"Bill Hammond."

"Does he tell the big men in Rupala what you write?"

"I don't know, but it's possible, yes."

"Do they know I'm coming to the capital with my *Open Letter*?"

"Not from me, no," I said.

When she said nothing to this, I made one final gesture. "You can still leave Lubanda and put the farm, all this business of growing teff or coffee, all this . . . struggle behind you," I said in a tone that was almost pleading.

"This 'struggle,' as you call it, is my life, Ray," Martine said. She lifted her basket into her arms. "I am going to camp here in the village tonight," she said, "then head down Tumasi Road in the morning."

"Tumasi Road?" I asked with a level of alarm I couldn't conceal. "Why aren't you going cross-country? It would be a lot faster and no one would know where you were at any given moment."

"Yes, but there are more villages along the road, places to stop and talk. I would like to spread the word a little on the way to Rupala. People will misunderstand what I am trying to do. I am white, and they will use that against me, too. But there may be a few I can make understand my hope for Lubanda."

With that she turned and walked away.

A few minutes later, I penned a last report to Bill Hammond, one that related this latest conversation with Martine, the fact that she'd written an "open letter," and that she was bringing it on foot to Rupala by way of Tumasi Road. When I'd finished, I folded the paper, put it in an envelope, then summoned Seso.

"Take this to Rupala," I told him with a nod toward the Land Cruiser. "To Bill Hammond." I glanced out toward where I could see Martine beginning to set up her camp for the night. "Martine has decided to take Tumasi Road into Rupala. He might be able to protect her."

Seso looked at me worriedly. "This is a bad thing," he said. "You should go with her. But not on foot. You should drive her to Rupala."

I shook my head. "She would never allow that."

Seso said nothing more, but simply took the report, the same troubled look still in his eyes.

By the time night fell, Martine had made a fire and was sitting beside it, her knees drawn up to her chest as she silently watched the flames. I was reluctant to approach her, but after a time, my unease gave way and I walked out to her.

"You probably don't want any company right now," I said by way of giving her the opportunity to dismiss me.

"Everyone wants company," she said, and nodded for me to join her. "When are you leaving Lubanda?"

"My year will be over in three weeks," I told her.

I didn't expect her to inquire further, and she didn't. Instead she leaned forward, poked briefly at the fire, then sat back and gazed out toward the road.

"There is a word I learned when I was in Kigali," she said. "My father had taken me there when I was a little girl, and on trips like that I always picked up new words from the various dialects." She smiled. "I wrote them down and later I put them all in a notebook." She shrugged. "I do not know why this one just came back to me."

"What's the word?"

"*Ihahamuka*," Martine answered. "It means 'without lungs.' It is used to describe the sort of terror that takes your breath away." She looked at me like one from the distant deck of a burning ship. "I am afraid, Ray."

"I'm sure you are," I said. "And you should be."

Her expression was as tender as any I had ever seen. "I wish it actually helped, the things you and the others do. And I know that here and there, it does." She shook her head. "But in the end, it hurts us more."

At that moment I felt my own version of *ihahamuka*, my dread of losing her so fierce, my conviction that she was the only woman I would ever love so absolute, it took my breath away.

"Don't go to Rupala, Martine," I said quietly. "You don't have to do this."

She poked at the fire again. "Stop, Ray, please."

"Or wait until Fareem gets back and the two of you can make the walk together."

"Fareem is already back," Martine said. "But this is not his fight."

"But he surely must have pleaded with you not to go or to let him come with you, because—"

"Of course he did," Martine interrupted sharply.

She was clearly not going to reconsider her decision to walk to Rupala, and so I made no further argument against it.

"No more about this, Ray," she said sternly, then gave the fire a final stir. "No more—I mean it."

She was silent for a long time, and I could tell that she was thinking of something. She was staring off into the middle distance, though it was only a wall of darkness now.

At last, she said, "It is strange, Ray, but do you know what really bothers me?" She looked at me very seriously, then said, "It is that no one will visit my father's grave." She drew in a long breath, held it for a moment, then very slowly released it, as if savoring the life she still had.

It was a vision of her that overwhelmed me, and so I released the one true thing I knew in vehement whisper.

"I love you, Martine."

She stretched her arms over her head. "I need to sleep now. I plan to leave at dawn."

I got to my feet. "Good night, then."

I turned and headed back toward the house. I got only a few feet before she called to me.

"Ray."

I faced her. "Yes."

"You will find her," Martine said assuredly. "The one for you."

"Sure," I said.

In the glow of her dying fire, her smile seemed almost transparent, as if she were already turning into a ghost. "I know you will," she said. "I really know you will."

I nodded. "Yes, I'll find her," I said.

But I never did.

# Twenty-three

It had all seemed so simple once, I thought as I continued my journey toward Tumasi. I would come to Lubanda and dig a well or build a school or plant trees or do some other goodly labor. But in the end, I'd done no good at all. Then after less than a year, and in drear admission of my failure, I'd gotten on a plane, flown out of Lubanda, and never put anything at risk again.

Now, walking across the empty plains, I thought of the last time I'd put myself in peril, remembered the red sun rising over Tumasi Road, where I'd endured a sleepless night, Martine's lifeless camp only a few yards from me, the embers of her fire long ago grown cold.

I'd stayed in my house, listening to the sounds of her awakening—getting water, lighting a breakfast fire. I'd waited until those sounds ended, then gone out, certain that by then she'd gone.

"Good morning," I said to Seso.

He was squatting a few yards from the house, drawing figures in the dirt with a stick, an idleness that was new to him. As I approached, he glanced toward the road, the dusty Land Cruiser he'd driven back and forth to Rupala.

"Did you give Bill my note?" I asked him.

He nodded in a way that struck me as moody, perhaps even sullen.

"So he knows that Martine is taking Tumasi Road?" I asked.

"He knows," Seso said crisply.

"Did he say anything about protecting her?"

Seso shook his head. "He would not tell me such things."

This was true, so no further comment was necessary. Besides, it was obvious that something was eating at Seso. It seemed better to let it go until he saw fit to tell me.

I had already turned and headed back toward my house when he suddenly got to his feet. "Why did she do this?" he asked in an angry voice, a tone I had never heard from him before. "Because she is white! That is why. She thinks she can do anything, and no harm will come to her because she is white." He suddenly slapped his chest. "But to *us* this harm will come!" he said in a despairing cry. "The ones who rule will take revenge. Mafumi will punish us for what this white woman does."

"Mafumi?" I said. "What makes you think Mafumi will rule Tumasi?"

Seso gazed at me as if I were a little boy in need of instruction. "Because he has the sharpest panga."

There it was, I thought, African politics as Seso knew it, triumph forever the misbegotten child of brutality.

"Martine doesn't want that to happen any more than you do," I said.

"But what weapons does she have to protect us?" Seso asked bitterly, then added with an even more bitter smile, "Little wooden shells?" He shook his head and looked defeated. "You should warn Fareem that she is taking Tumasi Road. Long before she gets to Rupala, bad men will know what she is doing. They will come for Fareem, and the color of *his* skin will not protect him."

In life, we expect a trumpet to herald the beginning of some great, life-transforming event, or a bell to toll at the end of it. But reality is more prosaic than that, and so I heard only the crunch of Seso's feet as he strode away.

One thing was certain, however. Seso was right in saying that every-one would be alerted to Martine's mission long before she reached Rupala, and so, yes, Fareem had to be warned that she had taken Tumasi Road.

Seconds later I was headed toward Martine's farm, the familiar plume of red dust following the rush of my Land Cruiser like a huge furry tail. I saw no one on the road or in the distance until I came upon Ufala. She was sitting at a rickety wooden stand, hoping for someone to buy any of the array of items she'd gathered around her—a few pots, some medicinal herbs, the crushed dried leaves she smoked and sold or traded for various other supplies.

"Have you seen Fareem?" I asked, thinking that he might have set out in search of Martine despite her insistence that none of this was "his fight."

Ufala shook her head, then waved her hand in the general direction of the farm, a gesture I couldn't read save its possible suggestion that the conversation was ended.

I arrived at Martine's farm a few minutes later. It looked more desolate than before, but I knew that this was only because she wasn't there. In fact, I saw nothing but her absence. It was in the empty table beneath the tree, the empty chair on her porch, the empty fields that swept out from all sides, even in the ghostly movement of the brush that shivered here and there when it was touched by a dry breeze.

"Is Martine still determined to make her way to Rupala?"

It was Fareem.

He was standing in the door, looking gaunt from his long walk back from the north.

"Yes," I said. "By way of Tumasi Road."

He looked alarmed. "Then everyone will know what she is doing before she gets to Rupala." He walked out to the table, where I joined him. "She told me that they are going to take her farm."

281

"They are."

"I told her that she could deed it to me," Fareem said. "Then she could stay here forever. But she said the farm cannot be deeded to me because Rupala says it is not hers."

"I'm afraid that's true."

Fareem stared at me darkly. "Martine said worse is coming, that she is no longer to be considered Lubandan."

"That's also true," I said, then risked another, yet more risky truth. "I offered her a way out, Fareem. A way out of Lubanda."

Fareem's eyes sparked with recognition. He knew a conspirator just as he had known a spy. "A way out for both of you," he said. "Together."

"Yes."

His lips curled into a sneer, and his eyes suddenly filled with a searing contempt. "Do you know what Martine thinks of you?" he asked. "She thinks that your head is full of wrong things. Full of errors. Like all the others in the Land Cruisers, bringing the money. She says you are like a man who puts food in a rabbit's hole and does not see that as long as you do this, the rabbit will never come out of its hole."

Suddenly his voice grew taut, and I could see how mightily he was trying to control himself.

"And this rabbit is Lubanda," he said. "We are always children to you. Helpless. We can do nothing if you do not help us."

I could feel his barely suppressed contempt like a heat. It came from him in successive boiling waves. But rather than attacking me further, he straightened himself and stared at me as if from a great height.

"You bind us up with your money," he said. "Every dollar is a link in the chain."

"Is that what Martine wrote in her open letter?" I asked.

Now Fareem seemed to come to a hard boil. I had never seen this rage that was inside him, nor guessed how deep it went, the fierce anger of a man who had known only the achingly opposite poles of condescension and contempt.

"Go home," he said. "I will go and find Martine." His tone was firm and commanding, a voice that drew a line in the dust. He would go in search of Martine and he would do so alone. I was no longer of any use at all in Lubanda.

He said nothing else, but took a long step and then another, and swept by me very quickly. I didn't bother to offer him the Land Cruiser because I knew he wouldn't take it. And yet, though he would have to move quickly to catch up with Martine, I felt so certain that he would, so confident that he would find some way to protect her, that a wave of relief settled over me as he grew small in the distance, and at last disappeared.

But in believing this, I was once again in error.

The news had come by way of Ufala, who'd heard someone moaning in the bush early the next morning. Fareem had gotten only a few miles down Tumasi Road before he'd been dragged out into the bush and beaten unconscious. Ufala had given him water and placed wet cloths on his swollen eyes. He'd moaned incoherently until he'd finally pulled the cloth from his eyes and uttered his first coherent word: *Martine.*

Ufala had told me all this that afternoon, after she'd helped Fareem back to the farm. She'd then returned to the village and told Seso about the beating. Seso had, in turn, come to me.

"It is as I told you," he said grimly. "Fareem's skin could not protect him."

He still seemed to believe that the whiteness of Martine's skin would somehow protect her, but I knew that this was not the case.

"I'll go find her," I told him, then rushed to my Land Cruiser and headed down Tumasi Road, toward Kinisa, the next village on the way to Rupala, where I thought it likely Martine might have stopped for the evening.

Twenty years had passed since the afternoon I'd rolled into Kinisa in search of Martine, and now on foot, with the memory of my meeting with Bisara still fresh in my memory, I entered it again. As a village it bore the same name and was located in the same place as before. But it was the same in only those two ways, because its people had been grievously punished by Mafumi for the crime of living in the same village as a young girl who'd rejected his advances.

Unlike the outrage at Janetta, which had been carried out hurriedly, Kinisa had met its fate some years after Mafumi had fully consolidated his power in Lubanda. Because there'd been no countervailing force, the savagery he'd ordered had been carried out at leisure and had known no bounds. Before it was over, nearly a thousand people had perished during a three-week carnival of blood.

Janetta had to some degree recovered, as I'd seen a week before. Kinisa, on the other hand, had not, and now it was only the charred remains of this once thriving village that greeted me. The circular mud walls of its huts still stood, but the roofs were gone, along with anything else fire could consume. The spare vegetation of the region now claimed the center of the village, and on either side there was nothing but the sweep of the savanna.

I stood amid this ruin, but only briefly, because the village itself urged me on, proof positive that if it were Mafumi's old cohorts who were now plotting against Fareem, then the horrors that awaited him could hardly be calculated. It would not suffice for such men merely to hang him or put him in front of a firing squad. They would first torture him in endlessly elaborate ways, or if not that, beat him in the unimaginably brutal way Patrice Lumumba had been beaten, his features no longer recognizable by the time they'd finally gotten around to shooting him.

On that thought I looked eastward, across a wide expanse, to where, in the distance, through the shimmering heat, I could faintly make out the red-clay gully that had once been Tumasi Road.

# Twenty-four

Ten years before, I'd attempted to reach Tumasi. The drive had been hard and I'd been threatened on occasion by fang-toothed thugs, but I'd managed to get halfway to my destination before a much greater risk had turned me back. In fact, I'd made it all the way to Nulamba, the little town where Seso had been taken for interrogation and where Fareem and I had found him locked in a storage closet. It was there that the dread of going farther had overwhelmed me and I'd turned back. But while there, I'd endured the puzzled glances of the villagers as I'd made my way toward the constabulary where I'd found Seso that night.

It was a village that had later turned to Mafumi, and thus it had been spared the sort of treatment Janetta and Kinisa had received. In fact, tattered posters of the Lion of God still hung here and there in the village, along with a long-outdated government newsletter whose first page was devoted to Mafumi's thoughts, such as they were: that AIDS was caused by a "Western poison" President Dasai had disguised as an antimalarial pill; that all art and culture had originally flowed out of Africa, only to be stolen by the West; that one day Lubandans would rule the world from a spacecraft launched from the solar system to which they'd gone "before this world began." Compared with such transparent lunacy, Nyerere's fraudulent weather predictions were the pinnacle of reason. And yet, it all seemed of a piece somehow, the magical thinking of a continent ravaged on all sides, first in the theft of its resources, and second, as Martine had written in her *Open Letter,* "in the theft of its will."

Little remained of the small, makeshift constabulary where Fareem and I had found Seso save for a single, crumbling wall, now overrun with vines, its cracked cement floor spouting grasses and one dusty fern. Still, it provided a step, or at least a marker, for it was here that I'd stopped ten years before, stopped and turned around and headed back to Rupala, then onto a plane that had returned me to my risk-aversive life.

After a moment, I headed back toward the road, but not before stopping to look more closely at one of the village's Mafumi posters, the Emperor of All Peoples sitting proudly on his elephant-tusk throne, a photograph I'd seen in *The New York Times* some years before. It was the last time any mention of Lubanda had actually appeared in the *Times,* in an article that had thoroughly chronicled Mafumi's authoritarian clownishness: his claims to have raised the dead, cured the sick, laid curses upon his enemies so that their arms had withered and their eyes had fallen out of their heads. One of the author's unnamed sources, a local named Bashir Rutani, had later been found hanging by his feet in a deserted playground. The sign dangling from his toes had said "Child Molester," but there was no record of his ever having been one.

"Who are you?"

I turned to see a tall, thin man standing just behind me, a panga dangling from his hand.

"I'm an American," I answered. "I'm headed north, up Tumasi Road."

He nodded toward Mafumi's presidential portrait. "Our chief made good magic."

I knew that he did not mean this as a joke. Mafumi's magical powers had long been an ideological pillar of his rule. The stories were printed as fact in the country's only newspaper, mainly in pictures. Films were also shown on Lubanda's only television station. Few Lubandans owned televisions, however, and for that reason VHS cassettes had borne the weight of propounding this grotesque mythology, transported in military jeeps to the remotest villages, along with a boxy old television and an electric generator that could produce enough electricity to play the president's miracle movies. There he'd been in living color, Mafumi blessing plants that abruptly sprouted, healing stricken livestock that instantly rose to their feet and galloped away. In Rupala, they'd been distributed by the Lubandan Youth Corps, the president's cadre of teenaged boys, some of whom had been fully armed. The single cassette I'd gotten my hands on had later been seized at the airport. "Not to leave Lubanda," the guard told me, then tossed the tape into a large plastic bucket filled with other things that were not to leave Lubanda: medicine, tins of food, foreign currency, pornographic magazines.

"But the new chief, he does not make magic," the man added contemptuously. "The new chief does not have big powers."

There was only one picture of Fareem, the "new chief" in this still Mafumi-intoxicated village. It hung from the side of a storm fence, a different portrait from the one I'd seen at the consulate office in New York, the president dressed casually in flannel shirt and trousers, his arms outspread as he welcomes a group of children. The legend said simply: *The President Embraces the Future of Lubanda.* There were slashes across his face, and his ears were gone, his eyes gouged out.

The man slapped his hand with the panga and stared grimly at Fareem's picture. He didn't need to say what he felt; it was obvious in the malevolent glitter of his eyes. He would have liked nothing better than to slice Lubanda's current president in two.

Ten years before I'd been pressed forward only by moral anguish, a wind whose force, as I'd discovered in that failed effort, is quickly dissipated. Now, however, was different, the purpose of my present journey not to redeem myself, but to save Fareem from the likes of the man who stood before me, glaring menacingly at this same portrait.

Surely if any man on earth deserved protection, I told myself, it was Fareem. But on that thought, I recalled the hatred in his eyes when I'd last seen him, his contempt for the hope I'd presumptuously believed myself to be bringing to Lubanda. Once again I heard his voice: *Do you know what Martine thinks of you?*

I did know now, and I also knew that she'd been right. But twenty years before, I'd been young and foolish and crazed with love. What mixture could have been more fraught with risk?

The final consequence of that lethal concoction lay before me, and so as politely as possible I said goodbye to the man with the panga and headed toward the road, walking neither hurriedly nor slowly, but at a moderate pace, like an animal determined not to let a far more danger-ous animal smell his fear.

The next village down Tumasi Road was little more than a collec-tion of huts. It was called Hanuma, and it was here I'd expected to find Martine when I'd gone in search of her twenty years before. In those days, it had been a village alive with children, where Martine was able to stop, trade her shells for food or water, perhaps camp for the night. It had always been an exceptionally friendly village as well, with much singing and dancing and good fellowship. Once welcomed as a guest, she would have been safe there.

I'd hoped to find Martine still in Hanuma when I'd arrived there late that afternoon. As expected, I'd found the villagers at their routine labors, their chief stretched out on the ground, very much the patriarch, with several women in attendance and two young men intently focused on everything he said.

"I'm looking for a white woman," I said. Then, with a strange ache of absolute recognition and acceptance, I added, "But Lubandan."

The chief turned to one of the young men and spoke to him in a language I didn't recognize.

"I speak English," the young man said. "Come. I will ask about this woman."

I followed him as he moved about the village, inquiring if anyone had seen a white woman. No one had, so it seemed clear that Martine had not made it as far as Hanuma, which could only mean that at some point she had decided to leave the road and head overland toward Rupala.

This would vastly decrease her risk, and because of that, I felt great relief at the thought of her moving across the savanna rather than so visibly and provocatively down Tumasi Road. On the savanna the Lutusi would receive her as a guest, give her food and let her camp with them at night. Within three days she would be in Rupala, and I'd already decided that I would drive there, wait for her, and then, if she would allow me, bring her back to her farm, where, I hoped, Fareem's anger would have subsided.

So I was in a less fearful state of mind by the time the young man escorted me back to my Land Cruiser. No one had seen Martine, and this was good news.

At that point, I'd planned to return to Tumasi, both convinced and relieved that Martine had decided not to take the far more dangerously exposed open road and was now walking overland toward Rupala.

"Thank you," I said to the young man, then turned back toward the Land Crusier, where, in the distance, I saw a woman moving toward us. She was walking slowly, in the way of someone exhausted, which suggested that she had been on the road for a long time, and thus might have encountered Martine.

We both approached her, and as we did so, her expression grew apprehensive, like one expecting harm. The young man spoke to her in a language I didn't understand.

"She is nervous because she has seen bad signs," he told me. "They are very superstitious, her people, always looking for signs."

"What did she see?"

"Shells," he answered, "but not from the water. Made of wood. That is why she thought they were bad signs." He could see that this information had thrown a shadow over me. "She thinks they were put there to trap her. That they were meant to lure her out into the bush. For this reason, she did not leave the road."

"Did you see a woman?" I asked.

The young man turned to the woman, spoke to her, received her response, then looked at me. "She saw only the shells."

*Only the shells.*

There are moments in life when you are forced to accept what De Quincey called "the lurking consciousness" of a terrifying truth, moments when you know that something has gone catastrophically wrong, and that you were an instrument of that wrong. Such had been that instant for me.

I'd recalled that terrible moment many times during the twenty years that had passed since then, but never more vividly than when I reached the place on Tumasi Road where I'd brought the Land Cruiser to a halt at the spot where the woman had seen Martine's shells. For that reason, only the pull of the macabre would have made me stop again and head out into the bush, as I had done on that heartbreaking afternoon. And so I didn't stop, but instead walked on through the morning mist, then on through the midday heat, and finally through the cool of approaching evening, when at last I reached Tumasi.

The entire village was in the same state of disrepair as Kinisa, save for a tall storm fence enclosure that had been erected near the road. It was here, I suspected, that whatever was valuable had to be kept in order to prevent its being looted. But there was nothing inside the fence, and beside it only a metal pipe that rose about six feet, then curled over in a spout.

To my immense surprise, Ufala, now impossibly old and shriveled, sat at a roadside stand not far from the fence. She was selling cassava and was obviously amazed to see a white man. But as I drew near, she recognized me, though with what level of suspicion or dread I could not imagine.

"It's been a long time," I said.

I could see that, like Bisara before her, Ufala was trying to decide if I could be trusted. And she was right to be cautious, for in a world of such dire risk, the most dangerous risk of all is the one it takes to trust someone else.

"I've come to talk to you about Seso," I said. "I'm sure you remember him."

Ufala nodded.

"He was murdered in New York City three months ago," I added.

Ufala stared at me silently, but I could see a tension building behind her eyes. Everything in life brought her trouble, and surely I was no different from the rest. But she had always been one to calculate the risks, then take the road least pitted with them, and I had little doubt that she was doing that this very moment.

"You remember that Seso was Lutusi," I said.

She nodded again, but remained silent.

"And when the Lutusi have something valuable to trade, they leave it with someone they trust," I continued. "Seso had something valuable to trade, and I think he left it with you."

I had started thinking this the moment I'd learned that Seso had not left whatever it was he had for Bill Hammond with Bisara. So there had to be someone else. It could have been anyone, of course, but surely Seso would have known that any close associate would have fallen under suspicion, and that for that reason it would be less risky to give it to a more distant acquaintance, and even better to leave it with a woman, whom no man would suspect of being trustworthy. If this was true, I reasoned, then Seso might possibly have left it with Ufala. It was a long shot, I knew, but it was the only shot I had.

I told Ufala all of this, though it was difficult to tell how much of it she understood. She was very, very old, after all, and suspicious by nature. Nor did I have anything to offer her, save what suddenly occurred to me—a threat.

"If you have what Seso gave you," I warned her, "some men are going to come here and they are going to do bad things to you."

Ufala remained silent.

"Seso is dead, and, besides, you don't owe him anything," I told her. "Why take a chance on being hurt?"

I couldn't tell if she believed any of what I'd told her, or even cared, since it was possible that Seso had never given her anything. But I had come all this way on unproven suppositions, so why not follow the road I'd taken to its end.

And so I waited. For a long time, Ufala stared at me in that inert posture I remembered from so many years before. Then, as if an answer had come to her in the wind, she rose and waved me to follow her. We walked through the old market, which was stirring a bit, past the little house in which I'd lived and worked, now filled with stacks of cassava and kindling. I saw again the stalls, the produce, the small milling crowds. I thought that a few of the villagers recognized me, but I wasn't sure. I had changed a great deal since then, grown older and grayer, and with a far less hopeful sparkle in my eyes.

At the far end of the village, we came to a hut. Ufala pointed to it, then to herself.

"Yours," I said.

She nodded, then bent down and went inside.

Waiting outside her hut, I could smell the various grains of the region, millet and fonio and teff. In the absence of aid, beyond the pressures of the global market, the people of Tumasi had returned to their ancient grains.

When Ufala emerged again, she was carrying a small sack. She glanced at the pots that lay about the fire pit just beyond the entrance, one of which I recognized as having once been Martine's.

When she saw that I recognized it, she said, "Men bring her back and put her on fire. They do this in the field behind her house. And when she burn up, they kick around the ashes."

*Such was the product of your error,* the Ancient Chorus sang to me, *yours and yours alone.*

I abruptly felt like Actaeon, the hunter, who turned into a deer and was set upon and torn apart by his own ravenous dogs. But such soul-lacerating thoughts were more than I could afford. Or at least more than Fareem could afford. I had come to save him, not condemn myself, and so I forcefully returned to my purpose.

I nodded toward the sack that dangled from Ufala's hand.

"Is that what Seso gave you?" I asked.

She nodded.

I took the sack from her, reached into it, and found a sealed plastic bag. The plastic was thick and almost opaque, so that I got only a glimpse of what was inside, a thin envelope stamped with the crossed pangas of Mafumi's old regime.

"Thank you," I said to Ufala.

I turned to leave, and once again noticed the storm fence that had been erected at the entrance to the village.

"The fence looks new," I said as I turned back toward Ufala. "What's it for?"

"Lutusi children," Ufala answered. "The trucks bring them here to drink and wash, then they take them to Rupala."

"Trucks take them to Rupala?" I asked "Why?"

Ufala shrugged. It had never been her habit to ask questions.

It wasn't until I'd gotten back to the road, slumped down in a small area of shade, and drawn out the contents of the envelope that it had been revealed suddenly, revealed in the way an image in a camera abruptly comes to sparkling focus, allowing me in that shattering instant to understand the hope Seso had had for Lubanda, and in just what risky, desperate way it had also been Martine's.

The children press in upon us as Fareem escorts me through the camp that now covers Independence Square.

"Most of these children are Lutusi," Fareem informs me.

"A noble people, but with a few strange customs," I tell him. "When they had something valuable to offer, they never brought it with them to the market."

Fareem smiles as if his spirit is lifted by a sweet memory. "That is true. They left it with someone they trusted. Martine often traded for things she'd never seen."

He kneels down and the children tighten around him. He cradles them in his arms, and almost immediately one of his aides steps forward and takes a picture.

"I did that once, remember?" I say as Fareem rises. "Took pictures of a president with children on his lap."

"President Dasai, yes," Fareem says. "We all went up north." He appears to recall just how risky that trip had been. "Dasai was brave, you have to give him that."

"Unfortunately, courage is never enough," I remind him. "One has to be aware of traitors behind the curtain."

Fareem nods sagely, a man who has learned this lesson well during his years of opposing Mafumi as comrade after comrade fell. "Yes, it is important to know who's at your back."

I think of Nulli Beyani, the shadows within which he may yet lurk. "Do you know who is at your back, Fareem?"

"I am watchful, if that is what you mean."

I think of my mission, the steps that have led me back to Lubanda once again, the report I'd given Bill after my return to New York, the way he'd stared bleakly at the photograph I'd given him, and which had surely been what Seso had wanted him to see. After that, we'd agreed on what should be done next, and on the fact that this action, like the ones before it, was fraught with risk, as all things human are, a decision whose consequences would be small for us, but great for Lubanda, and yet worth risking.

I glance about the camp and think of Seso's son, how his death must have severed that lonely man from his last hold on earth, set him to take the risk he took, knowing, as he always had, that the color of his skin would not protect him from murder, the fantasy of Negritude that had orphaned Martine no less a myth in his last hour, as the blows rained down upon his feet, than it had ever been.

Fareem sees some part of this playing in my mind, though he cannot know its terrible detail, and so he says, "We're doing our best to deal with the problem of Lubanda's orphans, but, as you can see, their numbers are quite overwhelming at the moment."

With that, he drapes his long arm over my shoulder. "Come, Ray, let's go now."

We walk back to the car and get in.

"Food and shelter are in short supply," he says. "Once these are secured, we can begin the process of returning these children to their homes."

We are moving swiftly now, down one of Rupala's rocky roads. The tumbledown city spreads out in all directions, looking like nothing so much as a vast pile of worthless goods, the remnants of an old largesse, a landscape littered with the spare parts of things that should perhaps never have been brought here in the first place, the shoddy treasure Mafumi came to seize.

"Everything is in disrepair," Fareem tells me when he notices me staring out the window. "Mafumi did nothing to maintain the infrastructure."

"He was waiting," I tell Fareem.

"Waiting for what?"

"Waiting for aid," I answer. "When people expect it, they wait, and so they don't initiate anything."

Fareem is clearly troubled by my remark. "Is that what the think tanks believe now?"

"No, it's what Martine believed," I answer. "She wanted Lubandans to be themselves, a people and a place with their own pace and character, one that shouldn't be distorted by foreigners."

"Ah, yes," Fareem says with a look that is surprisingly dismissive of the argument made in Martine's *Open Letter*. "But does it distort a people to give them running water, electricity?"

"Martine had neither," I remind him. "And 'give' is the operative word."

Fareem's eyes narrow somewhat, but he says nothing.

"I remember how she once positioned the hand of the giver over the hand of the receiver," I add. "The receiver's hand just waits for something to be dropped into it." I let this latest remark hang in the air between us, then add significantly, "Martine wanted to save Lubanda from people like me."

Fareem turns from me and stares out the window. He says nothing more until we reach the Presidential Residence, but I can feel the heat from his relentlessly calculating brain.

When the car pulls up to the Presidential Residence, he turns to me, and I see a great upheaval in his eyes. "I did love her, Ray," he says with great sincerity. "It wasn't easy."

"What wasn't easy?"

He seems taken aback by the question. "What happened on Tumasi Road. It wasn't easy for me to go on after that."

"You took a great risk," I remind him. "Leaving Lubanda, going to Europe. Coming back is an even greater one."

"Why?"

I draw in a long, hard breath. "Because you never know who's at your back. Someone you think a friend or a comrade in arms, but who is actually a traitor."

Fareem looks at me curiously, but with the intensity of old. "I trust you have brought something other than suspicion to Lubanda," he says with a quick glance at my briefcase.

"I have brought nothing but hope to Lubanda," I assure him.

With that assurance, Fareem opens the door and I follow him out into the bright sunlight. The new flag waves in the hot air as we mount the stairs, and I once more feel the weight of what I carry in my briefcase, the terrible risk that in this, too, I may be wrong. Still, I can see no other way, dark and unknowable as this way surely is.

"I have a private office," Fareem tells me. "Much smaller than the grand one where you waited. Let's go there. We can talk without fear of being heard."

"Is that one of your fears?" I ask him.

"No, why do you ask?"

"So you have complete trust in those around you?"

He nods. "Of course. That is important, don't you think?"

"I do, yes," I tell him. "Perhaps the most important thing of all. Without it, what is there?"

"Emptiness," he says.

"And fear," I add. "You are never afraid, Fareem?"

"Of what?" Fareem asks.

"That your country might not love you back," I answer starkly.

Fareem stops short, as if by the unexpected warning of a peril equally unexpected.

"No," he says confidently, though it seems to me an uncertain confidence because he knows that Lubandans, like most mortals, are limited in their judgment but unlimited in their violence, easy to fool, frighten, and enrage.

With that same uneasiness, he turns and we head down a long corridor festooned with the various artifacts of the former regime: portraits of Mafumi posed before iconic places he had never been, the Great Wall of China, the Eiffel Tower, and Mafumi himself, the poster child for idiocy.

"You're keeping all this?" I ask.

"We plan to build a memorial to Mafumi's victims," Fareem informs me. "There is to be a museum, and these things will be exhibited there." He smiles. "Along with what he thought was Hitler's pipe. Of course, Hitler did not smoke." He shakes his head at the sheer lunacy on display before him. "Mafumi spent millions on such fake artifacts. Paintings without provenance. A piece of the moon. Sand from Mars."

We are nearing the end of the corridor.

"Mafumi was a child of violence," Fareem tells me. A vague sadness settles over him. "A man is made by the violence done to him, Ray. Mafumi's parents were both slaughtered right before his eyes."

"I thought that was just part of his made-up biography."

We have reached the door at the end of corridor. Fareem opens it and waves me inside, where I take a seat in front of a small desk.

"No, that part of Mafumi's life is true," Fareem assures me. "We figured it was this scene of parental massacre that had so deranged him."

"We?"

"The people around him, I should say."

"You've met people who were around Mafumi?"

"Only when they were shooting at me," Fareem says with a dismissive shrug. "Or trying to run me down in a car."

"That's hardly a place where such information would be exchanged," I say.

Fareem now appears slightly tense, as if accused of something, under interrogation.

"What do you mean by that, Ray?" he asks.

I lift my briefcase, place it on my lap, open it, and draw out a photograph. "Do you know this man?" I ask as I hand it to him. "He's standing directly to your left."

Fareem glances at the photograph, then says. "We were in Janetta, to commemorate the massacre. That's Nullu Beyani."

"What is his position?" I ask.

"He's the head of the National Police," Fareem answers. He hands the picture back toward me. "Why do you ask?"

"He visited me in New York," I tell him. "He told me he'd come there to investigate the murder of Seso Alaya."

Fareem is clearly not surprised to hear this. "That is true. I sent him there myself."

"Why?"

"Because Seso worked under Mafumi," Fareem tells me. "In the archive. He may have known state secrets, and when such a person flees the country, and is then murdered . . . I'm sure you understand why we needed to get to the bottom of it."

"Did you know that Beyani went to Sura before Seso's murder?" I ask.

Fareem looks genuinely surprised to hear this.

"Why would he have done that?" he asks.

"He went there to talk to Seso's old friend Bisara. Do you remember him?"

"I met him a few times, yes. He sometimes came to visit Seso."

"They tortured Bisara," I inform Fareem. "Beyani and his thugs."

For the first time, Fareem appears disturbed. "Why would they have done this to Bisara?"

"Because they were looking for whatever Seso had to show Bill Hammond," I said. "You remember Bill, I'm sure."

"Of course," Fareem says. "He's now head of the Mansfield Trust." He looks confused. "What did Seso have for Bill?"

"Something important," I answer, then permit a dramatic pause to lengthen tensely before I add, "And so Nullu Beyani and some of his agents came to New York and they tortured Seso, but he wouldn't tell them where he'd left what he wanted Bill to see."

Fareem merely stares at me.

"He left it with someone Beyani would be unlikely to think had anything of worth," I add. "In the first place, someone who was not Lutusi. In the second place, a woman."

"Not Lutusi," Fareem repeats with a hint of self-accusation, as if this possibility should not have escaped him, but clearly did, a dreadfully unexpected turn in a plan he'd thought successful before now. "A woman."

Still, he only smiles. "Seso was always quite smart."

I let my gaze fall to the briefcase, consider my next move for a moment, then make it. "Anyway, I found what Seso wanted Bill to see."

Fareem watches me silently . . . and waits.

I take out the envelope in which Seso had sealed its contents and place them on Fareem's desk. "The pictures were taken many years ago and put away in some forgotten corner of Mafumi's archive. You might say they're part of the historical record."

"The historical record of what?" Fareem asks as he reaches for the envelope.

"The Tumasi Road Incident."

Fareem's hand snaps back from the still unopened envelope as if from a serpent, and stares at me silently. Then, as if in response to a dare, he picks up the envelope and spills the photos across his desk.

And so there it rests, fully exposed, the stages of Martine's torment, pictures taken from a distance but which nonetheless record with awful clarity the terrible choreography of her ordeal. In the first of these pictures, she stands alone as a noose of jeering men draws in around her. The pictures fully reveal the awful terror that gripped her, the *ihahamuka* she had so dreaded. The men are pointing at her, dancing around her. Like hyenas they rush in and yank her hair, then dart away, rush in and slap her, poke her with their crude spears, nip at her with the blades of their pangas, then retreat laughing. It is hard to say how long this goes on before the real assault begins, after which she tries to run, staggers, at last drops to the ground, where they fall upon her, ripping at her clothes, hitting her with stones, slashing her with pangas. The final photograph is a close-up of her barely recognizable face, the distinguishing feature of which remains the flaming red hair that must have given Mafumi all the proof he needed that the witch was dead. Like all the others, it is a perfect picture, save for one thing.

"Do you recognize that starburst crack in the lens, Fareem?" I ask.

He looks up from the photographs, and although there is a terrible acknowledgment in his eyes, I see also that he remains true to the risk he took.

"You will never understand Lubanda," he says, as if I were still the young man he'd so thoroughly deceived. His gaze is still and steady. "You will never understand my situation." His smile is rueful. "You could return to America, Ray, which is what you did," he reminds me darkly. "But I was stuck in Lubanda. Stuck with Lubanda . . . as it was then."

It strikes me that there are moments so desperate and hopeless that practicality merges with criminality so seamlessly and completely that it becomes all but impossible not to join the devil's brigade.

"And so you made your deal with Mafumi," I say.

It does not surprise me that Fareem makes no attempt to deny this. In Ovid's world of myth, it is possible to change. People turn into trees, animals, even mountains. But outside that classical world, we remain to the end the thing we were at the beginning. Martine, despite the risk, remained Martine, fighting for her dream. It is the same with Fareem. He was, at heart, a survivor, and as such, he'd keenly perceived the extreme risk of his situation, caught as he was between Gessee and Mafumi. I have little doubt that he must have tried everything he could to avoid the deal he made, but in the end, like an adept risk manager, he'd figured the odds and made his choice.

"It was never meant to go that far with Martine," Fareem tells me. "She was only to be frightened. I was to take pictures of it because that's the kind of proof Mafumi needed. I thought it would force Martine to leave Lubanda, which she had to do, because she was doomed here. You know that, Ray. You yourself tried to force her to leave, remember?"

I nod.

Fareem's gaze returns to the photographs. "But it got out of hand."

303

"It always does," I tell him gravely.

Fareem looks stricken. "I couldn't stop it," he tells me desolately. "I couldn't even stop taking the pictures. Mafumi wanted them, and so I had to do it. Later, when I tried to keep my camera, they beat me up and took it. That's when I got out of Lubanda, and after that I did nothing but oppose Mafumi."

It is certainly possible that all of this is true. Fareem may indeed have wanted to stop Martine's torment, but knew he couldn't, that the beast would have blood, and that he would have to make a record of it. It is also possible that he turned against Mafumi at that moment, fled to Europe, then watched with fear and trembling as the other members of his government-in-exile were stabbed or shot or beaten to death. Or he might never have broken with Mafumi and, instead, conspired with his agents to carry out these same murders. I have no way of knowing. At the heart of all risk management, I remind myself, there lies the ineradicable X of human behavior.

"And now, as president, I want to help Lubanda," Fareem assures me. He takes a deep breath. "Especially the orphans—most of whom, by the way, are Lutusi."

I cannot know what is in Fareem's heart at this moment. Perhaps he does, in fact, want to help Lubanda. But I do know that in the matter of the orphans, he is lying.

"The Lutusi don't have orphans," I say. "The word itself, 'Lutusi,' means 'family.' All the men are your father and all the women are your mother."

I watch as Fareem leans back slowly, his gaze very still.

"The Lutusi children in your camps aren't orphans, Fareem," I tell him bluntly. "You round them up and truck them into Rupala. It's just one of your tricks."

Fareem makes no effort to deny this. "This 'trick,' as you call it, is a small price to pay in order to get the help Lubanda needs." He studies my expression and seems to think that simply by being forthright, by denying nothing, he has found a way into me, a little door his argument can enter. "You should not punish an entire country for my mistake," he adds pointedly. "My mistake, Ray—an error of judgment the Mansfield Trust has no need to hear of."

I recognize that Fareem's strategy at that moment is a very risky one. And it does not work.

"I'm afraid it's too late for that," I say. "I've already shared this information with Bill Hammond." I take out the letter I have come to give him and place it on his desk.

He picks up the letter, reads it, then looks up. "Nothing?" He is clearly shocked. "The Mansfield Trust is denying all aid to Lubanda?" His gaze remains fixed on the letter like one dazed by a blow. Even so, it takes only a moment for his disappointment and dismay to transform themselves into contempt for those he had presumed to be his bene-factors. "This is the hope you have brought to Lubanda, Ray?" he asks sharply as he crumples the letter in his fist.

"It is, perhaps, Lubanda's only hope," I tell him.

Fareem smiles, but thinly. "Very well then," he says coldly. "Lubanda will do just fine without your aid."

I stare him dead in the eye. "That is my hope, Fareem," I tell him truthfully, "that is my one true hope for Lubanda."

My belief, as I leave him, is that Fareem's hold on the reins of power will not last very long. Without aid, he will not be able to buy weapons or fill the warehouses of Rupala with the goods others like himself have so often used to bribe local chiefs and pay for private armies. I fear that in desperation, he will pit one tribe against another, but with nothing to hand out as reward to those who do his dirty work, even this strategy may fail, and with that failure, some new direction may perhaps emerge, one that no longer waits for the distorting gifts of donor hands.

Such is my hope for Lubanda as I head back down the corridor, leaving Fareem still seated behind his desk. Admittedly it is a risky strategy, since other donors may fill the void left by the decision of the Mansfield Trust. The aid caravan is a long and complicated one, after all, and good intentions usually occupy the moral high ground regardless of the evil that they do. It will be easy to vilify our decision, dismiss it as a cruel experiment. Many noble causes have been ignobly buried beneath the murky flood of such high-minded rhetoric and this one, too, may fall victim to that drear fate.

But at the very least, Lubanda will be Lubandan, in ways both good and bad when seen through Western eyes. Without doubt its tribal rivalries will remain as real as they were before the first foreigners came. And yet, if Lubanda is truly left alone, it is possible that the weapons of mass killing, like the money needed to buy them, will be less available. If this is so, then conflict in Lubanda will become exclusively Lubandan, its people's evils and excesses, like ours, entirely of their own making, with no outside forces to stir the old poisons into some new and yet more lethal brew. In Lubanda, as everywhere, man will remain what man has always been, our lives, both individual and collective, eternally afflicted with the troubles we ourselves devise.

That Lubanda's joys and tribulations shall forever be its own is my hope for this country as I exit the Presidential Residence and move down the stairs to where one of Fareem's drivers stands at the ready. He nods and offers the big smile he has no doubt been told to offer such people as myself, foreigners he supposes to be bearing gifts. I smile back, but rather than take his car, I glance to my left where one a private taxi idles by the curb.

At my signal, its young driver throws the car into gear and inches toward me.

"Where to, sir?" the driver asks as I get in.

"The airport, please."

We arrive there a few minutes later.

"Thank you," I say as I pay the fare.

"I hope you have a safe trip home," the driver tells me, then briskly turns back to his work.

In the simple nobility of this young man's work, in his independence, in the way he does not wait for some proffered gift, I feel my deepest love sweep out to Lubanda with the same overflowing fierceness with which it had once embraced Martine.

An hour or so later, as my plane rises over Rupala, I recall the visit—or was it a pilgrimage—I'd made to Martine's farm after my talk with Ufala, by then carrying the heavy burden of what Seso had wanted Bill Hammond to see.

The ancient air had been aglow in one of the region's fabled sunsets by the time I'd walked out into the field where her ashes had been scattered. There was no grave, but a rough-hewn, wooden marker had been sunk into her native earth. It was hand-painted and it had once borne her full name, but the windblown sand had by then reduced it to *Martine A.*

I don't know how long I stood with my hands reverently folded in front of me. Perhaps a few minutes; perhaps a little longer. But I do remember—and always will—that at one point a gust of wind had swept the field and on its wings a delicate cloud of red dust had lifted and turned and danced, like a woman around a village fire. Some of those tiny particles had risen from where Martine's ashes had been scattered, and so it seemed to me that some part of her was actually held within the folds of that natural pirouette. I knew that they would float awhile, these particles, then return to earth, then be lifted again and returned, and lifted and returned, in a rhythm that would never end, Martine forever a dancer in the dust.

More than anything, I'd thought as I'd watched the slow twirl of that delicate red cloud, it was to be inseparably and eternally Lubandan that had been the dream of *Martine A.*

And now, at last, she was.